200

MW00413909

SANDOVER BEACH WEEK

A CHRISTIAN BEACH ROMANCE

EMMA ST. CLAIR

2018 Kirsten Oliphant, updated 2019

Warning: All rights reserved. No part of this book may be reproduced aside from small excerpts used in a review. Please contact Emma for permissions: emma@emmastclair.com.

This is a work of fiction. All characters, names, and occurrences are a product of the author's creation and bear no resemblance to actual people, living or dead. Any incidences resembling actual events or people are purely coincidental.

❀ Created with Vellum

CHAPTER ONE

E mily had been singing along with her Big Fat Breakup playlist and didn't see the toll bridge until she was approaching it, fast. Hitting the brakes, she barely managed to stop before the red and white striped barrier. Her heart pounded. Before rolling down the window, she wiped her eyes. Not that she was crying. Nope.

The tiny, gray-haired woman at the booth flinched as Emily opened the window, a sad song blasting through the night air. Emily smacked the power button, glad that the playlist was still in the ballads, not the angry revenge pop songs yet. That really would have shocked the woman. Emily practically had the whole playlist memorized. Like her modeling career, her love life lately had been a series of rejections. The breakup playlist might as well have been the soundtrack to her life.

"Two dollars for the toll." The woman smiled, looking a little like a wax figure, not a person.

Emily never carried cash. Why did a tourist island have a toll booth on the only bridge? "I'm sorry. I didn't know there was a toll. I don't have any cash. Can I charge it? I have a credit card."

"Cash only." The woman pointed to a handwritten sign taped to the window.

"Can I pay on the way out? I'm staying for a week. I promise I'm trustworthy." Emily made what she thought was the sign for scout's honor. That was never her thing as a kid. Her mom had been too busy dragging her around pageants or casting calls to let Emily do something normal or fun like Girl Scouts.

"Two dollars for the toll."

Emily stared at the woman. Could she say anything else? Was Emily being punked? No other cars were around. No other people hiding or cameras anywhere. It wasn't tourist season yet and this looked more like the start of a horror movie than anything.

She sighed. "Let me look in my car. Maybe I can find some change under the seats or something."

Emily unbuckled, digging around the console for change. Kim and the caravan of other girls who came up earlier that day for the bachelorette trip hadn't mentioned a toll. If Emily had been able to leave work and go with them, she wouldn't have had this problem. But her boss, who liked to stand over her desk and literally talk down to her, barely let Emily have the week off for this trip.

The company where she was a temp was in the middle of launching a huge campaign for a startup called Outdoor Access. The company was blowing up, in a good way. But Emily just answered phones and was, as Mr. Anderson liked to remind her, totally replaceable. During one of her lunch breaks, Emily had written up a solid proposal for the social media arm of the campaign. But Mr. Anderson held the proposal limply in his hand when she gave it to him, then

2

reminded her that she was a temp. Her hope that this job might help her get started with marketing seemed fruitless.

Emily had thought about making a dramatic quitting scene when she left for the beach at the end of the day. But those scenes only worked in the movies. In real life, quitting would mean she was no closer to moving out of her parents' house and away from their constant criticism. They were disappointed enough in her career choices and her perpetually empty bank account, even if they liked the control it gave them over her.

Her mother kept trying to push her back into the modeling world, but Emily had burned any connections she had when she fled New York the second time. She stayed only a few days and would never go back. Not for modeling. Not for fun. Not for anything. Mostly, she liked to pretend like that never happened.

At twenty-six, Emily was practically geriatric in the modeling world. There was some print work in Richmond—catalogues and such. But it wasn't a modeling hub or a big enough city to have much work. She was waiting to hear back on a big contract for a brand of women's clothing that she didn't really want. It was the kind of clothing women her mother wore: overpriced rich lady clothes. Nothing Emily would ever wear, if for no other reason than it was her mother's style.

The job would be boring, but good, consistent money. Until she knew if she got that gig, she didn't have the luxury to make a bold exit, no matter how great it would have felt to tell her boss where he could stick it. Not that she enjoyed modeling, but that seemed to be her only skillset, other than building a social media following.

If she pushed for it, she could get more paid campaigns as an influencer on Instagram. Brands contacted her all the time because of her substantial following, but she struggled to do paid posts that didn't feel fake. These days, even her personal posts on Instagram felt fake, like she filtered out her real self to present a character instead. No one wanted to see her real self, sifting through discarded coffee cups and other trash, looking for change in her car. She spotted a gleam of silver in the passenger seat under a fast-food wrapper.

"Look! I've got a quarter!" She handed it to the woman with a flourish and a smile, hoping she might dismiss her with a wink.

"Two dollars for the toll."

No such luck. Sighing, Emily got out and started searching the floorboards in the back seat. Underneath some clothes and a pair of high heels in the back, Emily found another dollar in change. "Okay, we're up to…$1.25. Can I get some grace? Or something? I literally have nothing else."

"Two dollars—"

"—for the toll. I know. I don't have it. Do I need to drive back until I find an ATM? Just tell me what to do."

Emily sounded as desperate as she felt. Tears pricked her eyes. She didn't even want to come on this trip, celebrating Kim's upcoming wedding. Every engagement, every wedding left Emily closer to being the last single girl in their group. Kind of like a game of last woman standing, but being the last one meant losing, not winning. With her most recent breakup only a few days old, the timing couldn't be worse.

The woman in the toll booth gave her a sympathetic smile but didn't offer any suggestions. Where could Emily find an ATM? The last twenty miles of the drive from Richmond to Sandover Island, North Carolina had been mostly country, with few lights and only an occasional gas station. Emily couldn't remember the last open business she had seen.

Maybe she could text the girls and someone could drive

out to bring her change. Emily didn't know why Kim had chosen this out-of-the-way island with a toll bridge for crying out loud when the more popular Outer Banks beaches were a few miles south. Or Virginia Beach, which would have been much less of a drive from Richmond. She only knew of Sandover because it's where Jimmy had moved.

She could always call Jimmy. Except that she couldn't.

The thought made her throat clog with emotion she didn't want to examine. Much more emotion than she felt over her most recent breakup. Her Big Fat Breakup playlist wouldn't touch the feelings she had about Jimmy, her best friend Natalie's little brother.

Three years ago, Emily wouldn't have thought twice about calling him. She would have already been on the phone, smiling at the sound of his voice. Within minutes, he would be here for her. He always had been. But he wouldn't be now and she had no one to blame but herself for the fact that their friendship ended. Her heart clenched and Emily turned away from the toll booth so the woman wouldn't see the emotion on her face.

Headlights approached from the road. A fire truck pulled up behind her car, engine rumbling. A broad-shouldered man in a uniform got out of the truck. Maybe she could borrow change?

He smiled as he got closer. Emily crossed her arms over her chest, steeling herself to fend off unwanted looks or comments. But his smile was friendly, not flirtatious. His eyes didn't travel up and down her body or look hungrily at her face. He had a kind expression and didn't shift his gaze from her eyes. Her shoulders relaxed.

"Let me guess—you don't have the two dollars for the toll?" he asked.

"I didn't know there was a toll. Any chance I can bum seventy-five cents?"

"I've got you covered. No worries." He handed the woman a five-dollar bill and then she gave him back a dollar.

"Thank you so much! I was pretty stuck here. I'm surprised they make firemen pay the toll. Seems like public servants would get a pass."

"Greta makes everyone pay the toll. She's very dedicated to her job."

"Thanks for helping me out. I was beginning to think I was going to have to drive back another thirty minutes to get cash. What kind of tourist destination has a toll bridge?"

"Yeah, the toll is … just one of those things about the Island. I guess you've never been here?"

"Nope."

He stuck out his hand. "I'm Beau."

Again, no flirting. Beau probably had a girlfriend. He spoke like someone whose heart was taken. It was always refreshing—and a little surprising—to talk to guys who didn't try to hit on her. Usually, men glanced at her, and only saw blonde hair and long legs. That was enough for them. Emily wore little makeup and dressed casually to tone down her appearance, but it didn't matter. Guys were just drawn to her. Well, not to *her*. Just her appearance. Once they got past the surface, they bolted.

Sermons and books and Bible studies all talked about the importance of inner beauty. Focusing on the inside, not the outward appearance. Without her outward appearance, Emily was beginning to wonder what she had left. She wasn't sweet or soft like a lot of the girls from church. She laughed too loudly and had more of an edge to her humor. Rather than radiating joy and peace, Emily was a bit more sarcastic and pessimistic. Sometimes she got lost in her dark thoughts and they pulled her down so hard that she couldn't break out of them for a few days. Depression, anxiety—there was probably some name for it, but so far it had been pretty rare. Emily fought it back with the sheer force of her will. If she ever couldn't, she would get help. That's what she told herself. If she didn't look the way she looked, often she wondered if she might be that weird girl in the corner everyone ignored. In any case, the "gentle and quiet spirit" used to describe a beautiful woman in 1 Peter 3:4 didn't really fit.

Which is maybe why she was the kind of woman guys dated, not the one they wanted to marry. Really, she had saved Jimmy the trouble of liking her when she shot him down at Natalie's wedding. He would have eventually figured out that she wasn't marriage material just like every other guy had.

It only took Hudson two months. He broke up with her a few days ago in an it's-not-you-it's-me speech. With the added bonus of saying that he thought God was calling him to something different. It was all Emily could do not to roll her eyes at the God comment. Such a cop-out. Sure, God could call you to different things. But she'd been dumped enough with that line to see it as an excuse. She would have appreciated honesty instead. Half the guys who broke up with her got engaged to someone else a few months later. The it's-not-you-it's-me thing didn't work. It was *definitely* Emily.

She pushed these thoughts away as she stuck her hand out to shake Beau's. "I'm Emily. Thanks again."

"I hope you enjoy Sandover."

"Thanks. Hopefully I won't see you again." He looked puzzled. She pointed to the truck, still rumbling behind him.

"Because if I do, I'm probably on fire. Firemen—get it? Sorry. My brand of humor is an acquired taste."

He laughed. "No, that was good. Okay, then, Emily. Hope I don't see you again, too."

He jogged back. The fire truck flashed its lights and gave a quick honk. Emily was still blocking the entrance to the island. She waved and got back in the car as Greta raised the barrier. Rather than putting the breakup playlist back on, she drove in silence over the bridge, watching the moonlight reflecting on the water. Less than ten minutes later, Emily pulled up to the three-story beach house.

Before she got out of the car, she rested her head on the steering wheel and closed her eyes. She could already hear the dull roar of the ocean. The sound soothed her, even though she wasn't much of a beach girl. It was time to put on a brave face and be the girl everyone expected her to be. The one who stayed up the latest and laughed the loudest and would take any dare. The strong, confident woman who dated casually and never seemed upset when it didn't work out.

Emily just needed to be able to turn it on for the first few days, when almost all the girls would be there. Sunday night, half the girls had to leave and get back to jobs and families. Things would quiet down after that. If Hudson came up, she would shrug it off and could spin it a different way—they broke up and it was a good thing. This weekend was about Kim's upcoming wedding, not Emily's sad life. If she could get out of her own head, this week would be a great distraction. She needed to get out of the funk she'd been in. Maybe a girls' weekend was just the thing. Somehow, though, the thought only made her sink further into her sad state. The last thing she wanted was to have an emotional breakdown in front of these girls, none of whom she felt very close to.

Lord, help me to let go. Get me out of this stuck place in my life. And help me get through this week with the girls.

Her silent prayer was interrupted as shouts came down from one of the balconies. "The life of the party is here! Whoop!"

"Emily! Get up here, girl!"

Emily took a deep breath. She stepped out of the car, shaking her hips and raising her arms above her head. "Who's ready for a bachelorette weekend?"

As cheers rang out from above, Emily began the climb upstairs, trying to prepare herself to be the version of herself that everyone expected her to be.

CHAPTER TWO

"You've been quiet since we got back." Beau's voice shook Jimmy out of his thoughts. "You okay?"

The guys were putting their gear up, after returning from what Beau called a "grilling situation." Which was a glorified way of saying a small and easily contained grill fire. Typically, this involved an embarrassed man and a bottle of lighter fluid. Most of their calls were for mildly serious things, at least until summer, which was a few weeks away. Now that Sandover was a growing tourist destination, there were more people, more drinking, and more accidental blazes during June, July, and August.

"He's probably thinking about the hottie on the bridge. I know I am," Robbie said, whistling.

"Shut up," Jimmy and Beau said at the same time.

"Can't a guy appreciate a beautiful woman?"

"You aren't appreciating, Robbie. You're objectifying. Learn the difference," Beau said. Robbie only rolled his eyes, but he didn't say anything more.

Neither did Jimmy. But that didn't mean he wasn't

thinking about the beautiful woman on the toll bridge. When he saw her standing there, Jimmy didn't believe it at first. But then she turned, her face illuminated in the lights of the fire truck, and it was like a giant hand grabbed him around the chest and began to squeeze.

Emily. He hadn't seen her in three years, other than photos on social media, which he mostly tried to avoid. She had like 40,000 Instagram followers, which made him equal parts jealous and proud. Every post had hundreds of likes and comments and heart-eye emojis. Seeing her made him sad all over again and then jealous and angry at all the comments from other guys telling her she was hot or asking her on dates. They didn't know her. Not the way Jimmy did.

It could be like a black hole, sucking him down as he scrolled through her pictures. Emily smiling with friends. Emily in full makeup on set for a photo shoot, making a silly face as if that could offset her beauty. Emily laughing at a party. Emily eating dinner.

In the early days after they stopped speaking, Jimmy drove himself crazy, clinging to every update, scrolling the comments to see which ones she responded to, always trying to beat back his jealousy and the heavy reminder that she wasn't in his life anymore. They had been so close for years. Now he only got the same access that those thousands of random followers got.

But her captions made him remember the sound of her voice and what it was like to have her random and hilarious commentary on everything:

Ramen for lunch. Don't be too jealous.

. . .

Do you think cats are planning a hostile takeover? Discuss.

To drivers who don't understand the purpose of a blinker: FIGURE IT OUT.

It had been weeks since he let himself scroll through her feed. But seeing her tonight brought everything right back to the surface. Jimmy leaned closer to Beau so Robbie and the other guys wouldn't hear. "That wasn't just any beautiful woman. That was the *one.*"

Beau's mouth dropped open. "That was *your* Emily?"

Jimmy nodded, and Beau ran a hand through his hair. "Man. Did you know she was coming to Sandover?"

Jimmy closed his eyes and tightened his jaw. "No. But she knows I'm here. My number hasn't changed."

"You sure? I mean, if you haven't talked in years, maybe she doesn't know."

"She's my sister's best friend. Like it or not, she knows pretty much everything I do. Can we stop talking about it? Please."

Jimmy had been so close to getting over Emily. He finally started to date again, even if he was struggling to feel something more than friendship for Amber. They had been on a handful of dates, but weren't officially dating. He couldn't seem to pull the trigger on an actual commitment. She was cute and nice and went to his church. The right kind of girl, he kept telling himself. But seeing Emily on the bridge reminded him that he was hopelessly and helplessly in love with someone who didn't love him back.

No. He wasn't in love with her now. Those were just echoes of his old feelings. He didn't feel that way now.

13

Keep telling yourself that, buddy.

"I'm here when you're ready to talk." Beau gave Jimmy a firm pat on the back and headed up to the bunk room.

Jimmy nodded, but he knew Beau. He wasn't the kind of friend to let things go. So, he wasn't surprised a few hours later when Beau sat down on the couch next to where Jimmy stared at a baseball game he wasn't really watching.

"Shouldn't you be asleep?" Beau asked.

"Shouldn't you?" Jimmy didn't turn away from the television.

Beau sighed. "I know you don't want to talk about it, but—"

"So then, can we not talk about it? I'd appreciate that."

"We don't have to beat it into the ground. But I think we should at least have a conversation. She's here. You're here. Clearly you aren't over her, so ... "

"I'm over her."

"You aren't even fooling yourself with that line."

"Fine. You want to talk about our feelings. Let's go deep. But fair's fair. I talk about Emily and you have to talk about Mercer." Jimmy turned from the screen to level his gaze at Beau.

He groaned. "Fine. I'll go first because there is so little to tell. You know this story—it's old news. Mercer is hot and cold. Mostly cold. I'm going slow because that's how she seems to want things. Trying to warm her up, one degree at a time. At this rate, we'll go on our first date in a decade. Your turn. What happened with you and Emily?"

Jimmy leaned back in the couch, letting his thoughts trace back to memories he had spent the past few years trying to lock away. "She was my sister's best friend. I had a crush on her basically since I was a kid."

Beau wiggled his eyebrows. "An older woman?"

Jimmy rolled his eyes. "A little less than four years. It mattered a lot when I was younger. I mean, a girl who's a junior in high school isn't going to date an eighth grader. Or even a senior girl and a freshman guy. It's weird."

"Yeah, but it shouldn't matter now. Did you ever tell her how you felt when you got older?"

"Not for years, but it was obvious. I was not very smooth. Or subtle."

Beau chuckled. "Knowing you, I can imagine."

Jimmy smiled, even if it was a little bitter. For years Jimmy had followed Emily and Natalie around the house, spying on them. He moved into teasing her or bringing her small gifts. When he was older and got serious about baseball, he started taking his shirt off unnecessarily whenever she was around. Natalie rolled her eyes and constantly shooed him away, but Emily never seemed to mind. She didn't lead him on, per se, but she treated him kindly and probably passed it off as a crush.

Maybe it had started that way. But it didn't take long for his crush to deepen. Anyone could see Emily's physical beauty. Jimmy saw the Emily that few other people did. She had a wicked sense of humor, but Jimmy knew that sometimes it just covered up her pain. Humor was a part of her, but sarcasm was also her armor. Underneath the surface, Emily had a tenderness that ran deep and a ferocious loyalty for the people she loved.

The years did nothing but increase his feelings. They simply grew up with him. From like to love. He'd dated other girls over the years. But his only serious high school girlfriend had nailed it when she broke up with him: "You *like* me, but it's clear you *love* someone else."

"Did you ever get the sense that she returned your feelings?"

"Yeah. I guess I was wrong, but I thought so at the time. I told you about my accident, right? The one that got me interested in being an EMT."

Beau nodded. The summer after his senior year, Jimmy had shattered both his legs jumping off a bridge into the river with his high school buddies. It was a stupid dare with lasting consequences, essentially ending his baseball career and his college plans.

"When I had my accident, Emily came to the hospital. It felt like something changed between us." Jimmy swallowed, remembering the worry on Emily's face and how she had climbed up into the hospital bed with him, snuggling close while they watched TV. He had been shocked. If he hadn't been so drugged up and in pain, he probably would have tried to kiss her. "She spent a lot of time with me after that since I didn't go off to school. Driving me to physical therapy, just hanging out. That kind of thing. It felt like friendship, but with ... potential."

"Then what happened?" Beau pressed.

Jimmy sighed. "I decided to tell her how I felt the next year at my sister's wedding." He launched into the story he hadn't shared with anyone, ever. He'd been over it so many times in his mind that it was just as fresh as it had been three years ago.

Girls got romantic about wedding stuff, so Jimmy had decided that Natalie's wedding was the perfect time for the conversation. Plus, he was the best man and Emily was the maid of honor. They would already be thrown together a lot just because of that. By the end of the night, Jimmy promised himself he would finally tell Emily that he loved her. It had long been an unspoken rule between them that they never addressed his feelings, even if they both knew.

He remembered imagining that Emily would, finally,

admit that she saw him as more than Natalie's little brother. She would look at him the way he always looked at her—with adoration and love. They would share a first kiss and that would be the start of their future together. He had really believed he stood a chance.

Emily had looked so beautiful walking down the aisle during the ceremony. Even though it was Natalie's day, seeing Emily coming towards him, her eyes locked on his, they could have been the only two people in the room. She had winked at Jimmy and he beamed back. He'd hardly registered his sister in her wedding gown. *One day that will be us,* he had thought to himself.

What a joke.

He stuck close to her over the next few hours, working up the courage to ask her to dance. When she agreed, he knew that it was time to stop stalling. Jimmy wasn't much of a dancer, even for slow songs, where it was just swaying. It was hard to think of anything coherent when his hands were on her hips and hers rested gently on his neck. Emily didn't seem affected by it in the slightest, playing lightly with the hair just above the collar of his suit.

"What's going on? You look nervous, Jimboy," Emily had said, using the nickname that he hated. Not how he hoped to start a conversation.

He groaned. "Don't call me that."

"Jimboy? I call you that all the time."

"I know. And I hate it."

"Really? Well, too bad. That's the perk of being like your big sister. I get to make the nicknames."

He had made a face. "You're not my big sister. You're hardly older than me."

"Four years."

"Three and a half. Practically nothing now that I'm out of

17

high school."

"You're still a teenager."

"I'll be twenty next month."

"Jimmy, what's the deal? I don't want to argue with you about stupid stuff. Just dance."

He had pulled back so they were eye to eye, then took a big breath. This was the moment. "I don't want you to see me as your little brother anymore. I definitely don't see you as a sister," he had said, his voice low and husky. He stared into her eyes, those gorgeous blue eyes, trying to project everything he was feeling into his gaze.

For a moment, Jimmy saw something flash across her face. His heart beat faster, fueled by the tiny hope her look gave him. Maybe ...

And then Emily stopped dancing. She pulled her hands away from his neck and removed his from her hips.

"Look, Jimb—*Jimmy*. You're too old to have a crush on me. Let's move on. I'm your sister's best friend and always will be, which makes you like my little brother. You're family. I don't feel any other way about you and I'm not going to. If you want to stay friends, you've got to grow up and stop this crushing thing."

"It's not a crush," he had said.

Jimmy meant that he felt something more and deeper. He meant to tell her that he loved her, but the words came out all wrong. Instead he just sounded like a whining, petulant boy. He could even hear it in his own voice. He wished he could pull back the words to say something coherent and eloquent. He had gone through this moment in his head so many times, where he would talk to her about his feelings and say just the right thing and then take her face in his hands and—

"Jimmy. We're friends. I care about you. Please don't ruin

what we have."

The music had changed to something up-tempo and couples around them began dancing. Emily patted him on the shoulder and didn't wait for him to say anything else. She disappeared into the crowd, leaving him standing there among all the moving bodies. He thought that pain was as bad as it could get. Until he had to watch her flirting with every other single guy at the wedding for the rest of the night. He called a Lyft and went home early.

That night, Jimmy made the decision to leave Richmond, destination unknown. He had finished up his EMT certification earlier that year and figured he could find a job anywhere. He had literally pulled out the map, closed his eyes, and put his finger down. Sandover Island. Two days later, he packed a few bags in his car, leaving most things behind. When he was three hours gone, he called and told his parents, afraid they would convince him to come home if he called before the halfway point.

He'd walked right into the fire station there, which happened to be hiring. Some firefighting training had been required with his EMT certification. Jimmy got hired, met Beau, and here he still was. Running. Hiding. Trying unsuccessfully to forget.

Which brought him right back to this couch, where Beau was giving him a sympathetic look. "Wow. I can't believe you hadn't told me the full story before now. But I can see why. That's harsh, man. But it's been three years. Maybe some things have changed?"

"She made it clear that she only sees me as her best friend's little brother. Emphasis on both *little* and *brother*. As far as I know, nothing has changed."

"So, it's an age thing? That matters so much less as you get older. You're twenty-two. She's...what? Twenty-five?"

"She turned twenty-six in February."

"You're going to let a few years stop you?"

"It didn't stop me. It stopped *her*."

"But it might not now. That's what I'm saying," Beau said.

"Say that's true. Then there's the other part of that—the part where she thinks of me like a brother. Nothing throws cold water on a guy. I don't know how time would have changed that."

"Again, it's been years. You don't know how that's changed or how she feels. You should give it a chance. It says something when you love someone this long."

"It says I'm an idiot."

"No, it says that your feelings matter. Emily matters. She's here. Track her down and give it a chance. You won't know if you don't do anything."

"So, why don't you ask Mercer out?"

"Touché. I will. In due time. But first—"

Beau was interrupted by the alarm going off. Both of them were on their feet and moving toward the truck bay and their gear.

"We've got a live call," Robbie shouted. "A balcony collapse on one of the oceanfront beach houses."

An adrenaline surge hit his bloodstream as the alarm continued to blare. Jimmy hated the thought of people getting hurt, but the feeling of danger and the rush of saving lives stirred his soul. He liked the feeling of doing good, of helping with something bigger than himself.

And selfishly, tonight he wanted something—anything— to push back the memories of Emily that had resurfaced. The vault where he had locked them up had cracked wide open tonight. It was going to take more than one emergency call to repair the damage, but it would be a start.

CHAPTER THREE

Emily walked out on the deck, alone and finally able to breathe again. The balcony had a gorgeous view of the beach three stories below. She leaned her arms on the railing for a few minutes, letting the ocean's roar overpower the noise in her head. After dealing with the girls for the past few hours, she needed this moment alone to recharge.

The hot tub called to her, steam rising and dissipating into the night air. Sinking into the almost too-hot water, she moaned. Yeah, she could get used to a house like this with a hot tub overlooking the ocean. But only if she didn't have to keep being the life of the party. It was exhausting. And it was a lie.

To these girls, that's who Emily was: a good time. Tonight, she felt like anything but the life of the party. She was depressed. It wasn't something she liked to admit. For a while, she hadn't recognized the dark feelings and the critical thoughts that assaulted her during the particularly low points. There was a critical voice in her head that listed off the mistakes she made daily. Sometimes she could tell it to shut up and that worked. Other times these critical thoughts and the heavy feelings overwhelmed her to the point she had a hard time getting out of bed.

She didn't know if she was depressed enough to need clinical help. A drug, a counselor. Mostly, she just tried to power through the low feelings, even the days when she lay in the floor of her room, curled in a ball, trying to hide the sounds of her crying with loud music. She definitely didn't want her parents involved. Her mom would just try to get her on some pill—she took enough herself. Or she would order Emily to pull herself up with her bootstraps, while also blaming her for letting her modeling career crash and burn when she left New York.

Those days weren't that frequent, usually triggered by some event. It could be as small as getting criticized by her boss, or if her mother's words didn't roll off her back the way they usually did. It had been much worse since New York. Her time there had taken the tiny fissures and cracks and made them into deep, gaping chasms.

When she tentatively touched on the subject once with this group of girls, no one took her seriously. As though the fact that she had a model's face and body meant that Emily couldn't struggle with feelings of self-loathing. A few rolled their eyes. Stacy had utterly dismissed her, saying, "Poor, beautiful Emily. Being a model isn't enough validation? You need us to stroke your ego too?" Emily's mouth had snapped shut and she never tried to talk about it again.

She understood, to a point. Her whole life people had been telling her she was beautiful. The words stopped having meaning after a while, though. Especially since it was all in her genes. She didn't even work out. How do you respond to praise for something you had nothing to do with? It was like people praising you for a gift someone else gave you. She didn't earn it and she couldn't give it back. But her looks did give her advantages and that's what other girls saw when she complained. Emily had something they didn't and was still complaining.

Emily didn't want to pretend anymore. She used to be that girl—the lively, fun one who made people laugh, but lately, it had all been an act. Echoes of the light, carefree girl she used to be. Inside, Emily had fallen apart and was desperately trying to hold the pieces of herself together. But these women had no idea. She wasn't sure they would care if they did. They weren't bad women. They became friends through church and the singles group, but the relationships weren't deep. For Emily, things had just never dipped below the surface.

Spending this weekend with them was the worst timing. Things had been rough with her parents and her job and then with Hudson breaking up with her. She wasn't so upset about him, specifically. In fact, if she was being honest, she didn't miss him at all. That was also a problem. She was dating guys that she didn't care about, so desperate to find someone who felt like Emily was worth something, or at least worth marrying. The problem wasn't that they didn't think she was worth marrying. She didn't believe it herself.

The answers were right in front of her: she needed to find her worth in God and not in what some guy thought about her. But she couldn't seem to break this cycle of feeling like not enough and hiding the struggle from everyone around her.

The door to the house opened and a handful of other girls splashed into the hot tub: Kim, the bride-to-be; Sarah, her best friend who was already married; Leah and Stacy, both single. There were still voices coming from inside the house and what sounded like 90s pop music playing. Water splashed and spilled over the side of the hot tub as they piled in. Kim settled next to Emily and Stacy took a seat across the hot tub, presumably so she could glare. Stacy had a crush on Hudson before he and Emily started dating and had been nothing but hostile since.

Stacy could have him now. Good riddance. He would probably marry her.

"Watch the drinks," Emily said, holding her wine glass high. "I don't mix chlorine with my Dr. Pepper."

Kim leaned her head on Emily's shoulder. The bridal tiara she wore on her head scratched lightly against Emily's neck. "Are you drinking Dr. Pepper in a wine glass? You're such a hoot."

"Just keeping it classy," Emily said.

Stacy snorted and Emily ignored her.

"How many people should be in this thing?" Sarah asked. The water level had risen to the very top of the hot tub. Their legs all tangled in the middle.

"It's fine." Kim waved a dismissive hand. "Stop worrying."

"I'm not worrying, I'm just concerned," Sarah said.

"Like there's a difference."

Sarah and Kim bickered constantly like an old married couple. They had known each other since they were little and been roommates in college. Emily wondered if Sarah fought the same way with her husband, Mitch.

"Better question—is it safe to have a Jacuzzi on the third-floor balcony?" Leah asked.

"I agree," Stacy said. "Is there a weight limit?"

"I'm sure it's fine," Kim whined. "Relax and enjoy. I can't have fun if everyone's complaining and worrying about every little thing."

"This just seems like a poor choice," Leah said. Stacy nodded, but Kim just rolled her eyes.

Emily raised her glass. "To poor choices and living dangerously!"

The conversation moved onto Kim's wedding and the date Leah went on last weekend and Sarah's husband's new job. Emily zoned out. The truth of it was that she didn't really care that much. If anyone noticed that she was quiet, no one said anything. She wished these women well, but it wouldn't matter to her when the friendships fizzled out. Which they would.

It reminded Emily of how much she missed Natalie. Technically, they were still best friends. But a lot had changed. The two of them had been inseparable for years—until Natalie's wedding. The dynamics of their friendship definitely shifted in a normal way after she got married, and especially after Natalie had her daughter, Scarlet. But the reason for the shift had more to do with a conversation about Jimmy on Natalie's wedding night.

"Leave my brother alone." The words shocked Emily into standing perfectly still in the bathroom. Natalie looked fierce and furious even in layers of satin and lace. "I won't watch you trash Jimmy's heart like you've done with other guys. It's time to stop leading him on."

The words had been like ice poured over her soul. Emily had no idea why this was on Natalie's mind on her wedding night. Or why she spoke so harshly. Wedding stress? Maybe it was just the last straw after years of Jimmy chasing Emily. She hadn't done enough to push him away, that was true. She had never closed the door on the idea of a relationship, probably because she had started to see that door as partway open from her end. Not that she had mentioned this to anyone, definitely not Natalie.

Maybe Natalie saw the way Jimmy had been looking at her all night. Whatever he had been holding back over the years, he had let it all go that night. He looked at Emily like he really saw her and loved every single part of her. It had made Emily's heart flutter. Every time he had touched her, she had felt her whole body react. When she had walked up the aisle during the processional, his eyes had never left hers. For a tiny moment, Emily thought about what it would be like to walk toward Jimmy, wearing a wedding dress. She didn't hate the idea. In fact, she kept thinking about it that whole night.

Until Natalie's words made her heart sink like lead. It was the perfect opening to confess that she had started to have feelings for Jimmy. But Emily couldn't do it. She had been terrified to make a mistake that would change things with Jimmy. Or Natalie. In the moment, it felt like loyalty to her best friend and, in a strange way, to Jimmy too. If Natalie didn't think Emily was good enough for Jimmy, maybe she wasn't. So, while it felt like her heart was shriveling up inside her chest, Emily promised her best friend to back off.

Less than an hour later, she had to put her words to the test when he asked her to dance. With Jimmy's hands on her waist and his face gazing at her with what looked a lot like love, Emily's mouth went totally dry. She couldn't deny her attraction to his tousled blond hair, wide smile, and eyes the color of summer sky. To his kindness, his strength, his humor. When had he grown up? When had she stopped seeing him as a brother?

Why had she told Natalie that she would back off?

The realization of her feelings terrified her, even as Jimmy's hands dropped to her hips. Heat had rushed through her body. Emily had worked hard at keeping her face from giving her away. And then he broke the rules by talking about his feelings for her. This was a line they never crossed. He flirted and she could flirt back. He could hint, but they did not say it.

That night, though, he said the words. Out loud. Not "I love you." Emily stopped him before he got that far, but she suspected it was where he was going. Keeping her promise to Natalie, Emily did what she did best—she slammed her walls into place. She brushed Jimmy off, telling him that she saw him like a little brother. And she hated herself as she watched the adoring look on his face disappear, replaced by pain and anger.

Natalie got her wish—Emily left Jimmy alone. But the price was steep. That night shifted all three of their relationships. Emily lost her two best friends while trying to keep them. The next week Jimmy moved to Sandover without a goodbye.

Emily ran too, all the way back to New York to work with an agency that had been interested in her. If her head and heart hadn't been such a mess, she might have vetted the company better and avoided the disaster that followed. When she came home less than a week later, Emily had been bitter and broken, filled with more shame and more regret than before. After that, her life fell into a slow decline that now felt like a standstill.

Jimmy was somewhere on this island. The thought wouldn't leave her mind and the urge to text or call him grew. But she couldn't. There was too much between them now. Too much space, memories, history, hurt. Her heart lifted at the thought of hearing his voice or seeing his face. But she doubted Jimmy would feel the same way.

Natalie mentioned he had started dating someone recently. Even thinking about it made sweat start beading on her hairline. Jealousy pooled in her stomach, hot and sharp. Maybe it was time to get out of the hot tub.

"You still with us, Emmie?" Kim nudged her.

Emily hated that nickname. Elle stuck her head outside before Emily could answer. "You guys ready to watch a movie?"

Kim stood. "Yes. I'm roasting in here. Let's go, ladies!"

Everyone started moving indoors except Emily. She wanted—no, needed—a few minutes of peace before heading back inside.

"You coming, Emmie?" Kim called from the doorway.

"Be right in! I need to simmer a little more. I'm still a little medium-rare."

Kim laughed and closed the door. Emily's shoulders relaxed as the laughter and chatter moved inside and the sound of the ocean again filled her ears. After a few minutes, she couldn't ignore the sheen of sweat that covered her exposed skin. She got out of the hot tub and stood again at the railing, letting the salty breeze brush against her skin. Below on the beach, she could see the ocean, black with white-edged foam in the moonlight. The view was mesmerizing. It reminded her just how small she was and just how big God was.

She leaned on the balcony, her feet on the bottom crossbeam and her arms over the rail. That's when she heard the sound that rose up louder than the ocean: a groan and then a splintering crack.

There was the sensation of shuddering and a jolt. *Earthquake* was all Emily could think as she clutched the railing. Her body froze in place, clinging to the wood as it moved. It *moved*.

She closed her eyes. There was a horrible crash, then another, and finally, a deafening thud and the sound of a splash that called to mind the water park she had gone to as a girl with her parents. At some point, rational thought told her that the balcony was collapsing. She heard screams from inside the house and the girls shouting her name.

Emily waited for the sensation of falling, but it didn't come. Opening her eyes, she felt the sway of the deck more strongly. When she registered her surroundings, Emily thought she might throw up.

The hot tub had fallen through the deck. And the one below it.

The flooring of the balcony had almost all been ripped away when the hot tub fell, leaving Emily hanging onto a very unsecure railing, almost ten feet away from the building. The overall balcony framework was still attached to the house and to the ground, but not by much. It swayed slightly, a movement not unlike riding on a boat, back and forth. Essentially, she was holding onto the equivalent of tooth-picks glued onto the back of the building.

Emily could see the ground three stories down, which seemed like an endless distance. If she hadn't had her feet up on the bottom of the rail, she would be on the ground along with the broken pieces of wood and the hot tub, which looked like it had imploded. Just seeing the distance to the ground made Emily feel shaky.

Her wine glass dropped from her hand and shattered below. She didn't realize she had still been holding it.

"Emily!" Kim screamed her name.

"I'm still here." Her voice shook and sounded unfamiliar.

"We're calling for help. Just hang on, okay? You're going to be fine! Just hang on!"

The thought struck her as so absurd. What else was she going to do—let go? A choking laugh came out of her mouth that turned into a sob. She couldn't cry now. She needed to be strong.

A gust of wind lifted her damp hair from her neck and the railing swayed, creaking. Her stomach lurched along with the shaky wooden structure. Emily could hold on … but the question was—would the structure stand long enough for help to come?

CHAPTER FOUR

J immy steered the big ladder truck in front of one of the new homes right up on the ocean. It wasn't the biggest on the beach, but still a million-dollar home. Like the On Islanders he spent most of his time with, Jimmy hated these rental properties that had popped up on the coast. They were like barnacles crusting over the hull of a beautiful boat, ruining the clean lines. And apparently not only built quickly, but cheaply if a balcony had collapsed.

"Pull the truck to the side in that empty lot," Beau said. "It's the back balcony. We've got someone trapped on it. Don't know how high."

"Sounds bad," Jimmy said.

"It might be. Jimmy, you'll go up. Robbie, can you handle the occupants? Whit, you're on ladder controls. This is one of Jackson's properties," Beau said.

"Did you call him?" Jimmy asked.

"He's on his way."

Jackson was a good friend of theirs, though he was a

decade older than them. The three of them met up once a week for Breakfast and Bible, as Beau called it. Often with Cash, a cop who would be arriving soon if he was on duty tonight. Jackson's father had been an investor and now Jackson ran Wells Development. He had his own house about five minutes away on the beach.

"If you stop right about there, we should be able to angle the ladder. It's a good thing this lot is empty."

"I just flattened the For Sale sign," Jimmy said.

"Least of our worries."

"I have a bad feeling about this," Robbie said from the back of the truck.

"Let's keep *Star Wars* out of this," Beau said lightly.

The guys joked around a lot back at the station and on some of the calls, but Jimmy could never get into humor on the more serious and life-threatening situations. Some of the guys said he'd get used to it, but after three years, he never had. Jimmy stopped the truck, the nose almost to the dunes in the driveway and lot next to the tall house.

A group of women stood around below the house, looking frenzied. Jimmy's stomach dropped as he saw the remains of a hot tub smashed on the cement below what used to be the balcony. A splintered mess of wood stuck up at odd angles below and around it. All that remained were the posts that went from the ground up, and some of the rails and framework.

And there, at the very top, a woman in a bathing suit clung to what was left of the third-story balcony, her blond hair whipping in the ocean wind.

Oh, God. No ....

"Isn't that—" Beau started.

"Emily," Jimmy felt a coldness spreading in his gut. "It's Emily."

For a moment he couldn't breathe. He said a silent prayer and forced his body to move on autopilot. He hadn't gone to a call like this one, but he had training on ladder rescues. His training made his feet move him to the back of the truck, next to the ladder.

Beau shouted orders to Robbie and Whit. Jimmy tried not to look up at Emily, because when he did, the sheer terror he felt seeing her hanging onto the frail structure was more than he could take. But he couldn't not look either, as though he could hold her there with his gaze. He clipped a belt around his waist that in a few minutes he would hopefully attach around Emily's waist. He could do this. He *would* do this.

God, please get me up there in time. Hold her there until I can reach her.

Robbie herded the women toward the road and away from the balcony. Just in case. Jimmy's stomach twisted. The hydraulic ladder began its climb, Whit at the controls. It seemed impossibly slow to Jimmy. His legs were filled with nervous energy and it was hard to stand still and wait for Whit to raise it and position it near Emily, but not touching the structure.

"Can this thing go up any faster?" Jimmy asked.

"Just another minute," Whit said.

Beau called to him from below. "Can you do this one, Jimmy?"

"Yes. I'll be fine."

"I've got you, Jimmy," Whit said.

Jimmy swallowed. He met Beau's eyes for a minute.

"Strong and courageous," Beau said.

"Strong and courageous," Whit and Jimmy repeated.

The two words had become their station motto. To most of the team, it was just an encouraging phrase, but to Beau and Jimmy, it was more. It was part of the charge that Moses

33

gave Joshua in the Bible. The rest of the passage talked about God going before them and being with them. To Jimmy, "strong and courageous" was a reminder that God was in control. He went before them and he was with them.

Even now, when the woman he loved was three stories up, holding onto a structure that didn't look like it could last five more minutes.

As the ladder neared the top, Jimmy saw Jackson pull up to the curb in his Jeep. He ran over to the truck. "What happened?" he said. Then he saw the remains of the deck. "Oh...God. Is anyone hurt?"

"We've got one still up there," Beau said. "Jimmy's going up. Jackson, man—head back out to the street, okay? We'll talk after we get her safely down."

Jackson nodded, looking miserable. "I had it inspected. Shouldn't they have caught something?"

"They should have," Beau said. "Let's talk about that after. For now, this isn't your fault. Okay? We're going to get her down. Wait out there with Robbie."

Jackson went back around to the front of the house, head down and fists at his side.

Red and blue lights flashed and a cop car pulled up to the curb behind the truck. Cash jogged over to them. "I got the call. Oh man—this looks bad. What do you need from me, Beau?"

"Can you head out to the street with Robbie? Keep the women out there and anyone else from coming back here," said Beau.

"You got it," Cash said.

Jimmy put a hand on the ladder, which was almost to the top. It had never felt slower. Beau moved around to the back of the house underneath Emily.

"Hey, up there!" Beau called.

Jimmy could hear Beau's loud voice, but not any replies from Emily over the wind and sound of the waves and the ladder's motor.

"I would ask how you're doing, but that seems like a silly question," Beau went on.

Emily said something and Beau laughed. Good. She still had a sense of humor about her. Knowing that gave Jimmy some small comfort. Emily was the strongest woman he knew. She was a fighter.

"We've got a ladder coming right now for you. It's going to stop as close as we can get and then one of my guys is going to come on up there and bring you down. No big deal. Tomorrow this will just be one of those stories you save for your kids and grandkids. Okay? You're just fine. In a few minutes your feet will be back on the ground."

Beau had a gift for diffusing situations and calming people. Jimmy felt like Beau was speaking to him as well, stilling the panic that threatened to rise in his throat.

Normally Jimmy was good in emergencies. Not at calming other people, but in maintaining his composure. Beau said it was because Jimmy never lost that sense of feeling invincible that teenage boys often have.

But Beau was wrong.

Four summers ago when he had jumped from the bridge, that sense of being invincible disappeared. He couldn't see the rock just under the surface of the river. The sound of his bones cracking and the feeling of his legs literally crumpling before he passed out—that moment stayed with him. Always. Sometimes he still felt the ache all along his legs. A ghost pain that reminded him he was very much human. If anything, he carried with him a sense of how fragile things were along with wicked-looking scars.

"That's as good as we're going to get," Whit said. "You think you can—"

"I've got it." Jimmy had already started climbing.

The ladder swayed as he ascended. He could see the wreckage of the deck below through the rungs. Jimmy didn't mind heights, but the feeling of the ladder moving with the gusts of wind and seeing how high he was above the ground made his stomach lurch. He could only imagine how Emily felt, so isolated out there on the unstable remains of the decking.

He looked up as he climbed the last ten feet. Emily's face was hidden by her hair. She had her cheek pressed into the top of the wood railing. Her muscles were shaking. He picked up speed, already planning how to get her over the railing to the ladder. He just needed the rest of the framework to hold long enough to clip a belt to her and get her over to the ladder.

"Hey," he said. Emily's head jerked, but only an inch off the railing. He could see tears in her eyes. She looked at him with relief and something else he couldn't quite read.

"Jimmy." A small sob escaped her throat. "Where have you been all my life?"

He grinned, feeling his heart swell. *Later. Focus.*

"Let's talk about that when I've got you down on the ground. For now, we've got some business to attend to. Mainly, we need to get you over the rail and onto this side with me."

"I don't know if I can move," she said.

"I'm right here and am going to make sure you're safe," Jimmy said.

"It's not just that I'm afraid—though I am. I think my muscles have cramped up. I don't know that I can loosen my grip."

"We'll take it slow. I'll clip a belt to you and then I'll help you to let go, okay?"

"Okay."

Jimmy positioned his feet firmly on the rung so he could lean over to get the belt around her without falling. But the angle was too difficult. She wouldn't be able to help clip it either, since she needed her hands to hang on.

"Scratch the belt. I can't get it from here. But don't worry —I can still get you. We'll loosen you up and I'll bring you to me."

He knew he had to keep her calm and do what it took to get her over, but even the word *slow* terrified him. They needed to get down now. The two-by-six boards she stood on were only loosely attached to the house itself. He could see the screws, almost fully undone from the socket at the point where they attached to the outside wall. Every gust of wind made the structure less stable.

"I'm going to touch you now, okay?"

"Don't get fresh with me, Jimmy."

"Can I save that for later?" He grinned.

"If you make sure I get a later, yes."

With each joke, he could sense her calming down. It was so easy to fall back into their old rhythms of light flirting. All Jimmy had to do was pretend Natalie's wedding night didn't happen. That and the past three years of silence. He pushed that hurt from his mind. He knew that this was the best way to calm her, but it hurt to think that this was only because it was an emergency. Probably as soon as she was back on the ground, she would shut him out again. For now, he needed to focus on getting her off the structure.

"Okay, now you'll feel my hand on your back. Let's start with your right hand. We're going to loosen one finger at a time until your grip is open. Then you can let go with your hand." He watched as she lifted a finger at a time until one hand no longer had a death grip on the wood. "Good job. You're doing great. Now, let's start loosening up your arm."

"I don't want to let go." She sounded panicked. It wasn't anything he'd heard in her voice before.

"Don't or can't? If you can't, we'll just do it slowly and I'll keep talking you through. If it's don't and you're afraid, I've got you, Em."

"I think I can lift my arm."

"Great." Jimmy leaned over further, careful not to put any weight on the wood, keeping his boots firmly on the ladder rung. "Just swing that arm over my back and see if you can grab onto my jacket, okay?"

"It's hard to get a grip. Your jacket's so thick."

"You're right. Try...here." He adjusted his feet and leaned a bit further over and reached one hand under her arm. "Can you get your arm around me now?"

She lifted up onto her tiptoes, shifting her weight toward him. The wood groaned and she flinched back.

"Keep coming," he said. "That's it."

Her right arm was now around his back, but her left still clung to the railing. He was either going to have to drag her up and over the railing, or she would need to step up and give herself a push. Either one, but it needed to happen now.

"Okay, Em. I've got you. But this last bit is the trickiest. We've got to get you up and over now."

"Jimmy—"

A sudden gust of wind rocked the ladder. It tapped the wooden frame. Jimmy felt it shifting. Emily made a small whimper. Her eyes were squeezed shut as she clung to him with her one arm.

"Don't think about that," Jimmy said. "Listen to my voice. I'm right here and I've already got you. Okay? Almost done. I'm going to lean over a bit more and grab you under your other arm. Hold onto me, even if your grip is weak. I've got you. I'll lift you and you're going to pull. Here we go."

He braced one knee against the ladder's side, firming up his footing.

"Steady," Beau called up from below.

Jimmy heard it for the warning that it was. Beau wouldn't make conversation while he was in the middle of a rescue unless it was necessary. He clearly didn't like how far Jimmy was leaning off the ladder or the state of the structure itself. He meant both *hurry* and *be careful.*

"Grab onto me and pull while I lift you."

"I can't. I can't let go," she said, her voice shaking. "I know I have to. I feel stupid, but I can't do it."

She was almost frozen in terror. He could see her hand, white-knuckling the railing. He could pry her hand loose, but that would mean letting go of the hold he had on her. If she couldn't loosen her grip, he didn't think he could get her over. He had to get her to relax, a task that felt as impossible as physically getting her over the rail itself. This had already taken too long. Jimmy tried to relax and keep his voice light.

"You know, I shouldn't be surprised that you're the one up here."

"What?" Emily looked shocked, then narrowed her eyes. He could feel the slightest release in tension from her body.

He grinned. It took effort and everything in him to force a natural smile. "You always were the drama queen. All-the-Attention Emily." This was a nickname he and his sister Natalie had teased Emily with over the years. It wasn't completely untrue, and Emily hated it.

"*James,*" Emily said. Her grip loosened. He felt her body relax just enough.

EMMA ST. CLAIR

"Only my sister calls me James." Before she could react, Jimmy hoisted Emily up.

For a moment she resisted, instinct and fear kicking in. But then she grabbed him tighter. Jimmy dragged her over the rail, hoping the wood didn't cut her on the way. Her feet kicked out, jockeying for a toe-hold to push against the rail.

That's all it took for the rest of the structure to crumble. Jimmy felt the railing disappear as a sickening crash sounded. Screams rang out from the front of the house.

Emily clung to him. The momentum of that final push with her toes almost made Jimmy lose his footing, sending them sliding and tumbling down the ladder, but he grabbed the side. She held him so tightly that he knew she wasn't going anywhere.

"He's got her!" Beau called out and there was a cheer from the other side of the house.

And then Jimmy was able to breathe and focus on Emily. Her face was only inches from his, buried in his chest. Her whole body pressed up against him. He couldn't move. Or didn't want to. He pulled her even closer in a one-armed hug, keeping them steady in place as his other hand gripped the ladder.

"You know, you could have just called me." Jimmy's lips brushed over her ear.

Emily threw back her head and laughed then, a sound that made his chest ache. He had missed that sound. He also ached with the desire to kiss her, right where her jaw met the soft skin of her throat. He swallowed. Every feeling he had been trying to keep at bay for the past three years had come flaring up with even more intensity if that was possible. All the hurt too.

"Thank you for saving me," she said in a breathy voice.

Her gaze locked on his and he felt his whole body wake

from just the look in her eyes. It was not the look you gave your friend's little brother. It held passion and something deeper. Hope stirred from a flicker to a roaring flame in his chest. His heart felt like it was burning in his chest with each moment she held his gaze.

"Anytime," he said. "Every day if you need it."

Emily leaned closer, so close that he felt her breath tease his cheek. Jimmy froze, his eyes on her lips.

She leaned closer still. Closer. Was she going to kiss him? This was a moment he had been hoping for his entire life. Jimmy closed his eyes, lips parting.

Not like this.

Just before her lips reached him, Jimmy turned his head slightly. Her kiss landed on his cheek. They hesitated there for a moment, but he felt her stiffen in surprise.

Jimmy tasted disappointment. And when Emily pulled back, he could see it etched in her face, along with hurt and confusion. She ducked her head, trying to hide it, but it was unmistakable. His heart sank. The last thing he wanted was to push her away.

But he knew that she had just been through something traumatic. It felt a little like kissing someone who had too much to drink—the things Emily felt right now might be because of the circumstance or the heightened emotion in the moment. How would she feel when they were back on the ground, when adrenaline wasn't coursing through her? Plus, there was Amber. He hadn't committed to her, but it felt wrong to kiss his dream girl without telling Amber he didn't want to date her.

"Can we get down now?" Her voice was soft, hard to hear with her chin still tilted down.

"Of course." He gave her arm a gentle squeeze, but she didn't respond or move.

Jimmy's stomach twisted. Had he just killed their chances? He really thought that he saw—just for a moment—the same intense feelings he had for her reflected in her eyes. He wanted it to be real, not a product of the moment or of her reaction to being saved. Hero complex was a real thing, but it wasn't uncommon for people to fall for someone who saved them. He wanted Emily. But he wanted it to be real. Right now, he couldn't be sure of why she was interested in him.

He shouldn't even be thinking about that right now. He needed to focus on the job. It wasn't over until she was on the ground, safe.

Get your head on straight.

"Are you two coming down?" Beau shouted up. "We've got some anxious people down here."

Jimmy went back into job mode. He hated to release Emily, but he did, stepping to the rung just below.

"I've got you," he said. Emily nodded, but still did not look at him. As they began the long climb down, Jimmy wondered if he would still have her when they returned to the ground and to reality.

CHAPTER FIVE

Though Emily hated it when Jimmy pulled away from her, it gave her a little space to recover from her embarrassment. What had she been thinking trying to kiss him? And why hadn't he let her? Emily wanted to kick herself. She had just almost *died*. Her emotions were heightened, tearing her barriers down and allowing her feelings for him to bubble up to the surface, spilling over into an impulsive action.

She couldn't even say that she did it without thinking. Emily had absolutely thought about kissing him. The way his lips would feel against hers as his strong arms surrounded her ... No. Right now she needed to stop thinking about it. Because they were still on a ladder suspended three stories up. Emily shuddered, returning to the present moment, where the wind from the beach made the ladder rock and the splintered remains of the deck were visible below them.

Thank you, God. Thank you that I'm not splattered down there on the concrete. Emily closed her eyes, trying to focus her breathing. Whatever else she felt for Jimmy, she was so glad that he was here. This all felt like some kind of cosmic wake-up call, but she didn't know what she was supposed to wake up from, or what she should do about it.

The rich timbre of his voice cut through her disjointed thoughts. "You ready? I'll be right below you, so you're safe. We'll go at your pace. Just hold onto the handrail and keep your feet steady. Try not to look over the side."

His voice soothed her. He was really good at his job. She felt a surge of pride. Jimmy—her Jimmy—had grown up and was doing good things. Not that she had ever expected otherwise. But to see him in action gave her a ridiculous sense of happiness. It almost smoothed over the other zillion thoughts in her head. Almost.

Jimmy had probably been right to turn away, even if her disappointment threatened to crush her. Even if kissing your rescuer in the heat of the moment was how it always happened in the movies. In real life, things were more complicated. With so much history between them, a kiss would need to have a conversation come first. Maybe a few conversations. If he even wanted to kiss her. Maybe he didn't anymore.

Had he turned away because he didn't want to kiss her? Or because he didn't want to kiss her while they were on a ladder after almost saving her life?

"Emily?" Jimmy had moved a few rungs down while she had not moved. He stared up at her, making her cheeks flush.

"Right. Sorry." A gust of wind made the ladder shudder. Her fingers tightened on the railing. "Do we really have to climb down? They can't just lower it like an elevator while I stand here?"

He chuckled. "Nope. Sorry. The hard part is over. We can take this as slow as you need to. I'm right here."

Emily nodded. He was right there. But where she wanted

him to be was right *here*, with his strong arms around her and her face back into the solid muscles of his chest. He smelled so good and felt like home. Her eyes stung and she blinked back the stupid tears threatening to fall.

She needed to get back down on solid ground and get her head back on straight. Taking a shaky first step, Emily began to move. Heights had never bothered her before, but they did now. Would this be a permanent thing? She ground her teeth at the thought. There were few things Emily hated as much as feeling scared and out of control. She felt both now. Her muscles shook and her heart had not yet returned to normal speed. All she wanted was to ask him to stop moving and to wrap her up in his arms again.

"That's good, Em. Just one at a time and we'll be down before you know it."

His voice coaxed her toward him, bathing her in a security that contradicted her surroundings. Emily couldn't fight the pull. It was more than just the fact that she needed to follow him to get down. She needed to be closer to *him*.

Emily could still feel the slight bite of stubble against her lips when she kissed his cheek. A connection hummed between them. Or she thought it had. Did she imagine it? Could Jimmy still feel the same way after all this time? If anything, seeing him made her realize that she felt more. Her feelings had matured and bloomed into something much stronger than what she felt a few years before. It seemed strange that her feelings could grow, since she hadn't seen him. But they definitely had.

Her legs shook as she stepped from one rung to the next. Jimmy had said not to look down, but the ground was visible beneath the rungs. The whole ladder swayed with every gust of wind. The sound of the deck crashing to the ground played again and again in her ears.

45

"How are you doing?" Blue eyes twinkled up at her and she gripped the rail tighter.

"On a scale of great to smushed-on-the-pavement, I'm in the alive-and-kicking category." Emily gave him a small smile. He grinned up at her and her stomach flipped. Emotion choked her throat. She had missed that smile. Slightly crooked, with a hint of mischief behind it.

"I think you're doing amazingly well, all things considered," he said.

"Do you have a good basis for comparison? Have you rescued a lot of girls from balcony collapses?"

"This is my first. And hopefully last."

"So far, I haven't died. I'd give this rescue a five-star rating."

"You'll leave a review on Yelp, right?"

"We'll see if that rating holds. I'm still not down."

Jimmy laughed. Emily warmed at the sound, not wanting it to end. She could hear the voices better from down below and glanced over to see her friends standing near the road with a few guys in uniform. Her shaking legs wanted solid ground, but the rest of her didn't want this time with Jimmy to end.

"You're halfway now. I knew you'd get through this. You always were the strongest girl I knew."

Emily focused on the rung below. She couldn't look at him. Not when it felt like her emotions were spilling over onto her face. She was already in such a vulnerable position. Letting Jimmy glimpse the depth of her emotions would be too much. She needed a wall between them. A wall and a moat and maybe a ring of fire to keep him back.

As her feet touched down on the truck, she felt an intense relief that was beyond words. She understood what people meant when they said they wanted to kiss the ground.

Instead, she planted her feet on the top of the truck and took a deep, shuddery breath.

Jimmy stood before her, eyes tracing over her features as though looking for wounds that needed to be healed. He put a hand on her shoulder, like he wanted to pull her into a hug, but he didn't. Everything in her ached to hug him, but she didn't.

He was still Jimmy, but he was more grown up. Not a boy, but an achingly handsome man. He looked finished some-how, with his square jaw and muscular shoulders. He was solid, exuding a trustworthy strength. He always had, but there was now a confidence to him, a sense that he had grown into himself. Emily realized her heart was racing as she stared at him and her face flushed. His hand dropped away from her shoulder and she immediately missed the contact of his skin on hers. She wanted to throw her arms around him and press her face into his neck, but it felt like a yawning distance now stood between them. Was it because of their past? Was he trying to be professional? Or was it something else?

"Can I give you a hand?" Beau called up from the ground.

Emily moved to the steps that led down the back. Jimmy pressed a hand to the small of her back to steady her. But it had the opposite effect as the skin of his palm met the bare skin of her back. She still wore only her bathing suit. Emily suddenly felt exposed and self-conscious. Jimmy must have felt her stiffen, because his hand disappeared. She wanted to tell him that it wasn't because of his touch, but Beau was right there so she didn't say anything.

"Glad you're okay, Emily." Beau smiled warmly as she climbed down.

Emily crossed her arms over her chest. "I thought I said I didn't want to see you again."

47

Beau smiled. "At least our second meeting ended happily, right?"

"Very. I'm never leaving the ground again."

Jimmy climbed down behind her and stood a few feet away. She'd never known him to be shy, but he suddenly was. All the bravado and intimacy and joking on the ladder was gone. The shock of it hit her like a cold wave.

"Why don't you hop up on the bumper so we can check you out," Beau's voice was slow and kind. Both he and Jimmy were so good at their jobs. Emily was glad Jimmy had found a place where he belonged. She felt suddenly jealous. Her emotions were all over the place. Tomorrow she was going to wake up with an emotional hangover.

Jimmy reappeared with a canvas medical bag. He had taken off his bulky jacket. Underneath, he wore a tight navy T-shirt that showed off his broad chest.

Beau patted Jimmy on the arm and stepped back. "Jimmy's going to take a minute to check your blood pressure, vitals. Just to be sure you're okay, officially speaking. Then I know your friends want to see you."

Emily sank down and for the first time, realized how exhausted her entire body was from the mental and physical stress of what she had been through. Her knees shook. Jimmy put a hand on her arm. His touch had her body vibrating even more.

"I'm going to take your blood pressure now, okay?"

Emily nodded and he wrapped the cuff around her arm. She was able to watch his face because he wouldn't look at her now. His eyes were fixed on the white face of the dial as he inflated the cuff. Every brush of his fingers made her skin light up. She bit her lip and flinched slightly back.

"You're shaking. Are you cold?"

"I don't know what I am. I think I'm just ... overwhelmed."

"I can get my jacket if you'd like."

"That's okay."

"You sure?"

Emily thought about being surrounded by the scent of Jimmy. "Yeah, okay. Sure."

She barely caught his grin as he darted back to the open door of the truck and returned with his heavy jacket. When he draped it over her shoulders, his fingertips grazed her collarbone and she shivered again. Having the weight of the jacket and his smell surrounding her was almost as good as being in his arms. Okay, no—not even close. But as good as she could get apart from Jimmy holding her.

He used a pen light to look in her eyes and her throat. Emily wondered if all this was necessary, but she didn't care. There were so many things she wanted to say and ask, but she was having trouble with her words.

"You're awfully quiet." He smirked. "For you."

Was he flirting? Emily cocked her head to the side and gave a little grin. "Maybe I've changed in the past few years."

The words were out before she fully realized the weight of them. Emily wished she could suck them right back into her body. Bringing up the time that had passed meant reminding them both of *why* so much time had passed and the way Emily had treated him that last night.

Jimmy made a humming sound as he rummaged through the medical bag. Emily closed her eyes. She managed to screw things up quickly.

"Jimmy, I didn't mean—"

"It's fine. I'm going to listen to your heart and breathing now."

Emily snapped her mouth shut. The stethoscope was cold

against her chest and she again felt self-conscious of how little she wore underneath the jacket. Her legs were still bare. She caught him looking down at them and then he jerked his gaze away.

Every nerve in her body was firing. The silence between them felt like a living thing. A hard, painful thing. It was all her fault. Back then and now. One careless phrase and she had shoved him away. This time, though, she didn't want him to run. She wanted to pull him close, but she was afraid.

Summoning her courage, Emily grabbed Jimmy's hand. He met her eyes, finally, his gaze holding a depth of emotion that almost made her breathless. Just the feel of his hand in hers made her skin flame.

"Hey," she said, in a low voice. "Thank you. You saved me from splattering to a bloody pulp all over the concrete. Also? It's really good to see you again, Jimmy. I didn't realize how much I've missed you. I'm sorry for bringing up the past. Maybe ... maybe we should catch up on the past few years?"

Without knowing she was going to do it, she brushed her lips against his fingertips in a soft kiss. Jimmy pulled his hand away. Emily had to look down at the ground so he wouldn't see the tears that filled her eyes. Rejection was a familiar friend. But the pain of this was so much more than anything she had felt before.

"Your vitals look fine. I think you're going to make it." Jimmy took the medical bag back to the truck as hurt coursed through her.

Kim and the other women rushed her as soon as Jimmy gave Beau the okay. No one questioned the fact that tears ran down her face. It was expected for the trauma she just went through. Only, the trauma of the balcony collapse didn't even compare to the wracking pain assaulting her heart.

"I'm so glad you're okay," Kim said, sobbing. "This is all my fault."

Emily patted Kim's back. "That's just bad logic. You're getting married and we all came down to celebrate you. Maybe we had too many people in the hot tub. That's not on you. I'm fine. And what if it had happened when we were all in there? We got lucky."

"But now we don't have a beach house," Stacy said. "Do we have to go home?"

Voices raised around her, but Emily wasn't listening. She tracked Jimmy with her gaze as he moved away, talking to Beau and another man, not in uniform. Two cops also had joined the conversation, one white-haired and another who looked like their age with dark hair and a close-cropped beard. Jimmy glanced back at her but turned away when he saw that she was looking at him.

He can't even look at me.

Emily shrugged off Jimmy's coat and let it fall to the truck behind her. She whispered to Kim, "Can you get me a T-shirt or towel or blanket? A mumu? A ski parka? Anything, really."

Kim hugged her again and then disappeared up the stairs.

One of the other firemen moved closer to Stacy. She was also still in her red bikini. He didn't hide the fact that he was eyeing her body. Gross. "You definitely can't stay here," he said. "But if you need a place ..."

Beau stepped closer with the only man who wasn't in uniform and looked miserable. Jimmy stood some distance away, his jaw tight. Looking at him, her hurt joined forces with anger. He seemed fine one minute and then flipped a switch the next. Three years had passed. Was he really not mature enough to move on, even a little?

Emily's feelings were too volatile. They were volcanic.

She needed to get some rest and sort out how she felt in the morning before she said or did something truly awful that she couldn't take back.

"Ladies," Beau said. "I'm so glad we have a happy ending to this night. But the thing is this—we can't let you stay here. Not with the doors from the house leading to a direct drop to the ground. This place will be condemned until further notice."

"Where are we supposed to go?" Stacy whined. "We have a full week at the beach planned."

Kim returned with an oversized T-shirt that Emily gratefully threw over her suit. "We can't stay here? Where are we supposed to go? We paid for a full week! This is my bachelorette party!" She looked close to tears again and Emily tried hard not to roll her eyes. She almost died. Where they would stay just didn't seem like that big of a deal. Maybe she should go home.

"Definitely not. But we've got a great option for you. This is Jackson," Beau said, pushing the other man forward. "He owns this property. But before you start sharpening the pitchforks, this is a new rental property and it seems the inspector clearly didn't fulfill his duties. We will definitely be following up about that. But for now, he's got a potential solution."

Jackson cleared his throat. "I have a home a few miles up. Right on the beach. A bit bigger than this one. I'd like to offer you my home for the rest of the week. And I'll of course refund your payment. I feel terrible about this and plan to make sure the inspector is held accountable. I'm just so glad you're okay."

Kim squealed and hugged Jackson. He looked distinctly uncomfortable until she pulled away. "Thank you!" She hugged Beau now. Emily looked down at her feet so she wouldn't have to watch her hug Jimmy.

"There's plenty of room, but there is a small issue," Beau said. "You'll have roommates. Me, Jackson, and Jimmy. We'll be at the station a lot, so we won't be around that often."

Sharing a house with Jimmy ... Emily's stomach dropped even as her heart sped up. Would he even want her there? She gave him a sideways glance and he still leaned up against the truck, arms crossed and shoulders stiff. It could be really awkward.

Or maybe it would give her a chance to regain his trust. His friendship.

Or more ... a tiny voice whispered in her head. She tried to ignore it. With the way he was acting right now, she'd be lucky to get casual friendship from Jimmy. Hoping for more was ridiculous.

There was a moment of silence and then squeals from the girls.

"Are you sure you have room for us?" Emily asked.

"It's a big house," Jackson said. "We can bunk together in the master and give you girls the rest of the house. My daughter has a room there, but she's only here on some weekends until summer. There are four total bedrooms you can share. It should be plenty of space."

"We just moved in temporarily," Beau said. "Our rooms are pretty empty anyway. And clean. Jimmy and I only stay there the nights we aren't working, so you won't see us every day."

"That's really generous," Kim said.

"It's the least I can do," Jackson said. He met Emily's eyes with a tortured expression. "I am so sorry that happened to you. I'm really glad you're okay."

Emily nodded. "It's not your fault. Thank you." He seemed a little relieved.

"As long as we don't have a call, we can help you guys carry things over to Jackson's house. Why don't you start getting things packed up."

Most of the girls disappeared up the stairs. Emily felt frozen on the back of the truck in the too-big T-shirt. Her mind was still spinning, her emotions a volatile cocktail. An ache started in her head, just behind her eyes. Jimmy had disappeared somewhere. Probably anywhere he didn't have to see her. Stacy and Kim were the only two women left down there. Kim seemed to be waiting for Emily, while Stacy hadn't moved more than a foot from the fireman who had been drooling over her.

Stacy smiled up at him. "When do you guys get off work? Or when does your shift end?"

"We're off around eight a.m. tomorrow for twenty-four hours," he said.

"Let us treat you to dinner and drinks tomorrow," Kim said, looking between Beau and the other guy. "Please? It's the least we can do?"

Jimmy walked back around the front of the truck, but stopped a good distance away when he saw Emily. She cleared her throat. "We were supposed to do your bachelorette thingy tomorrow night, weren't we?"

"What better way to spend a bachelorette party than with a bunch of hot firemen?" Stacy said.

"I don't mind," Kim said. "It will be fun and we owe you a big thanks. Please say you'll come? We're going somewhere called Mo's."

Beau looked at Jimmy. "We'd be happy to join you. Tomorrow night it is."

Jimmy's jaw clenched as he looked at Beau. He began

putting gear back on the truck. One of the other guys lowered the ladder and another wrapped caution tape around the building. Emily could still see the tension in Jimmy's shoulders even as he turned away. Things had felt so good between them for a few minutes, so normal. One comment about the past and he was shutting her out. And now they were going to be sharing a living space. This was going to be a long week.

CHAPTER SIX

Within an hour, the girls had moved all their bags and groceries to Jackson's house. The firefighters helped them load up and then headed back to the station. Jimmy mostly ignored Emily as he carried bags to their cars. She didn't know how to be around him now and it was killing her.

Should she ignore him right back? Pull him aside and apologize? Confront him angrily? Ask him to talk later? A big part of her felt scared to even try. Hudson's rejection was fresh on her mind. If Jimmy rejected her, she would be devastated. Beyond devastated. Maybe it would be better not to try. When he and the other guys left, he hadn't even waved goodbye.

Sarah leaned forward between Emily and Kim to get a better look through the windshield as they pulled up to Jackson's house. "*That*'s where we're staying? This is quite the upgrade!"

"Oh my goodness," Kim said.

Oh my goodness was right. This was less of a beach

house and more of a beach mansion. Jackson's house was three full stories on top of stilts with parking underneath. The outside was gray and weathered and looked like the classic beach house. He met them at the bottom of the stairs, waving them into parking spaces underneath and in front of the house. It was enormous and beautiful, right on the water with a public beach access and parking next door. Much of the house was glass—picture windows and sliding doors out onto balconies that Emily definitely wouldn't be setting foot on.

Jackson stood in the driveway and smiled. Now that they were away from the wreckage of the other balcony, he seemed calmer and more friendly. He was probably terrified of getting sued. "I can help you ladies with your bags. There's an elevator on the bottom floor to make things easier. Just don't open the door while it's moving. I know that sounds obvious, but it's happened before."

"Not to be a diva," Emily said. "But can I call dibs on a room on the lowest floor?"

Jackson chuckled and grabbed her suitcase. "I think you've earned the right to call dibs. The top floor has the kitchen and the master, where the guys and I will sleep. The other two floors have four bedrooms and plenty of beds. There's also a couch on the bottom floor common area."

Emily followed Jackson up the stairs to the front door. He was probably about ten years older than she was, still youthful, but with deeper smile lines around his eyes. He seemed close with Beau and Jimmy and they were temporarily living here. She wondered how well they knew each other. Despite the fact that Jimmy was currently shutting her out, she had so much curiosity about his life. "This is a really great house. Thank you for taking us in."

"It's the least I can do. I can't tell you how sorry I am."

He set her bag down outside the first bedroom door. "This is one floor up still, but as low as you get. These oceanfront homes are almost all on stilts. Just because of the potential storm surge."

"Elle and I will take the other room," Sarah said, shoving by them with her luggage. The room Sarah picked faced the ocean, but Emily didn't feel like fighting for a view.

"That's fine," Jackson said. "It's my daughter Megan's room, but she hasn't fully moved in so it's pretty empty. She is particular about her things, so try not to mess with any of the things that are in there. And that means you'll get this room if you want to be on this floor." Emily nodded and Jackson opened the door. "This is Jimmy's room, so he'll probably want to grab a few things when he gets off shift. If you guys are old friends, I'm sure you won't mind."

Jimmy's room. She would be staying in his room. In his bed. Emily pressed a hand to her stomach to calm the riotous butterflies. Then her eyes flicked to Jackson. "Wait—did he tell you about me? You know that we knew each other?"

Emily hadn't mentioned to the other women that she knew Jimmy yet. She would ... but she hadn't been in a good mental state earlier. The last thing she wanted was to answer questions about him or their past. She had no answers right now and wouldn't be able to talk about him without crying or saying something she would later regret.

Jackson ran a hand over his jaw. "Beau told me when I got there tonight who you were." Emily got the sense that there was more, but that's all he said before backing toward the door. "I'm going to go help with the groceries. Make yourself at home."

As the other women filed into the house with their bags, Emily walked into Jimmy's room and closed the door behind her. She'd probably end up sharing, but needed a moment to decompress. And, if she was being honest, to snoop. Just a little bit. She was surprised at how sparse the room was, even though Beau had told her that it was temporary.

"Our lease ran out and Jackson said we could stay while we find a new place," Beau had told her while he helped them pack up the other house. "He's getting married soon and his daughter is moving in over the summer. For now, though, it's high living with low rent. Most of our stuff is in storage."

The closet had a few boxes in it and there were a few clothes in the dresser. Emily remembered Jimmy's room as a kid. He had baseball posters, trophies, and clothing strewn all over the floor. The only personal thing here was a framed photo of Beau, Jimmy, and Jackson on his dresser. All three had aviator sunglasses on and were smiling on the beach. It could have been a photo from a calendar with all the ripped abs.

Emily had seen her fair share of six-packs in the modeling world, but these guys were something else. Especially Jimmy. He was so much broader than he had been back in high school, though he looked good back then too. She smiled, thinking of how he liked to take his shirt off when she was around, trying to impress her. It did impress her, though she never would have told him back then. Now he looked more powerful, with massive shoulders and more than an eight-pack. She tried not to let her eyes linger on the line of his Adonis belt. Dang. He had been a cute boy, and had grown up into a handsome man.

It was his smile that got her the most though. Emily traced a fingertip over it. That grin had always washed over her like a happy drug, lifting her spirits when she was having trouble with her parents. Even when she had guy trouble. Jimmy had hated it when she talked to him about her boyfriends, but he would listen anyway. Sometimes she'd catch a muscle ticking in his jaw or see his hands clench into fists. Rather than using names, he would call them all Jerk.

"Still with the Jerk?" he would ask.

"Nah, I broke up with the Jerk," Emily would answer.

"Good riddance. That Jerk was a real jerk," he'd say.

Emily hadn't thought about that in years. Her eyes stung with tears. They pooled there, but she held them back. What would it take to get back to that place with Jimmy? Could they go back? Maybe she couldn't fix their past, but it had been a few years and they had both changed. Would it be possible to start over?

The one question that had haunted her for years settled into her mind, right alongside her headache. What would have happened if Natalie hadn't told her to leave Jimmy alone?

Emily could picture an alternate universe briefly, one in which Jimmy finished telling her how he felt, right there on the dance floor. In that world, she would have been brave enough to tell him that she had feelings for him too. They would have kissed under the lights, with the band playing soft music nearby, music they wouldn't even hear because they were so caught up in each other. They would have broken all the rules and still ended up okay.

Even imagining it made her whole body warm. Emily ached with longing for a reality where she and Jimmy would have gotten together. She wouldn't have gone back to New York and come home more broken than before. She wouldn't be living with her parents, trying to stave off depression and a desperation to be loved. And Jimmy wouldn't be living here, with a whole life he'd built four hours away. A life he likely didn't want her to have any part of, based on his actions tonight.

Emily turned the picture frame around on the dresser. Too bad her alternate universe wasn't reality. The reality was that she found Jimmy and then lost him all over again. Tonight, for a few brief moments on the ladder, it seemed like they had returned to what they had. He joked with her, smiled the way she remembered and loved.

Then she had almost kissed him. The memory made her wince and close her eyes. What had she been thinking? But she hadn't been thinking. The emotions of the moment combined with all the emotions she had been trying to ignore the past three years had erupted into a moment of stupidity. She didn't blame him for turning his cheek. Though it felt like more of a rejection than any of her breakups.

Whether because of the almost-kiss or something else, by the time they reached the ground, things had shifted between them. Maybe he just did what he needed to. He knew her well enough to calm her with jokes and teasing. Once she was safe, he closed himself back off.

She couldn't look at his crooked smile without loss choking her. Emily felt gutted as she stepped away from the photo and the deep sense of loss.

A Bible, book, and journal sat next to the bed. Emily rested a hand on the leather-bound journal. It was scuffed and worn, soft under her fingertips. She ran a finger along the edge of the book. As far as she knew, he'd never kept a journal. Or he hadn't back then. Emily was nosy. Curious was a better word. It was so tempting to get a direct line into Jimmy's thoughts. But there were some lines she wouldn't cross. Reading his private thoughts was one of them. Even if it was tempting to think about.

"Snoop much?"

Emily startled and jerked her hand away from the journal.

Stacy stood in the doorway. Emily moved away from the bedside table as Stacy wheeled her suitcase in.

Emily wanted to groan. If Stacy was choosing to share a room, it was solely to torture her. "Just looking around."

"Sure. No judgment here." Stacy stopped at the dresser and turned over the photo. "Yowza. These guys are smoking. Even Jackson. Though he is a little old."

"He's engaged," Emily snapped.

Stacy shrugged. "That's fine. Plenty of other guys for me. Too bad you're with Hudson, huh?"

"Yeah, too bad." Now wasn't the time to have a conversation about her breakup. Stacy was the last person she would talk to anyway. Emily wanted to yank the photo out of her hands and smack her with it. Deep breaths. Deep breaths. "Why are you in here?"

Stacy smiled. "All the other rooms are full. Lucky you! We'll be bunkmates. Don't mind me, though—you can keep looking through his things. I can't blame you."

Emily felt rage bubbling up inside of her. "I wasn't—whatever. I'm going to check out the rest of the house."

She needed to calm down. Stacy just loved getting under her skin. The best response was no response. Or just escape.

Outside the two bedrooms on this floor there was a small sitting room with a couch and two chairs. Maybe Emily would just sleep there. But then the thought of Stacy sleeping on Jimmy's sheets made her stomach lurch. Nope. Definitely not leaving her alone in there.

The next floor up had more bedrooms, but no common area. Emily followed voices to the top floor of the house. It was a large open room with a kitchen, dining area, and sitting area. A closed door near the kitchen must have led to the master where the guys would be staying with Jackson. Kim and Sarah were unpacking their coolers, moving drinks and food they had bought into Jackson's mostly-empty fridge.

"Can I help?" Emily asked.

Kim smiled. "Isn't this place amazing? I'm going to run back down and make sure we got everything out of the cars. You and Sarah can finish up all the food. Jackson's fridge is totally empty. Single guys clearly don't understand how to eat."

"If I didn't feed Mitch, he'd starve," Sarah said, rolling her eyes.

Emily held back a comment about grown men. She began pulling lettuce and deli meat and other things from the cooler. Megs, Elle, and Leah were out on the balcony. The glass doors were open and the sound of the ocean came in. The sight of the girls leaning on the railing made Emily feel almost physically ill. She honestly didn't know if she could ever set foot on a balcony again.

Jackson came up to the top of the stairs with Stacy and Kim, all three carrying boxes and bags for the kitchen.

"Ladies, let's keep this party going, shall we?" Stacy said. "The night is young!"

Emily glanced at the clock on the microwave. It was after eleven. She wondered what time Jackson went to sleep. Emily met his eyes. He looked like he already regretted the decision to let them stay here. The master bedroom was up on the top floor just off the kitchen and living room, which would be the loudest area in the house.

"I hope you have a sound machine or something," Emily muttered to him.

He smiled. "Probably going to need one, huh?"

"One? You'd be better off with two."

Jackson chuckled. "I'll take that under consideration."

"Let's finish watching the movie!" Kim said. "We barely started."

"I'll make popcorn!" Megs said.

"Need me to help you with the TV?" Jackson asked.

Emily waved him off. "We'll figure it out. Thanks again, Jackson."

He nodded and headed into the back bedroom. "Goodnight, ladies! Make yourselves at home. If you need anything, just let me know." He closed the door behind him.

Emily watched the other women settle into the sofa for a movie. The emotional weight of the day hit her—the dread of coming, the balcony collapse, the joy at seeing Jimmy to the confusion as he pulled away. She just couldn't sit on a couch right now, staring at a screen.

No one noticed Emily slip downstairs to Jimmy's bedroom. Stacy's things were still neatly in her bag, though her makeup was strewn all over the counter in the Jack-and-Jill bathroom connecting the two first-floor bedrooms. There was a stick of men's deodorant next to the mirror, which Emily held up to her nose. It didn't smell like Jimmy. Maybe Beau?

But when she slipped into Jimmy's bed, taking the side where his journal and Bible sat just a foot away, his scent rose up to greet her. Emily fell asleep with her face pressed into Jimmy's pillow, tears dampening her cheeks.

CHAPTER SEVEN

J immy had hoped the rest of their shift would have some action, though it was doubtful. They'd already had two calls—the grill fire and the balcony collapse —which was a lot for the off-season. It was past midnight by the time Beau filed the report and they had cleaned and put their gear away again. That gave them a bit of time to sleep, but Jimmy tossed and turned in the bunk room. The adrenaline was still coursing through him, leaving him too wide awake to even attempt sleep.

He finally got up and went back out to the common area, putting the TV on but not watching. The baseball game that he'd watched earlier—had that really been the same night?? —was over. He couldn't even remember who had been playing. Maybe he should hit the gym. He'd already done a workout earlier in the day, but another might help exhaust the muscles still twitching. Not even that would calm his racing thoughts, though.

"Can't sleep?" Beau walked into the common room.

"I can't seem to come down," Jimmy said. "The adrenaline is still going."

Beau sat on the other end of the couch. "It was an intense day. That rescue would have been a lot had it been a normal person, not Emily. I wouldn't be sleeping either. Want to talk about it? I'm happy to debrief. Professionally or personally."

Jimmy sat for a few minutes. He did want to talk. And he didn't. It took him a few minutes to form words and decide to say them. "I think I messed up."

"How so?"

"It was unreal to see her again. I mean, even in that moment, which was terrifying, she was just Emily. We were like we used to be. And then ... I think she was going to kiss me."

Beau's eyes got bigger and he grinned. "That sounds promising."

Jimmy shook his head. "I freaked out. I turned my head. She kissed my cheek."

"That's not so bad. I mean, you are dating Amber."

"That's not even why. I mean, Amber and I aren't committed. I wouldn't say we're dating."

"Does Amber know that?"

Running a hand through his hair, Jimmy closed his eyes. "We probably need to have a conversation. I've been trying to let her down easy."

"By avoiding her?"

"Basically. Real mature, huh?"

"Those conversations are never easy. Okay, so how did you mess up? So far this doesn't sound bad."

"I was feeling good. I mean, I wanted to kiss her so bad. I've dreamed about that for years, but that just didn't seem like the right moment. I don't regret it, but I do. Anyway, then we were just talking. I joked around with her to help calm her down."

"You did a great job. I don't think anyone else could have done what you did and gotten her off the balcony before it fell."

Jimmy swallowed. The seriousness of the situation hadn't been lost on him. "Thank you. I don't know what I would have done—"

"Don't think about it. You did it. She's safe."

"Yeah. You're right. So, we're coming down the ladder and things are fine. She made a comment about the past and how things have changed and ... I don't know. I couldn't just talk to her normally anymore. All I could think about was her rejecting me. All the hurt and anger just came rushing back." Jimmy paused, waiting for the knot of emotion in his throat to ease. When he spoke again, it was hardly more than a whisper. "I don't know how I can stand to see her again. I wish she'd never come here."

Beau seemed to know just how much time to give Jimmy before he spoke again. His tone was even and soothing. "Look, you saw the woman you have loved for years in a life-threatening situation. You had the responsibility of getting her down—which you did quite excellently, by the way—and that's a lot. To say that situation was emotionally charged isn't doing it justice. It's normal that you're going through a whole range of emotions."

Jimmy had thought so much about Emily the past few years. He had imagined running into her somewhere. But in his daydreams, everything was simple and easy. He would sweep her off her feet. She'd forget all the reasons she thought they wouldn't work together. They'd put the night of Natalie's wedding so far in the rearview mirror that it wouldn't even be a thing.

Tonight would almost fit the first part of his daydreams—he swept in and literally saved Emily's life. Though it felt nothing like he would have hoped. He had been completely terrified and shaken seeing her up on that balcony. He still felt the tension lodged in his chest, remembering. He knew she was safe now, but even thinking about her up on the remains of the balcony made his stomach clench.

And what about that almost-kiss? He knew that he just panicked in the moment, but he didn't want to take advantage of Emily in any way. Maybe he was seeking a perfect moment, when perfection didn't exist. Now that the moment had passed, it still felt like the right decision. Yet he longed to crush Emily to him and release the passion that had been simmering inside him for over a decade.

A *decade*.

He had held on too long. This was just a childish dream. Though everything in him felt drawn to Emily, maybe it was time to let go. To finally say the goodbye he thought he already said.

"I think ... I think I need to just let her go." The words tasted wrong in his mouth. Jimmy tried to muster up an inner strength. He could do this. He *should* do this. It was time to move on.

Beau touched his arm. "Hey. I can't tell you for sure what to do. But I think making any decision after a night like tonight is a bad idea. She's here for a week. Sleep on it. Pray about it. See what unfolds."

"It hurts too much," Jimmy ground out, his voice raw. "I don't know how I can be her friend. I don't know if I could be more, but I don't think I can do less. I've only always loved her. I thought maybe I was doing okay. Getting over her. Moving on. Now I feel like ... I'm back where I started.

But worse. So much worse. I'm angry with her. And with myself. I'm just angry."

"Let's get you to bed. I really think a little sleep after this day would do you good. Right now, you're emotionally vulnerable. It's understandable."

"Maybe I'll stay here at the station for the week. I don't know that I can be around her right now."

"That's not going to happen." Beau stood and pulled Jimmy's arm. "Come on. At least try to sleep. See how you feel in the light of morning. Fresh start tomorrow. We'll revisit this conversation. Okay?"

Jimmy let Beau pull him up and followed him numbly out of the common room. "I could go stay with Cash."

"Not gonna happen. You can't keep running, man. Worst case, nothing happens. She leaves Sandover in a few days. You go back to life as usual, but maybe less hung up on this one woman. Or maybe this is your second chance. Be vulnerable. Be open. You'll never know if you decide beforehand what you think will happen."

"I don't want to be open. I don't think I can be. Too risky."

Beau pulled him to a stop outside the bunk room. Robbie's snores came through the door. He dropped his voice to a whisper. "Three years later after you last saw Emily and you still feel this strongly. You clearly need some resolution. Not to be a walking cliché, but pray about it. This is that kind of love that's either going to wreck you or the kind that's meant to last."

"It already wrecked me. I don't know that I can take any more." Jimmy turned away from Beau and pressed his forehead to the wall. It was cool against his skin, but did nothing to calm the fiery emotions raging in him.

Beau put a light hand on his back. "You know it's a myth that God won't give you more than you can handle, right? People say that, but the truth is he gives us more than we can handle so that we'll turn to him. You can't carry this. But do you think it's a coincidence that your Emily ended up on that balcony tonight and that you were on call? That you are our ladder guy sent up there to rescue her? God is giving you more than you can handle. Trust him. Don't be rash. Ask for his help and see what he has for you, Jimmy. You know his plans are better than ours."

Jimmy balled his hands into fists. "Don't tell me God planned this. That feels like a cruel joke."

"I don't know God's plans for your future. But I know that the girl you love is sleeping in your house for the next six days. I do believe he planned this. This is a gift." He patted Jimmy's back and then stepped away. "I'm going to bed. This isn't like you, all this doom and gloom. I think you need to get out of your own head, man. Let go of the past. See what future God will write for you."

"Thanks for the pep talk." Jimmy knew that Beau was right. About all of it, really. But he didn't feel ready to accept that yet.

Beau sighed. "Get some sleep. You need it. See how things look in the light of morning."

Jimmy didn't turn and heard the door to the bunk room close as Beau went to bed. He turned and leaned his back against the wall. Closing his eyes, he pressed the heels of his hands over his eyelids until he saw stars. He could hear how his words had sounded: bitter, ungrateful, stubborn.

This was a gift. It didn't feel that way, but he knew that it was. Maybe the gift would be getting the girl in the end, though Jimmy hardly dared to hope. Maybe the gift was finally and completely letting go of Emily to move on. It was all or nothing. He didn't think just friendship could be on the table. Not with the turmoil in his head and his heart.

As much as he hated to admit it, if Emily would have him, he would be down on one knee tomorrow. He would give her forever and chase her down rather than running away like he had three years ago.

But Jimmy didn't want to be that guy—desperate for a woman who didn't love him back. It made him feel weak and foolish, young and stupid. Beau was right about waiting until the morning, but Jimmy didn't want to wait. What he wanted was to force himself to move on. He had to cut off these feelings before they killed him. Before Emily broke his heart for a second time. He needed to get over her once and for all. He just needed to figure out how.

Jimmy knew he should go to bed, but instead went back to the common room, letting the TV color his fitful sleep with sitcom laugh tracks and the false promises of infomercials.

CHAPTER EIGHT

Beau had been wrong. Waking up after a night's worth of sleep didn't clear Jimmy's head. Maybe part of the problem was that he hardly slept, tossing and turning on the couch with the TV on. But still. Jimmy felt just as conflicted and upset as they drove back to Jackson's beach house the next morning.

As he had hoped, the house was quiet. Trashed but quiet, littered with red cups and open bags of chips. A few pieces of clothing and towels were scattered around on the backs of furniture. "I thought girls were supposed to be neat. This looks worse than it does with the three of us bachelors."

Beau shrugged. "You know my sister. She's a huge mess and I'm the neat one. Guess you just don't ever know."

"This is going to make Jackson all twitchy."

Beau chuckled. "I'm sure he's just glad not to be sued. That could have been a really big mess last night at his rental house. I want to follow up with him today and see about who inspected the place. If someone isn't doing their job, it needs to be addressed. Are you going to hang out with Emily and the group today?"

"I'm going to take a nap," Jimmy said.

Beau gave him a pointed look. "Just don't hide out all day. And remember I'm here if you want to talk."

Jimmy didn't answer. He spent the rest of the morning away on an air mattress in the master bedroom. Some sleeping and some tossing and turning, trying to tamp down his emotions. When he woke up after a fitful sleep, it was after lunch and the house was quiet. Jackson must have still been at work and the rest of the house seemed empty. Looking through the glass doors of the balcony, Jimmy could see a big group on the beach in front of the house. It looked like Beau, Robbie, and Whit were out there as well. Jimmy didn't look too hard, not wanting to pick Emily out of the crowd. He knew he would have to see her later, when they all went out to dinner, but he wanted to put it off as long as possible.

His stomach turned, thinking about Emily and about his conversation with Beau the night before. He had to face this —whatever this was and whatever it would become. Knowing that Emily—*his* Emily—was here and would be sleeping under the same roof was almost too much. What if she was staying in his room? The thought sent his heart racing.

He needed to shower and wanted to pick up a few things from downstairs before the girls came back from the beach. Jimmy had already stepped inside his room and flipped on the light when he saw movement in the bed. A woman sat up, brushing her dark hair out of her eyes and blinking sleepily. A thin tank top covered her, one strap falling down her shoulder.

Jimmy started to back away, kicking his laundry basket on

the way. "Oh—sorry. I thought everyone was on the beach and I just needed a few things from my room."

"Don't go." The woman jumped up and grabbed his arm. Jimmy froze. "It's okay. I was just taking a nap. I'm Stacy. I guess this is your room?"

She blinked up at him through her lashes. Rather than looking demure, it seemed like a calculated and practiced look. Only then did he realize that she only had on underwear below her tank top. He could feel his face turning red.

"Oh sorry." She giggled and let go of his arm to pull down the hem of her tank top. "Don't worry. It's more than what you'd see on the beach."

But it wasn't the beach; it was his bedroom. And nothing about this felt accidental. Jimmy practically ran out of the room as soon as she had dropped his arm. "I'll come back later for my stuff. Sorry again."

As he ran back up the stairs, Jimmy thought he heard Stacy call, "Come back anytime!"

Jimmy hid out upstairs in Jackson's for most of the day. He hadn't wanted to venture back down to his bedroom after the encounter with Stacy, so he borrowed a few things from Jackson's closet. They were roughly the same size, though Jackson's T-shirts stretched tightly over Jimmy's chest. In the past, this might have been an intentional move. But tonight, he just didn't want to chance running into another half-naked woman.

From the start of the evening at Mo's with Emily and her friends, Jimmy was itching to leave. He'd tried telling Beau beforehand that he was too tired, but Beau just leveled a gaze at him. He wasn't going to let Jimmy get out of this. Or out of dealing head-on with the Emily problem. Jimmy definitely wasn't ready to deal with it, so he would keep avoiding until something made him face it. If he still didn't know how he felt, he couldn't know what to say to Emily. But he was completely aware of her presence across the table and just to his left.

Mo's was a noisy American restaurant with a full dinner menu and a dance floor. Waiters had to pull a few tables together to fit their big group. The place was packed with On Islanders and some tourists who were getting an early start on the season. A few couples were already moving to pop and country music on the dance floor.

Jimmy didn't want to look at Emily. But of course, every time he did, she was looking at him and just as quickly, looked away. Clearly, he wasn't the only one struggling with whatever this was. Or … maybe it was something else. She seemed a little off. They hadn't talked in three years, so it could be what happened the night before or anything. Her Instagram feed didn't tell the full story and Natalie hadn't supplied him any information. Maybe she was struggling with something else. The thought started to soften the anger and hurt.

Looking at her also wore down the hard shell he was trying to put over his heart. Not because she was so beautiful —though she was—but because when he looked at Emily, he remembered. Not just remembered, but he *felt* the past wash over him with the intensity of a wave. It woke the emotions that had been sleeping, the ones he thought he had left behind. When he met Emily's gaze, Jimmy felt home. Longing. Love.

Nausea clawed at his stomach. He didn't want to feel those things. He wanted to close himself back off and pretend like he could make it work with someone like Amber.

Though just thinking about Amber and their three dates felt like an unfair comparison. He had never felt like this for anyone but Emily. He couldn't wish away the feelings, but for tonight, he could ignore them. Jimmy focused on eating and drinking and didn't talk unless someone asked him a direct question. Which, of course, kept happening.

"So, Jimmy, was Emily your first balcony rescue?" One of the girls—he thought her name was Elle—smiled at him.

His eyes flicked to Emily's. "She was. Hopefully my last."

"We were so scared," Kim said. Jimmy knew her name because he remembered that it was her bachelorette weekend. "We were so lucky. Emily was so lucky."

"Hmm." Jimmy made an agreeable sound but turned back to his hamburger, though he wasn't remotely hungry.

"I don't think it was luck," Beau said. "I mean, what are the odds that it was Jimmy on that ladder?" An awkward silence descended on the table. Jimmy looked up at Beau, who seemed confused by the reaction. "Considering Jimmy and Emily knew each other."

"What?" Kim practically gasped and clutched Emily's arm.

Jimmy's eyes snapped to hers. He caught a fleeting moment of panic before she steeled her face into a controlled casualness. She hadn't told them? He tried not to let the hurt and anger overtake him again.

Stacy clucked her tongue, looking smug. "Wow, Emmie. Guess you like to leave out a lot of the details. Is that why you didn't tell us that Hudson broke up with you?"

Again, a flash of emotion moved over Emily's face, too fast for Jimmy to categorize it. Her cheeks flushed pink, but she kept her eyes half-closed, like she was bored. The other girls' heads whipped to Emily. Stacy had that kind of sly smile that Jimmy hated on women. A catty look.

79

It shouldn't change everything, but that tiny hint of emotion on Emily's face hit Jimmy in the gut. Very few things really rattled her, but he could see this—or something about this—had bothered her. He felt a surge of anger and protectiveness. That was the last thing he needed—to try to rescue her again.

This whole conversation was apparently news to Emily's friends, who were all speaking at once. "You and Hudson broke up? When?"

"Why didn't you tell us?"

"How do you and Jimmy know each other?"

"What happened with Hudson?"

"It happened early this week," Emily said, yawning. "You'll have to ask him what happened. He said, and I quote, 'It's not you; it's me.' And something about God's will. Standard breakup fare. It's not like we were together that long."

Kim patted her arm. "I'm so sorry."

"I'm really okay with it. But thanks."

Emily didn't look okay. She was covering and in a big way. Jealousy burned through him. Maybe she really liked this Hudson guy. But more than that, Emily didn't like baring her soul. This was the kind of conversation she would have saved for Natalie, or even Jimmy. Not at a big table full of people, a few of them strangers. Stacy clearly seemed intent on dragging her into the spotlight to be examined. Unless she had fundamentally changed, Emily would hate everything about this conversation.

Stacy tilted her head in mock sympathy. "I know that has to be hard, though. I mean, every guy you've dated has dumped you. After a while, I'd start to feel like the common factor was me."

"Stacy," Kim hissed this across the table, but Stacy only

shrugged. Robbie practically hung over her chair, not bothered by the catty comments. Those two deserved each other.

Emily rolled her eyes, but Jimmy saw the way her hands clutched the edge of the table. He wished that he sat close enough to reach for her.

"You got me! I've been dumped by all my boyfriends. Big deal. But hey, maybe Hudson will go out with you now, Stacy. You're welcome to have him. Quite the catch."

Stacy narrowed her eyes. Emily stood, pushing back her chair. She held out her hand across the table to Jimmy. "Want to dance, cowboy?"

Dancing with Emily. His mouth went dry as he stared at her hand, frozen.

For the past few moments, Jimmy had been firmly rooted in the present, his heart twisting as he watched whatever weird dynamic was going on with Stacy and Emily. But at the mention of dancing, he shot back in time. His hands on Emily's hips as she told him that she thought of him as a little brother.

Everything in him screamed that he should take her hand. His heart was doing a crazy rhythm in his chest. He still felt the desire to protect her, but it wasn't as strong as his need to protect himself from being shattered by her again. He couldn't move.

"I'm not much on dancing. Remember?" Jimmy dropped his eyes to the plate in front of him where his half-eaten hamburger looked completely unappetizing. He felt like a world class jerk.

A chair scraped back as Beau stood. "I'm game, Emily. Anyone else coming?"

Most of the table followed, leaving Jimmy and a few other women. He swallowed, trying to tamp down the emotions raging up in him: hurt, anger, jealousy, shame. One of the women moved to the chair next to Jimmy. He took a drink of water and forced his eyes away from the dance floor.

"I'm Elle. How did you end up being a fireman?"

From across the table, Kim chimed in. "And how do you know Emily? I can't believe she didn't tell us you guys knew each other!"

"Normally it's pretty boring," Jimmy said. "We put out a lot of kitchen fires and grill fires. You'd be shocked at how many people can start a fire in something fireproof like a grill."

Elle and Kim laughed. Jimmy glanced up, unable to hold back any longer. Beau twirled Emily on the dance floor to an upbeat country song. Her smile was wide. Beau met Jimmy's eyes for a moment and gave him a look. *Get out here,* it said.

"Well?" Kim's voice startled him back to the conversation at the table. Elle and Kim were both looking at him.

"I'm sorry. What did you ask?"

"If you guys are all single," Kim repeated.

"Oh." Jimmy looked down at his drink. "Sort of. I've been dating someone but it's not serious or official. Beau is ... complicated. Whit and Robbie are both single." Beau gave him another look over Emily's shoulder. "I'll be right back."

Jimmy made a beeline for the bathroom in the opposite corner of the restaurant. The noise of the restaurant faded once the door closed behind him. He splashed water on his face, leaning his elbows on the sink. What was he doing? He should be thrilled to have Emily here, asking him to dance. But now he could only think of the last dance they shared and how that ended.

Beau had said that he needed to stop running. He definitely didn't feel any better after rejecting her. He couldn't keep raising up this wall. It felt painful and wrong. And was Emily even okay?

He had sensed pain underneath the carefully crafted cover. Maybe it was the breakup with whatever guy. That would be hard to hear about. But maybe it was something more. Natalie said that she and Emily had been drifting apart the last few years. Was she even okay? There had been a time when she trusted Jimmy and let her walls down. He wondered if she would again. He didn't think he could just be her friend, but if she needed someone, he wanted to be there. Even if it left him crushed again at the end of this week.

He needed to get over his fear and his pride and his hurt and just over himself.

"Strong and courageous," he said to his reflection, feeling silly talking out loud. But the words were enough to get him out of the bathroom and to the dance floor. Beau and Emily were still dancing and laughing as he walked right up to them.

"May I cut in?" He held out a hand with his most charming smile. Emily blinked at him in surprise and dropped the hand she had on Beau's shoulder.

"Of course." Beau winked and backed away.

When Emily didn't move, Jimmy took a breath and her hand. The touch started his body humming. They just stood there, hands clasped together, staring.

"I thought you didn't like dancing," Emily said.

"I don't. But I *can*."

Jimmy grinned and lifted his hand, sending Emily into a spin, and then caught her in his arms, dipping her low. He pulled her back up quickly and spun her again. She laughed, her face open and bright. So beautiful. He had missed the sound of her laugh, deep and full. The sound made his chest ache.

A slow song came on over the speakers. With no hesitation, Jimmy pulled her closer. If he shut out the fears and the overthinking going on in his head, it was much easier to just follow his instinct. And everything in him wanted Emily closer.

The smell of her and the feel of her lower back underneath his fingertips was intoxicating. She had on shorts and T-shirt for what looked like a band he'd never heard of. Even in something casual, she looked stunning. It was the light within her that made her so, not just her long legs and deep blue eyes. He squeezed her closer, but kept her back enough that he could see her face.

"A slow song. This seems more your speed. Though I'm impressed by the moves you've picked up."

"I've got moves you've never seen," Jimmy said, grinning. This was a quote from *My Best Friend's Wedding*, a movie that Natalie and Emily had made him watch dozens of times.

Emily tipped her head back and laughed. Jimmy wanted to press a kiss to the center of her throat, but kept his distance. When she stopped laughing, she met his eyes with an intensity that shook him. "I bet you do. A lot can change in three years."

And suddenly they were back in serious territory, where things had been derailed the night before. Her eyes softened with something that looked like regret. Jimmy took a deep breath.

"So—" he began, just as Emily said, "I'm sorry."

They both laughed, a little awkwardly.

"What were you going to say?" Emily asked.

"You first."

Emily pressed her lips together and looked away. Without warning, she pulled closer to him, nestling her head into her chest. He couldn't see her face but the warmth of her body spread through him like a fire. Not just a physical heat, but something deeper. He wanted to ask her if she was okay, but found it hard to even breathe. She trembled slightly against him and he brushed his lips against her hair. Not quite a kiss, but almost. Jimmy felt like all his self-control, all his walls, had been smashed to bits. Just a few moments close to her. That's all it took.

He loved her. Still. Just as much as he had. More, maybe. So much that it hurt him to hold her this close without knowing if she felt the same. If they didn't talk about it and he just held her, then he could pretend for a few minutes, imagining what could be if she loved him back.

He swallowed and swayed with the music, running his palm up and down her back, smoothing and soothing. She sighed and relaxed deeper into him. Her fingertips brushed over his collar, lightly touching the hair at the base of his neck. Whatever they wanted to say could wait. At least for a few minutes. Maybe at the end of this song, it would all be over. Jimmy wanted—no, needed—this dance.

"I'm sorry I didn't call you to let you know I was coming. I should have called you." Her breath tickled his collarbone when she spoke.

"You're here now. And—" Jimmy swallowed. "I'm glad. Really glad." He pulled her closer still, their bodies lining up perfectly. "Out of curiosity, why didn't you call?"

She was quiet again. Her hand moved further up the back of his neck, giving his hair a gentle tug. "I didn't know if you'd want to hear from me." Her voice was small and unsure.

"Why did you think that?"

"I guess because of Natalie's wedding and ... everything. All the things I said then. I'm sorry for that too. I was a huge jerk."

"You weren't—"

"I was. Let me own it. I was a jerk. And I didn't tell you the complete truth then."

He wanted to press her, to demand that she explain. What didn't she tell him the truth about? Her feelings? Something else? He wondered if she could feel the way his heart had kicked into overdrive. Emily didn't get serious often, he knew. When she took her shields down, it was worth waiting and listening. He fought the urge to question her and simply waited.

"When you left, I thought you didn't want to be friends anymore. I guess it seemed like I should let you go since you wanted to run."

Jimmy swallowed. "I did run. I didn't know what else to do. But that didn't mean I didn't want to be friends."

Emily pulled away from him then, meeting his gaze. Her eyes held more emotion than he'd ever seen there. "Really? Because you never talked to me again after Natalie's wedding."

Jimmy looked away and Emily pulled close again, pressing her forehead hard against his chest. "It wasn't like ... I mean, we mostly just talked through Natalie. We didn't, like, hang out that much."

"We did after your accident. Then after that, too. We were friends on our own, apart from your sister. Until you left. I texted you. I called. You didn't answer. Leading me to believe that you didn't want to be friends. It was like you just disappeared from my life." She dropped her hand from the back of his head to his shoulder, then brushed down his arm. Her touch made it hard to think. Jimmy closed his eyes. "I really missed you, Jimmy. I know that I messed everything up and I'm sorry."

A lump formed in his throat. Jimmy didn't know if he could speak around it. He had not ever until this moment felt bad about leaving Richmond. It felt like the right choice, though made in the wake of Emily's rejection. But the pain in her voice filled him with regret. She missed him. Emily had missed him and was sorry. She had texted and called after the wedding and he simply ignored her because he was hurt.

He brushed his hand over her hair. When he spoke, it felt like he was dragging his voice over rough gravel. "Emily, I couldn't—"

"Jimmy!" A bright voice cut him off and sent his heart slamming into his chest at a dead stop. No. Not now.

He pulled back from Emily as a hand tugged at his arm. Amber stood beside them, smiling, but clearly annoyed. Her face was full of possession. She looked to Jimmy and then to Emily. And the expression on Emily's face ...

Amber stood on tiptoes and kissed Jimmy on the cheek. "Whit said you guys were up here," Amber said. "I tried you, but you didn't answer your phone! Aren't you going to introduce me?"

Emily pulled away and stood with her hands awkwardly stiff at her sides. She had made herself vulnerable to him and now she was doing her best to pull the mask back on. Jimmy saw the hurt there before her control snapped back into place.

When neither Jimmy or Emily moved, Amber put one hand possessively on Jimmy's chest and held the other out to Emily, who shook it limply. "I'm Amber, Jimmy's girlfriend."

Emily nodded, her face impassive for a moment. Then she broke into a big smile that looked completely forced. He wished he could make Amber disappear. He'd been trying to do that indirectly the past few weeks by letting things fade out when he should have just addressed it.

"It's not ... we aren't—"

"Jimmy's an old friend," Emily said, interrupting his faltering explanation. "We were just catching up after a few years on old times. He told me all about you! Thanks for loaning him to me for a dance. He's all yours."

Emily spun away in the crowd as Amber grabbed Jimmy's hand. "I love dancing! Why didn't you call me to meet you?"

Jimmy couldn't answer. His eyes followed Emily, who grabbed her purse and stormed to the door. Everything in him screamed that he should chase after her. But he hesitated long enough for Amber to grab him in a tight hug, trapping him there with his regrets, past and present. Then Emily was gone.

CHAPTER NINE

She should have worn more sensible shoes. Within a block of leaving the restaurant, Emily had taken off the strappy sandals that were cutting into her heels. She carried them now, walking over the cracked asphalt on the way back to the beach house. It was a much longer walk than she thought when she ran out of the restaurant. At this point, she hoped that she would even recognize Jackson's house. They all kind of looked the same in the dark, big homes lined up along the ocean.

Overall, this was really poor planning. But she wasn't thinking clearly after Jimmy's *girlfriend* showed up.

Of course he had a girlfriend. He was a great guy. A total catch. He had a spark about him that made it easy to smile. He was kind and thoughtful, funny, and strikingly handsome. Why just now was she realizing this? She felt like crying. She had missed her chance with him. Obviously. It was unfair to think that he would wait for her to come to her senses. It probably wouldn't have worked anyway. They had been friends. If they had tried for more, chances are he would have found her lacking, just like all the other guys who had passed in and out of her life.

Even with her doubts and feelings of self-loathing, she had hoped that Jimmy would run out of the restaurant after her, explaining everything. Heck, she would have taken a kiss instead of words. At this point, she was desperate. She would take anything. But Jimmy didn't follow her and Emily kept on walking.

This was better, though. She couldn't really fall for Jimmy. Natalie had made it clear that she didn't approve. They hadn't talked about it since, but nothing made her think that Natalie would trust Emily with Jimmy any more now than she did back then. Plus, he lived here now, four hours away from her. It was stupid and impossible.

Emily shivered. It was a warm night, but the ocean breeze lifted the hair from the back of her neck.

She tried to conjure up the images of Jimmy as the annoying little brother who had followed them around when they were younger. Anything to not think of him as the handsome, grown, amazing man she had just walked away from. Emily could still picture him when she and Natalie became friends—a kid with a crooked grin and a mess of blond hair needing to be brushed. But that image kept being replaced with him now, grinning at her while he held her close on the fire truck ladder. Broad shoulders, an amazing smile, those blue eyes. Arms that made her feel safe. Wanted. Loved.

But was she still wanted? Or loved? For a few minutes, she thought she felt something ... but then his girlfriend showed up. The girlfriend that he hadn't mentioned. Which seemed odd considering the conversation she had with Beau while they were dancing.

As Beau had led her out to the dance floor, she had almost

cried from relief. It had been humiliating to have Jimmy reject her. She turned to humor, always her savior. "You're not, like, into me or something, are you? You keep showing up places."

Beau had laughed. "Sorry—I shouldn't laugh. I didn't mean that to be rude. I am not, in fact, into you. Though you seem like a great girl. I'm rooting for Jimmy."

"Wow. You cut right to the chase, huh?"

"I also don't beat around the bush, if we're going to talk tired clichés," he said, spinning her around the dance floor.

She laughed. "Touché."

"No, *cliché*."

Emily shook her head, smiling. "Has anyone ever told you that you're kind of a dork?"

"Never. But my mom tells me that I can't leave well-enough alone, though. So, back to you and Jimmy. I see why Jimmy likes you, Emily."

"Who says he does? Did he ask you to talk to me? Because I just asked him to dance and he totally rejected me."

Beau made a face. "I know. And I bet he already feels terrible about it. He'll probably kill me if he finds out about this conversation also, so let's keep it between us."

"Trust me—he and I are not going to talk about this conversation," she had said.

"Maybe you should."

"Look, Beau. I like you. But why are you pushing this? He's not out here talking to me himself about it. He's hardly talking to me at all. Why are you?"

"Because I love Jimmy. He's like my brother. And I know how he feels about you. I don't know how you feel about him, but I have a guess. Our pastor at church always does the same benediction every week: You go nowhere by accident.

What are the odds of you being trapped on a balcony and getting rescued by Jimmy?"

"You're saying God almost killed me so I could see Jimmy again."

"When you put it like that, it doesn't sound so Biblical. I'm just saying that you're here for a few more days. Keep an open mind. And if it doesn't work or you don't feel the same way, go. But at least think about it."

Then Jimmy had asked her to dance. And now she was walking along a deserted beach road alone and barefoot.

Emily didn't want to think about Jimmy. The way he had looked at her. The feel of his hands on her hips. The way he smelled when she leaned into him ...

The way his girlfriend interrupted them.

A horn honked next to her. She jumped. Her nerves were still shot from the night before. "Get in, loser."

Sarah was behind the wheel and Kim had opened the back door of the SUV. Emily waffled for approximately half a second, then decided her feet were not going to make it.

"Why are you walking?" Elle asked.

"Exercise," Emily said. "I've got to keep my girlish figure."

Stacy snorted from the front. "Feeling fat? Is that why you're not in New York anymore?"

New York. Emily's stomach turned. She shoved away those memories.

"Stacy!" Kim said. "That's enough. You've been a jerk all night."

"Kidding," Stacy said. "Gosh. Emily knows I was kidding. Right, Em?"

"I knew exactly what you meant," Emily said.

Kim clapped her hands. "So, back to important business. Show of hands—who had chemistry with a hot fireman tonight? An almost-married woman has got to live vicariously."

Stacy giggled. "I might have seen a little action."

"Of course you did," Emily muttered.

"What about Jimmy, Emily? Old friends reunited— anything going on there? You sure looked cozy dancing."

"Until his girlfriend showed up," Stacy said. "That's why you left in such a hurry, right Emily?"

Emily leaned forward to the front seat, until she was practically breathing down Stacy's neck.

"Stacy—in the interest of your self-preservation and also for Kim, who's the VIP this week—would you mind dialing it back a bit? I mean, obviously, I'm not your favorite person. But your comments are getting tiresome. Give it a rest."

The car went silent. They had just pulled up to the parking space under Jackson's house. Emily hopped out. "If you need me, I'll be on the beach."

The house was next to one of those wooden crosswalks that led from a public parking lot to the beach, but there was also a trail in the sand that led directly through the dunes. She passed a punching bag under the balcony. Might have to revisit that later. Emily took the trail, the sand soothing her feet.

The beach at night looked like a black and white movie. The ocean was coal-black with glints of white from the moon. The foam a stark contrast against the gray sand. It felt peaceful to Emily. Enough that she could ignore the stickiness in the air that had always bothered her at the beach. Salt air did crazy things to her skin and to her hair. And the sand. Oh, how she hated sand. But since she got here, the ocean seemed to call to her. Even after spending the afternoon on the beach today, she hadn't minded the feel of the salt on her skin or the sand that she still found places even after a shower.

"You go nowhere by accident. Is that really how it is, God?" The wind and pounding waves swallowed up her voice in the night. Praying out loud had always felt uncomfortable and awkward to her. But standing on the beach, feeling small, it felt strangely okay. "Why am I here? I just need ..."

Emily's voice trailed off. She didn't know what she needed. Maybe that was the problem—she had thought for too much of her life that she did know what she needed and made decisions without praying or asking God. She didn't ask for directions so much as she just forged her own way. Look where it had gotten her: single, living with her parents, in a job that she hated. Not even a blip on the horizon of something to look forward to. Yeah, she definitely hadn't done well on her own.

"I need your direction," she spoke in the direction of the waves, feeling small and silly. "This is me, giving up. I don't really know how to do it. But I'm trying."

She hadn't expected an answer, but still stood there for a few heartbeats, letting the edge of the waves move over her toes. Asking seemed like a good first step, but she didn't know what to do next or how to even let God direct her. Sighing, she stepped back from the waves.

She had thought about taking a walk, but her feet were raw from walking barefoot on the asphalt. Instead she made her way over to the wooden crosswalk next to the house and sat up on the railing, trying to shake the memory of the balcony railing from the night before. It was hard to believe that even happened. That morning she had woken up, sweaty and tangled in the sheets on Jimmy's bed, dreaming she was falling from a car that had been driving down a highway at rapid speeds before veering off a cliff, the wheel spinning uselessly beneath her hands. Thankfully Stacy had slept through her nightmarish sleep. Emily didn't want that girl having any more ammo on her life to use.

Maybe she should just go home. It wasn't fair for her to feel jealous of Jimmy's girlfriend, but she did. Being with him, having his arms around her—it felt so safe. So right. Except that it wasn't right if he was dating someone else. Now she had just interrupted his life, which seemed to be going in a perfectly fine direction, unlike hers.

"Want some company?"

Emily almost fell off the railing at the sound of Jimmy's voice. He stood on the crosswalk a few feet behind her, his hands in the pockets of his shorts. He didn't step closer.

"Jimmy. *James.* You can't do that. Where did you even come from?"

"I just dropped Amber off. I saw you out here when I pulled up."

"Oh." Amber. His girlfriend. Emily swallowed back the bitter taste of jealousy.

"Can I join you? I'd really like to talk."

"I'm kind of sick of talking, actually. I'm all talked out."

Jimmy moved closer until he was leaning on the rail next to Emily. She could smell him—the mix of his cologne and just ... Jimmy.

"What do you want to do instead?"

Coming from someone else, this might have been flirtatious, but Jimmy was genuinely and carefully asking. He leaned against her, tentatively, and when she didn't pull away, he leaned a little more. She should push him away. He had a girlfriend. But she felt starved for his touch and his nearness. More than she wanted to admit to herself.

Emily looked up at the moon. It was three-quarters full, that last chunk cloaked in darkness. That piece, the invisible black one—she totally related to that bit. All hidden in the shadows and lost next to the bright, clean white of the visible surface.

She really needed to get out of her head.

"I really want to eat a big breakfast," she said.

"Breakfast. Right now? It's almost midnight."

"This dinky little island doesn't have anywhere that will serve waffles and eggs and grits and bacon at midnight? Because I don't know how you could stand to live here if that's true."

Jimmy grinned. "Well, there is this diner."

Emily hopped down from the rail, feeling reckless, but lit up inside. "Take me to this diner of which you speak. I want to stuff waffles into my face like tomorrow is the zombie apocalypse."

She held out a hand. He looked at her, a little like she was crazy, but he was still smiling like he had just won the lottery. Instead of taking her hand, he hooked his arm through hers. They began the walk back toward the house.

"Do you need to let your crew know where you're going?" he asked.

She groaned. "Probably. But they'll just talk about me and the hunky fireman. That's all they do. Talk talk talk."

"Hunky fireman, huh?"

"Their words. Not mine."

"Of course not."

"I'll text Kim. I don't have a key, though, if they all go to bed."

"I just happen to have a key."

"That's right. Well, then let's get our waffle on, Jimmy. And don't get any untoward ideas. I mean 'waffle' quite literally."

Jimmy smiled. Even though she didn't look at his face,

she could hear it in his voice. "I'm taking you at your word, Emily. Literal waffles you shall have. And the island's worst coffee."

"Oh, how I love terrible coffee. The gas station variety is my standard."

"Then you will not be disappointed."

Emily grabbed her shoes where she had left them next to Sarah's car. Jimmy held the car door for her, then closed it when she had her legs safely inside. As she waited for him to come around the back of the car, she realized something: this was the happiest she had been in three years.

Too bad it couldn't last.

CHAPTER TEN

A few hours before, Jimmy would not have imagined sitting across the table from Emily, watching her devour waffles almost as fast as she threw back coffee. After Amber showed up at Mo's, he honestly didn't know if Emily would ever talk to him again. It never looked good when you were having a potentially romantic moment and someone showed up claiming to be your girlfriend. Even if that wasn't the case.

He and Emily hadn't talked about Amber—or anything else of importance. Not yet. Instead, they slid back into the comfortable banter that had always existed between them, before everything changed.

"You're drowning a perfectly good waffle, Em." She just rolled her eyes. He grabbed her wrist, stopping her fork halfway to her mouth. "Stop—listen! I can hear its tiny screams."

Emily shook off his hand and continued to eat. "I'm just putting him in his natural habitat. Before I eat him. Good waffle. You have served your life's purpose."

She stuck a fork in the waffle again, syrup dripping from her chin. Somehow, even this was adorable on her. Jimmy wanted to reach out and wipe it off with his fingertip. Better yet, to lean across and kiss it away. How would she respond? His breathing hitched in his chest.

He looked down at his rapidly disappearing eggs, trying to shift his focus. He hadn't realized how hungry he was when Emily mentioned breakfast but might be ordering seconds.

"If you don't drown them in syrup, how do you eat your waffles?" Emily asked. "Please share your superior waffle-eating ways."

"First of all, I don't eat a lot of carbs." Emily rolled her eyes at this and he smirked, flexing his bicep. She rolled her eyes harder. "But if I were to enjoy a waffle, it would be only if every square was filled with butter."

"That's acceptable. Loads of butter or loads of syrup. We aren't so different after all."

"What about both?" He grinned wickedly.

Her eyes got wide and she clutched his hand. She flagged down the waitress. Eileen looked both shocked and exhausted by Emily's constant coffee refills. Jimmy knew her from the frequent Bible and Breakfast meetings with Beau, Jackson, and Cash, but she was much perkier in the mornings.

"I'm so sorry to bother you again. I'd like more coffee and one more waffle, please. With extra butter. Extra *extra* butter. Like, a bowl full of butter please."

Eileen stared. "I think we'll need to make another pot of coffee. I'll have to charge you for that."

Emily pointed to Jimmy. "Put it on his tab. He's a firefighter. Plenty of dough. And I'll drink whatever coffee you make."

"Sorry, Eileen," Jimmy said. "We're a little hungry

tonight. Don't worry—I'll tip as good as I eat. Um, could I also get two more eggs, scrambled? With another side of bacon. Please."

He smiled his winningest smile and Emily giggled. The sound moved through Jimmy like sunshine, lighting up his dark corners. Eileen shook her head as she walked back over to the cook, who glanced over at them like he couldn't believe it either. Emily realized that she was still grasping his hand. She pulled back and gave him a small smile. Jimmy immediately missed the feel of her skin on his and resisted the urge to take her hand again.

Jimmy watched Emily as she finished off the syrup-soaked waffle. A few hours before, he watched her bolt from Mo's and wondered if he had blown it. Again. He knew he needed to go after her, but had to first address things with Amber. Her possessive display clearly showed him that they were not on the same page.

Amber cried, which made Jimmy feel bad. It also seemed a little too much since they had been out like three times. He hadn't even kissed her. She definitely thought they were dating, as in, that they were in a relationship. Jimmy thought they were dating, as in going on dates—very big difference. While he tried to awkwardly pat Amber's back and say the right things, all he could think about was finding Emily before too much time had passed. It was like his heart was a ticking clock, booming out the rhythm urging him to go to her. Hurry, hurry, hurry.

Before she was gone again.

Jimmy still felt terrified about what would come next with Emily. He had no idea what to say or ask, or how to address their past. But if he had been unsure of his feelings, seeing her walk out of Mo's had made it crystal clear. He couldn't face the gigantic hole that she had left in his life.

Not again. But that might be the case at the end of the week. Unless she felt the same way or unless he could win her over.

Eileen reappeared with the waffle and a small bowl filled with butter. "This enough?"

"Could we get more?" She kept a straight face and Eileen looked shocked until Emily giggled. "Kidding. Thank you, this is perfect. You are a saint."

"I'll be right back with the eggs and coffee."

Emily took a knife and began methodically filling each hole with butter. "How's this, Jimmy? More? Less? I want it just perfect for you."

"I think that's excessively sufficient." Every square held butter, some melting all the way to a golden liquid. His stomach should have felt full, but rumbled.

Emily handed him the metal carafe of syrup. "Let's make this *our* waffle. Want to do the honors?"

Jimmy blinked. She had no idea the effect her words were having on him. *I want it perfect for you. Our waffle.* He felt like he was reading into every little thing. He flooded the waffle with syrup and then they both examined it seriously for a moment, like they were in the middle of some kind of ritual, not eating breakfast in a diner at midnight.

"It's perfection," Emily breathed.

Jimmy cut away a piece with the fork and pushed it toward her. Emily took a bite and rolled her eyes back in her head.

"I may die. This is the best thing ever." She spoke around a full mouth of food.

"Maybe I need to rethink my stance on carbs."

"Clearly."

They polished off the waffle in minutes, both stabbing the last piece at the same time with their forks.

"A gentleman would let the lady have the last piece," Emily said.

"Who said I was a gentleman?" Jimmy grinned, but then held up his fork in mock surrender. Emily ate the last bite, then scraped her fork on the plate, licking off the butter and syrup that had pooled on the bottom.

"This might be the best part. Do you frown on licking plates? Will I get you in trouble with this establishment? I gather that you're a regular."

"I am. But I'm happy to claim you, whether you lick the plate or not." She had no idea how much he wanted to claim her.

He could see the debate in her mind as she held the plate. Half of him wanted to see her do it. Eileen returned and picked up the plate, making the decision for Emily. She handed Jimmy his eggs.

"Are y'all done? Or should we make a few more waffles?"

Emily laughed. "I'm not sure any more waffles could fit in my body. Even if I tried. But thank you. You've been a peach to put up with us. Is the coffee ready?"

"Still brewing." Eileen actually groaned as she walked away.

"Doesn't that keep you from sleeping?" Jimmy asked.

"Nah. I don't sleep much. Plus, I'm kind of immune to caffeine. I can drink a pot and go to sleep. I've got long days of photo shoots to thank for that. We couldn't eat, but no one stopped us from drinking coffee. As long as we could brush our teeth before getting in front of the camera."

"That much coffee can't be healthy."

Emily shrugged. "We're all going to die one way or the other. I'd prefer to die caffeinated."

For the first time, silence descended on the table. Emily shredded a paper napkin into a snowy pile. He knew that it was time to address some of the big elephants in the room. It had been so nice to just … be. He hated to mess that up. But it was time.

Jimmy touched her hand. "We ate. Up for a talk now?"

Eileen delivered a fresh mug of coffee. Emily dumped three creamers in and took a sip. "Sure. That'd probably be good. I'm less hangry now. Let's start with Amber."

His stomach dropped. "Look, about Amber—"

Emily waved a hand dismissively, which did nothing to calm him. "You have a girlfriend. I'm glad."

She was glad. She was *glad*? Now his stomach had fallen through the floor to basement levels. "You—what?"

Emily touched his hand. "Jimmy, you deserve someone special. As long as she's good for you, I'm cool. If not, she'll have me to deal with. I'm happy for you. We can be friends, right?"

Jimmy fiddled with his napkin, trying to figure out how to respond. After all this, Emily wanted to be *friends*. She was *glad* that he had a girlfriend. So casual about it all. Too casual. She had been anything but casual when she stormed out of the restaurant. Her words might be saying one thing, but he felt like that wasn't the whole story.

"Amber isn't actually—"

"Jimmy. I don't want to talk about Amber. If she doesn't mind that you're hanging out with an old friend this week, everything is fine. We're good." She leaned across the table toward him and whispered. "That friend being me, of course. Can we hang out this week? If Amber is cool with that. I'll be honest—she did not seem that cool tonight."

"Amber would not be cool with that."

"Oh." Emily played with her silverware for a moment on the table, then put her hands in her lap.

"Em?" He kept his eyes fixed on her as she looked up at

him. Her eyes had a vulnerability to them that made him want to move to her side of the table and wrap her in his arms. "Amber isn't my girlfriend."

She blinked and he thought he caught a small smile before she steeled her expression. She cleared her throat. "Does Amber know that? She seemed pretty convinced otherwise tonight."

He rubbed a hand over the back of his neck. "The truth is that we went on three dates. Three. I wasn't interested in more and she was. I should have made myself more clear before, but I did tonight."

"Oh?"

"Yep. Still want to hang out this week even if I don't have a girlfriend?"

Emily smiled and then bit her bottom lip. "I guess that's okay with me."

"Good."

Emily seemed to relax in the booth. "Great. Now, about the fact that we haven't talked in three years—that's something we need to address. I miss being friends. The last few years sucked, to be frank."

"I agree. We should do something about that."

"Can we put an end to the years of silence? Even if we aren't living in the same place. There are phones. Email. Social media even. If we must."

"I'm good with most of those. Maybe not so much social media. Though I do follow you on Instagram."

"You do?" She looked shocked and pleased.

"Along with half the world, it seems like."

She rolled her eyes. "It's not that many. And you aren't half the world. You're Jimmy."

Her words made his cheeks warm. "Forty thousand people is a lot."

She grinned at him. "James, have you been stalking me? You know how many Instagram followers I have?"

"Forget social media. I've been told that I'm a pretty fantastic texter."

"I remember that about you," she said. "It's one of your best characteristics."

"If that's one of my best, I'd hate to hear my worst."

Emily threw her head back and laughed. She patted his hand and he resisted the urge to curl his fingers around hers. Friends. He needed to act like they were just friends. For now.

"I feel like I haven't laughed in years. Not like this. Thank you, Jimmy. It's been a pretty bad week. Month. Years."

"You had a breakup, huh?" He tried not to let the feelings of jealousy show in his face. Even if they were broken up, he hated thinking of Emily with a boyfriend.

She made a face. "It wasn't that big of a deal. Not even big enough to talk about. Didn't like him that much; now it's over. The end. Let's skip me. My life is seriously boring and ridiculous. Tell me everything about you."

Knowing Emily, that meant there were some private things she didn't want to talk about. Yet. "Not much to say here. I work at the fire station, which I love. You've met most of my friends—Beau, Jackson, and Cash. He was the cop the other night."

"A huge improvement from your high school friends, who were all idiots. I don't remember Cash."

"I'm not surprised. You had a lot going on. Honestly, I can't believe how well you handled any of the other night."

"You doubted my strength of character? I'm hurt."

"You're the strongest woman I know," Jimmy said. The compliment seemed to make her happy, but she looked down to hide her smile. "It was a traumatic event and would have been for anyone. Have you had any nightmares?"

She shifted in her seat. A tell. "No."

"Emily. You should see someone when you get home. They have counselors who specialize in post-traumatic events. Even just once might really be helpful."

"I don't need a shrink. It was one thing. I lived. It could have been bad, but wasn't." Now she was angry.

He sighed, recognizing that he needed to back off. Even if he was right, pushing wouldn't change her mind. She seemed angrier than she should be. Was there other trauma she was dealing with? "Okay."

"New topic of conversation: why did you move? Natalie and your parents were worried sick. And I mean, of all the places, why here?"

Now Jimmy found himself looking down. How to explain this and keep the conversation away from his feelings? She had to know why he left. He didn't know how much to say.

"I left because I needed a change of scene. I honestly don't know how I ended up here. I kind of picked a random spot on the map started driving. Here I am."

He waited for her to launch into the third degree on his story, which did not really explain anything. Obviously, the wedding and their conversation was why he left. She had to know. Didn't she? Emily only nodded.

"Your turn," he said. "Catch me up on the last three years."

She took a sip of coffee. "So, um, I gave modeling another go and then quit. I dropped out of dental hygiene school because it turns out I hate touching the inside of people's mouths. Who knew? I'm a temp at a marketing firm where I thought I could move up and do some digital marketing and stuff, but that's not going to happen. I still live with my parents and they're as awful as they ever were. I'm waiting to hear back about a big modeling job that I'm pretty sure I'm not going to get, so I'll be stuck at the job I hate even longer. Oh, and as you heard, every guy I ever date breaks up with me. That's basically my life right now. Sorry you asked?"

"I would never be sorry to know what's going on with you." He tried not to let his face show how much he hated hearing all that. He knew she wouldn't want anything that looked like pity.

She looked down at the table at the pile of shredded napkins. "You seem to have a good thing going here. Any job openings at the station?"

His eyebrows shot up. The idea of Emily moving here made his heart race. "You looking to move here?"

"I don't know where that came from," she said. "I'm maybe a little overly caffeinated."

"I wouldn't complain. I could talk to Jackson. He owns a grocery store here and also about a billion properties."

"I was kidding, Jimmy."

"Okay. But if you change your mind, I'm not kidding."

"Thank you."

She touched his hand and it sent heat traveling up his arm. He looked up at her. Not for the first time, looking at Emily made his heart skid to a stop before it began a slow, throbbing rhythm. She was so incredibly beautiful. But it wasn't her full lips and high cheekbones or her brilliant blue eyes. Emily's beauty came from deep within and lit up those classic features. Her fierceness and her strength and her sharp wit. Those qualities made her face more than traditionally beautiful. She became impossibly beautiful.

There was vulnerability to Emily that he rarely saw, but he knew existed underneath the sarcasm and quick quips. He had glimpsed it a few times over the years and wanted nothing more than to be the one she trusted enough to share it with. He wanted to spend the rest of his life waking up to see her face.

That thought felt like a knife in his gut. She didn't feel the same way, so he couldn't either. He pulled his hand back across the table. They sat in silence for a few moments. It wasn't uncomfortable, exactly, but it felt like something hung there between them.

"Hey, can I go to church with you tomorrow?"

"I'd love that." He couldn't stop himself from grinning.

"If it's cool, I'll invite the girls."

"Your friends go to church? They seemed really, uh … "

She laughed. "Wild? Not so church-y?"

"Little bit."

"I met them at church, actually. Singles group—worst name for a group ever. Anyway. You ever notice how there are kind of two camps of Christians? There are the ones who follow rules to the point that it just seems to be about rules. And then the other ones who embrace the whole freedom in Christ thing a little too hard?"

Jimmy laughed. "Yeah. My high school friends were in that second category, if you remember. Seems like they'd be in good company with your friends."

"Definitely. They aren't all so bad and they can be fun, but it's kind of gone too far over the line for me. People aren't great at balance. Do you remember my strict rule following period?"

"You deleted every song from my iPod. Even Skillet." Jimmy smiled.

"In my defense, I didn't realize Skillet was a Christian band. I actually liked their music so I thought it couldn't possibly be Christian. I should really pay you back."

"Yeah, you should."

"I'm probably not going to though."

"I know," he said.

"Anyway. I had just become a Christian, so getting rid of anything that didn't seem Jesus-y enough helped me really embrace that change. I thought I was helping you do the same. I did get better at finding the happy medium. I don't always get it right."

"No one really does."

"Yeah, but your friends seem balanced. This group I'm with doesn't help me much. With people like Stacy around, it can also be pretty miserable. She hates me. And she's kind of a terrible person."

Jimmy thought about when Stacy had paraded in front of him in her underwear. He felt heat rising in his cheeks.

"Why are you blushing?"

"I'm not blushing."

"Your face is the color of a fire truck, Jimmy. Out with it. Please just don't tell me you like Stacy. I would die. No—I'd kill you. Or her. Or both."

"Definitely not. But I feel weird saying it."

"Spit it out. It's me, remember?"

"Fine. So, she's staying in my room, I guess. I walked in earlier and she was still in bed."

"Yeah and?"

"And she got up just wearing her underwear."

Emily stared at him for a few seconds without speaking. He watched her work to swallow, her delicate throat bobbing with the effort. "She knew you were there? And she did that?" She looked like she was going to set something on fire.

"She said, um, I shouldn't worry about it. That it was just like a bathing suit."

Emily rolled her eyes. "I mean yeah—technically. But it's about context! Being on the beach in a swimsuit is different than being inside a bedroom just in underwear. That girl. It's not surprising. She asked me if you and I were together so she could make a move if not. Stacy couldn't wait to gloat to me about your girlfriend."

"What was she gloating about?"

"Your girlfriend—or, not so much girlfriend, as it turns out—showing up while you and I were dancing was great ammo for Stacy to use against me."

"Wow. Some friend."

Emily made a face. "Yeah, I'm not super close with any of them."

"Speaking of your friends, I think you might turn into a pumpkin if we don't get you back." Jimmy stood and set down some bills on the table. "Keep the change, Eileen! Thanks for putting up with us."

Eileen waved. Jimmy held the door of the diner for Emily and then opened her car door as well. As she got in, she turned to look up at him. "What about after church? We could get lunch, hang out, whatever. I want you to show me around your island. I mean, if you want."

His mouth felt dry and chalky. More than anything, he wanted to spend more time with her. But every moment he spent with her sent him spinning closer and closer to the familiar edge he knew so well. The one where he fell hard and fast and completely for a woman who made him feel so good, but also didn't feel the same way about him. Was he willing to basically repeat his past actions, even if it meant being friend-zoned … again?

Strong and courageous. Anything worthwhile was worth taking risks for. Right?

He smiled down at her, the decision made. "I've got the perfect place. You'll love it."

Emily smiled up at him and his heart did a flip. "Yay! I'm so glad we're friends again, Jimmy."

As Jimmy shut the car door, he wondered if she could hear the hollowness in his voice as he echoed her words. "Yes. Friends."

CHAPTER ELEVEN

"So where are you taking me?" Emily looked across the front seat to Jimmy.

The truth was that she didn't actually care where they were going. Jimmy was behind the wheel, the windows were down, and it was a gorgeous day. Emily felt giddy. The beach may not have been her happy place, but it was growing on her. The smell of the salt and her hair whipping around her face as he drove made her think of summers in high school: carefree days with warmth and sun and no sense of time. No heavy sense of responsibility that hung on her shoulders.

"Off Island, actually, to one of my favorite spots."

"I thought you were going to show me around Sandover? And what is this 'Off Island' business?"

"It's just how people talk here," he said, grinning. "Well, the On Islanders talk like that."

"Are you officially an On Islander? Do you carry a membership card?"

"No card. But I think I'm pretty official. I've been here

three years and working at the station means I'm pretty entrenched in the community. Plus, I hang out with On Island royalty."

"Beau?"

"Yep. And Jackson. He owns Bohn's, a grocery store that's been the only one On Island forever. Until Harris Teeter came along."

The disdain was obvious in his voice. "Oh my gosh, Jimmy. You drank the Kool-Aid. You *are* an On Islander. So then, why is an On Islander taking me Off Island?"

"This is one of my favorite spots on the coast. We don't have anything like it on Sandover. Hopefully, you'll like it as much as I do."

Emily closed her eyes and leaned back in the seat. If she was a cat, she would be purring. Being with Jimmy was a stark contrast to how she felt with the women she had come with. With the other women, she felt like she had to be on all the time. She was the high-energy, life-of-the-party Emily.

With Jimmy, she could just be. The way she felt when she was with him was free, easy, content. She was already dreading the drive back to Richmond at the end of the week. Back to work. Back to singles group and normal life. Back to ... nothing. Somewhere in the last few years, she had lost her joy. Until these last few days—until *Jimmy*—she hadn't realized it.

Jimmy had a light about him, always had. He drew people in without trying. They followed him because they wanted to go wherever he was going. Guys wanted to be him. Girls had always loved him. But it never went to his head. He'd been a little cocky when he was younger, but it was more a maturity thing than a character thing. Typical teenage boy. When it came down to it, Jimmy was humble and kind.

Pushing him away had been a mistake. She should have

been honest with Natalie that she had feelings for Jimmy. At the time, she had been scared to admit the feelings or to see where they went. She was still terrified. Natalie gave her an easy out. A cowardly way out.

Natalie. Even though they didn't talk as much now as they used to, Emily should at least tell her that she was hanging out with Jimmy. Or that he'd saved her life. A few times in the last day, she had pulled out her phone to text Natalie, but something always held her back. She expected another lecture, another warning to stay away. This time, Emily wouldn't say yes if Natalie said to leave Jimmy alone. She wasn't going to back down.

Jimmy hadn't been the only one to get hurt when they stopped talking a few years ago. Even if it was her fault and her choice to step away. She felt his absence like a wound, sharp and tender for months. Over the years it became like scar tissue. She almost didn't notice, only thinking about it whenever she tried to casually pump Natalie for details on Jimmy. Then the ache came back.

That morning in church, it had felt so familiar sitting beside him. She'd grown up going to church with Natalie, sitting right between her and Jimmy. Their dad had been the pastor, so it was just the three of them and then their mom. Emily's parents didn't go to church. Sunday mornings were for golf and pedicures.

It wasn't even that they didn't go to church—they didn't approve when she started going to church in high school. Though her mother never came out and said it, Emily thought she was jealous of how much time she spent with Natalie's family. She never had anything nice to say about Natalie or her parents. But Jimmy was handsome and athletic and had won a baseball scholarship, never mind that he never ended up going to college. Her mother was okay with Jimmy at least.

It was all about appearances to her parents. The right house in the right neighborhood with the right interior decorator. The right cars. The right clothes. The right daughter.

Except she hadn't been the right daughter. Again and again she felt like a disappointment to them until she stopped trying altogether. Now it was just a constant understanding that she embarrassed them. She could have been a model—beautiful, well-known, respected, dressed in fashionable clothes. Instead she dressed conservatively, wore no makeup, worked as a temp, lived at home. At worst, her mother cut her down. But mostly both her parents ignored her. It wasn't abuse or neglect, but a lack of actual care.

Jimmy and Beau's church, Hope, was a bit more informal than what Emily was used to. Most people wore jeans or shorts or just typical beachy clothes. Even the pastor wore shorts and sandals while he preached. Kim and Sarah had come, but everyone else wanted to sleep in or hit the beach early since so many of them were leaving. Beau played guitar up front, the instrument looking small against his big build. Every so often, Jimmy's leg would rest against hers. Sometimes an accidental brushing, and sometimes an intentional jab, like a poke to the ribs. One more thing she had missed: his way of teasing.

"What kind of music are we listening to?" Emily asked, extending an arm out the car window.

Jimmy smiled. "You don't know Chris Isaak?"

"Clearly not."

He turned up the volume. A man was wailing over the sound of a smooth electric guitar, something about flying. "You should appreciate this, Em. He's a legend."

"So you say."

"It's about meeting and connecting with a woman while he's on tour, but then having to fly away from her the next day. He's full of regret because he didn't tell her he loved her." Jimmy began to sing softly along with the words. If he realized the connection between the song and the two of them, he didn't show it in his face.

The song grew on her and Emily found herself tapping her fingers on the car door as they passed over the toll bridge. It felt like perfect sunny-weather music. Twenty minutes later they crossed another bridge. "Are we on Nag's Head?"

She had been here once as a little girl, but hardly remembered. Her parents weren't big beach people either. They both worked a ton and didn't take a lot of family vacations, but when they had, it was to mountain lodges or cities. Her mother described herself as "posh." Emily just thought of her as snobby. She liked wearing heels and designer clothes on vacation.

"It is." A few minutes later he turned into a parking lot. A sign read Jockey's Ridge State Park.

"Are we ... hiking? You know I'm not much for athletic feats."

"I remember. It won't be so bad." He grinned.

"What about food? I'm starving."

"You're hungry after last night's wafflefest?"

"Um, yeah. That was like twelve hours ago. Aren't you hungry?" With his massive muscles—not that she was checking them out—he had to put away a lot of calories.

"No. But we'll eat after. I promise you food." Jimmy ran around the car and opened the car door for her before she could do it herself.

He held out a hand and Emily let him pull her to her feet. She expected Jimmy to drop her hand, but he held on. Their fingers weren't intertwined, just palm to palm, which felt somehow more platonic. Though Emily felt anything but platonic about it. Her skin felt electrified from the touch, like her nerve endings had turned into live wires, humming and buzzing from their contact. She resisted an urge to curl her fingers around his and lean closer to him. Hand-holding could be just friends, right? It couldn't mean anything. Even if it did to her.

Did she want it to mean more?

Emily swallowed down the question. She didn't want to admit her answer. *Friends.* They were just friends. Jimmy took them down a path through some scrubby bushes. Huge sand dunes rose before them. They were more like rolling hills of sand than dunes, really. Someone was hang-gliding down from one of the higher hills. So much sand.

"What is this? Are we climbing these?" Emily asked.

"We don't have to go to the biggest one if you don't want to. I mean—if you can't handle it. But I want you to see the view from here. This is like the thinnest part of the island. You can see the sound on one side and the ocean on the other from here. It's really beautiful."

He dropped her hand as they started to climb and Emily immediately missed the contact. But it was actually a little more difficult than it looked just because of the way her flip flops sank in the sand. Her calves were burning by the time they got to the top. But Jimmy had been right about the view. The park stretched out with sand all around them, leading into low scrubby vegetation on the sides. She thought she saw a rabbit hopping among the bushes. The water of the sound sparkled behind them and in front of the dunes across the road and past a shopping center, she could see the ocean.

"Wow. This is really beautiful. It's so thin." The island couldn't have been more than a mile across at this point.

"It's amazing any of these islands are still here. They may not be forever. There are a lot of projects underway bringing in new sand to revitalize the beaches. It's a losing battle against erosion, I think. Then again, look how long this thin strip of land has been here."

"You sound like you're in love."

He laughed. "Maybe a little. I didn't really like history ever, but I think it's fascinating. Pirates called this place home. Real pirates."

"Blackbeard?" she said with a laugh.

"Actually, yes."

"Wait—was he real? I really thought Blackbeard was just a legend."

"Legendary, but a real guy who lived here. Pretty crazy, right? There were even some women pirates."

"Really? I definitely missed that in history class."

"I may have gotten a little nerdy on my pirate kick. I've got lots of time when I'm not on shift."

"Wow. Jimmy doing pirate research in his spare time. I never would have guessed."

"I'm full of surprises." He smiled, sending her heartrate skyrocketing. How could he do that with just a smile? Whatever she was trying to convince herself about friendship with Jimmy was utterly ludicrous. Her brain and body were totally not on the same page.

He bumped her shoulder with his. "Are you ready?"

"For what?"

"We're going down."

"Why wouldn't I be ready?" She narrowed her eyes.

"Because the best way down is like this."

Jimmy leaped downward, taking giant running strides down the front of the dune hill. He almost made it but just before the bottom, he tumbled into the sand, laughing. Emily paused for a moment, trying not to think of all the places sand was going to end up, then took a deep breath and followed him down, shouting as she went.

The speed was exhilarating. It felt a little like flying with each big leap down. Even though she fully expected to wipe out, she managed to keep her feet.

She stood above him, blocking the sun over his face. "I did it! And didn't eat it at the bottom, unlike some people."

"You sure about that?"

That was the only warning she got before he grabbed her legs, pulling her down in a heap with him. She laughed and swatted at him. He lay back in the sand, arms near his head and knees bent, feet flat. She could already feel sand in her shorts. But she didn't want to move away from him. Leaning back, she came to rest against his legs.

They sat there quietly, a peaceful silence stretching between them. It wasn't awkward, but felt like one of those spaces waiting to be filled. She could almost hear the questions between them, ones aching to be talked about.

Hesitantly, Emily reached out and touched the scars on the front of his leg. There were a few—long, thin, and white compared to his tan skin. Some from the accident itself where the bones broke through and some from the surgeries after.

"That was the scariest night of my life," she said, surprised at the emotion in her voice. "Natalie sent me a text saying you had a bad accident, but didn't really say much. I was really afraid we'd lose you."

"Impossible. I'm invincible," he said.

"No—you aren't. That's the thing. I bet you still think you are. Being a fireman: running into burning buildings, climbing up tall ladders to save damsels in distress. It's a good fit for you. But I bet anything that you're not nearly careful enough."

Under her fingertips, the scar tissue was smooth. She traced the line down the front of his shin, remembering Jimmy in a hospital bed, pale and pumped full of morphine. The memories of that night and the thought of his injuries made her feel sick. He had been so pale and in so much pain. And then he struggled so much after: losing his scholarship, having to spend months in a chair. He missed going to college completely and Natalie gave up law school to stay home and help him.

"You sound ... bitter.

"Maybe I just worry about you. Is that bad?"

"I don't mind," he said. "It means you care."

"Did you doubt that?"

"No," he said, but she didn't believe him. Not for the first time, she thought about apologizing for how she acted at the wedding. She couldn't bring herself to say the words.

Emily knew she should probably stop touching his leg, especially if she wanted to keep to the party line of just friendship, but she was fascinated with the scars. They were like a map that she wanted to study. He had grown still under her touch, as though afraid if he moved, she would take her hands away. She wondered if the touch had the same effect on him it had on her. He seemed totally calm on the surface, like this was something they did every day.

"You want to know the scariest moment of my life?" His Adam's apple bobbed heavily as he spoke. "When I recognized you up there on that balcony. And it continued until the moment you were safe. I don't know what I would have done if you hadn't gotten off that balcony in time."

"But I did. Thanks to you. I don't know if anyone else

could have gotten me to let go of that railing. I'm really glad it was you on that ladder."

They were both quiet for a moment.

"Have you told Natalie I'm here?" she asked.

"No. Didn't you? That's the kind of thing you usually share with your BFF."

"I haven't talked to her in a while."

"That's crazy. You guys used to talk all the time. Did something happen?"

Just that she didn't think I was good enough for you.

"She's so busy with Scarlet. It's been harder to catch up. She's still my best friend. Our lives are just ... kind of different speeds right now."

"I can see that. Scarlet is the cutest little girl in the whole world. But a wild one. I think Natalie's exhausted."

"She is. I bet you're a great uncle."

"If I saw her more, I would be. It's hard to get away. I haven't been able to convince them to come down enough. I'll have to call her later and tell her about this week. She won't believe it."

"Yeah," she said, but the word sounded flat.

He didn't seem to catch the hesitation in her voice. "Unless you want to?"

"That's okay. You can."

She and Natalie may not be as close, but her best friend always saw through her. If Emily called to say that she was spending time with Jimmy, she might tell her to back off again. Or she might hear the conflicted emotions Emily was fighting.

What did she want from Jimmy? She knew her feelings ran much deeper than friendship. Attraction didn't seem like a strong enough word. Everything in her felt like it was gravitating toward him. Like she was caught in his orbit. The thought made her feel panicky. Did she ... love him? Was that even possible after not seeing him for three years?

Maybe she *should* call Natalie. That would be a quick way to get over whatever crazy things she had. Natalie would remind her not to lead him on and then Emily could manage to keep Jimmy at arm's length. Somehow. She sighed and pulled her hands away, putting them in her lap.

"So, what'd you think?" Jimmy asked.

"About?"

"Jockey's Ridge. It's one of my favorite places on the Outer Banks. Like a beautiful desert plunked down into the middle of two bodies of water. Crazy."

Emily bit her lip. "Here's a little-known fact about me. I hate sand."

"You hate ... sand?"

"Yep."

Jimmy began to laugh. He laughed so hard that his body shook against hers. His eyes were closed, tears running down his face.

"What?" She couldn't help but giggle a little herself. He was hysterical and couldn't speak for a few minutes.

"You hate sand," he said, "and I brought you to the largest natural sand dunes this side of the country."

This threw him into another fit of laughter. She laughed along with him, then stood up.

"Now that I've confessed that I hate sand, let's get out of here. Wasn't there a promise made about lunch?"

He hopped to his feet, brushing sand from his legs. His cheek had a fine dusting of sand and she reached over to brush it away. It was a mistake. As soon as she touched his face, she felt breathless. She didn't want to just brush away the sand. She wanted to trace his cheek and the fine blond stubble along his jawline and down his neck.

Her eyes met his for a moment and she couldn't take his gaze. There were years of memories in the deep blue and a heat that she couldn't be imagining. She pulled her hand away and turned back toward the car.

No more. This can't—and won't—work. We're just friends. We're just friends.

These little speeches to herself weren't working anymore. Why couldn't she and Jimmy be more?

Because he's your best friend's little brother. That excuse wasn't enough either. So, why was she fighting this so hard?

Emily swallowed, thinking of Hudson. And the guys before that. She had never been enough for them. None of the guys she had dated could remotely compare to Jimmy. He was miles ahead of them in terms of his looks, his character, and just how much of a connection she felt. If she wasn't good enough for them, how could she possibly be enough for Jimmy? He deserved a sweet Christian girl with no baggage in her past. Someone more pure, more kind, more of that Proverbs 31 woman people loved going on about, the one who made Emily feel so inadequate.

When Jimmy realized, just like every other guy did, that Emily wasn't sweet enough or whatever enough to be marriage material, she would get the same speech from him. Emily didn't think she would survive hearing those words from Jimmy's lips. Whatever feelings she had beyond friendship, she needed to lock down tight. Before she ended up broken-hearted. It would be best for both of them if she saved him the trouble of finding out that she wasn't the right girl for him. She began to walk faster.

"I can't believe you hate sand," Jimmy called, jogging to catch up with her long strides.

Her mouth felt dry as she walked quickly ahead of him

toward the car. Emily swallowed down. "Maybe you don't know me as well as you think."

~

Jimmy shouldn't have been surprised at Emily's appetite after the waffles the night before. But he still stared in awe as she polished off the Manhandler, the biggest sandwich on the Country Deli menu. Watching her consume enormous amounts of food gave him a surprising degree of pleasure. She shouldn't be able to look so good and eat so much. It was amazing.

"They have foosball!" Emily said, wiping her mouth.

His eyes caught on her lips and it took a moment for her words to soak in. He stood. "I challenge you to a game. I'll go easy on you."

She rolled her eyes at his smirk. "No need. I'm pretty good at foosball. I don't need your patronizing, sexist 'help,' James."

And she didn't. Jimmy played his best and she pummeled him the first two games. Admittedly he'd been a little distracted watching her play, but she would have beaten him even with total focus. She made the cutest face when she was concentrating, chewing one side of her lip while she expertly turned the handles. She had a killer left-handed goalie shot that went straight to the back of his goal with a thwacking sound every time.

"When did you get so good?" he asked as she scored on him again. She was up two games to nothing and the score was nine to two in this third game. He didn't have a chance.

"We had a foosball table in the New York apartment after high school. Which makes no sense, as the apartment was

125

barely bigger than a foosball table. Anyway—foosball table but no TV. We were bored. So, we all got to be pretty good."

For as long as he'd known her, Emily almost never talked about her time in New York modeling. Jimmy wasn't sure why, but she seemed to skirt around that period in her life. This was the most detail he had ever heard about it. A tiny detail, but still. He didn't know if it was because she couldn't make it as a high fashion model in New York or something else.

"You were living in an apartment full of models who played foosball?"

"Yep. I know. It should have been a reality show." She flicked her wrist and the ball cracked against the back of his goal again. "That's game!"

She ran around the table and grabbed him in a hug. Though he'd known her for years and they'd been close, there hadn't been a lot of hugging or physical touch. Back then he would have loved this—and really, he still did, but it was fairly killing him now: the light floral scent of her lotion or perfume, the way her body easily folded into his. He hoped she couldn't tell how his skin started to smolder when she touched him. Being close to her felt good. Too good. Jimmy wanted to soak up every touch, while at the same time, every instinct of self-preservation he had told him to run. He had done this before and still remembered how it ended. Instead of pulling away, Jimmy found himself dipping his head slightly so that his nose was buried in Emily's hair.

She froze and pulled away, blinking, like she wasn't sure how she ended up in his arms. Clearing her throat, she turned away, moving back to the table where she took a long sip of her soda. Jimmy joined her at the table and finished off his water before throwing away their lunch trash.

"Thanks for lunch," Emily said.

"Thanks for schooling me in foosball."

"Don't take the loss too hard. I don't want you to lose respect for yourself."

"Ha. I have very little respect for myself."

"Really? Huh. The Jimmy I used to know was full of swagger, loved to strut, loved to take his shirt off. Show off all his attributes." She wiggled her eyebrows at him.

Jimmy ran a hand over the back of his neck. "Uh, yeah. I did that. I'd like to think I've grown up a little bit since my taking-off-my-shirt-to-impress-you days. Not that it worked," he muttered.

His eyes fell down to the floor, so it surprised him when Emily's fingertips grazed his arm. "You'd be surprised how effective it was," she murmured, pushing past him to the door.

His heart skidded to a stop. Did she just—was she ... flirting? When he didn't follow, too startled to even move, she turned back at the door and gave him a wide smile. "You coming, Jimmy?"

"Yep." He jogged after her and managed to open her car door.

"So, I think despite my hatred for sand, I need to spend some time on the beach. That's what the girls were up to, so I should probably make an appearance. Want to join us?"

He wanted to crack a joke about impressing her by taking his shirt off again, but couldn't quite muster whatever swagger she thought he used to have. "Sure."

Emily yawned and lowered her seat, nestling back into it, turned slightly toward him. "Wow. All the exercise has me exhausted." Jimmy snorted and she smacked him on the forearm. "Hey. That was exercise for me."

"Climbing the small sand hills or playing table soccer?" Jimmy asked.

"Both. This?" She gestured to her body from her toes all the way up to her head. Jimmy swallowed and tried to keep his eyes on the road. "Is all genetics and exactly zero exercise, Mr. Muscles."

Jimmy grinned. "You noticed my muscles, huh? Even with my shirt on?"

Emily groaned and threw a dramatic hand over her face. "Your muscles are probably visible from a space station. Happy? Now, I'm going to take a little nap. Wake me up when we get back." She yawned again. When he went to turn the music down, she touched his arm again, softer this time. It sent waves of heat rising over his skin. "Leave it on. I like your weird music."

Jimmy rolled his eyes and put both hands back on the wheel, trying not to notice the way her shorts rode up a little, revealing more of the creamy skin of her legs. Within moments, she was asleep. Her eyes were hidden behind sunglasses, but at a stoplight, Jimmy could see the even rise and fall of her breathing. Hesitant at first, Jimmy reached out his hand to thread fingers through her hair. When she made a soft sound and leaned into the touch, he firmed his touch, letting his fingers work through her hair, gently massaging her head.

By the time they pulled up to Jackson's house, Jimmy had a cramp in his arm and a burning in his gut. It didn't matter how much that fearful part of him said to back away, he felt pulled into Emily's inescapable orbit. Again. Or had he ever really left it? Suddenly his move to run away and move to Sandover seemed as ineffective as holding a newspaper over his head in a rainstorm. He still loved her. The big question was: how did Emily feel about him?

Emily stirred as he removed his fingers from her hair and threw the car in park. She groaned and stretched her arms above her head, revealing a tiny sliver of pale skin at her stomach before she tugged down on her shirt. "Thanks for letting me nap. Sorry I was such bad company."

"You're fine," he said. "I did keep you up pretty late last night."

"I think that was me keeping you up."

"It was an equal partnership of non-sleeping. You needed a rest."

She cocked her head and tipped her sunglasses up, revealing her startling blue eyes. "Did I dream you giving me the best head massage of my life?"

Jimmy couldn't read the intense expression in her eyes. "Guilty as charged. Is that ... okay?"

"Okay? I'm thinking now of how to pack you in my bag and take you home with me."

Her tone was light, which just made Jimmy's heart ache more. He didn't want it to be a joke. Though he wouldn't want her to take him home. He'd like to keep her here with him. The very idea got him too excited, too hopeful. She was being lightly flirty, but she had always been just at that edge of friendly and flirty with him. It didn't mean anything.

"I'm staying in your room. Need me to get you clothes or anything? I can keep you safe from Stacy."

"You're staying in my room?" He hoped his face didn't show the crazy feelings coursing through him at the thought of Emily in his bed.

"Yep. I hope that's okay."

"Sure. Yeah. Could you get me a bathing suit? Second drawer on the left side."

"You could always come and get it yourself?"

Jimmy knew she didn't mean anything by that, but the thought of being alone in his bedroom with Emily made his heart go a little too wild. "That's okay. Just toss one out to me and I'll change in Jackson's room."

When Emily threw him his least favorite swim trunks, bright red with turquoise sharks and purple hearts all over them, he rolled his eyes. They had been a gift from "Scarlet," aka, something Natalie picked out from his niece. Closer to a gag gift than anything, he hadn't been able to throw them out. Emily grinned. "Those looked like just your style."

"Scarlet picked them out. According to Natalie."

Emily laughed. "That makes total sense. Okay. I'll see you out there, shark boy."

Despite the fact that he had to climb up and down more flights of stairs, Jimmy beat Emily out to the beach. Robbie was trying to give a few of the women body surfing tips, while Beau and Whit had set up a net for beach volleyball and were playing a rousing game of two on two. Jimmy had promptly forgotten all of the women's names, other than Stacy and Kim, the redheaded bachelorette. Hard to miss her, as she was still wearing a bachelorette sash over her bikini. He chuckled and set up two chairs he'd carried out from under Jackson's house. He waved to Beau and sat down in one of the chairs, just watching all the activity.

As soon as Emily arrived, it was like the tone of the group shifted. The volleyball game came to a sudden halt and women congregated around Emily, like they were waiting for her to decide what to do next. Except Stacy, who left for a walk with Robbie. Within minutes, Emily was organizing a human pyramid in the shallow waves for a photo. Beau and Whit had what seemed like a thousand phones, snapping photos for the giggling tower of women. They got taken out by a rogue wave and all came up, sputtering, laughing, and hair plastered to their faces, Emily laughing harder than all of them. She moved next to the volleyball net, picking up a big beach ball instead of the actual volleyball, leading to a humorous game that looked like it was in slow motion due to the lightness of the beach ball.

Jimmy felt oddly introspective, happy to watch despite Beau and Emily both waving him over. Though their outward personalities were very different, Emily was a lot like Beau. He was the glue not only for Jimmy, Jackson, and Cash, setting up and keeping up their once weekly coffee and Bible study, but even in the station with the guys like Whit and Robbie. Beau had an easy leadership that people looked to without him demanding it.

He wondered if it secretly wore on Beau the way it seemed to in Emily. By the time she fell into the chair next to him, she looked exhausted. Emily did seem exhausted by it. Clearly these girls looked to her, but they also expected her to be on all the time. They all scattered once she sat down.

"Maybe the beach isn't so bad," Emily said, flicking droplets of water on him from her hair. After the volleyball game, which no one seemed to win, she had led a mad dash into the ocean. "I've never been crazy about it, but I like it here. Despite the sand."

"I'm glad. I really love it here."

She leaned sideways in her chair, curling her legs up and facing him. "Do you think you'll stay here forever? Or will you ever come back to Richmond?" Her voice was soft, curious.

"I'm not sure. But I really have come to think of this as home."

"It suits you. I don't know if this makes sense, but you seem more ... you." Before he could think of how to respond to what sounded like a compliment, Emily nodded to his bathing suit. "The shark and heart trend also suits you."

"I'm not sure that sharks and hearts are a trend."

"It beats out high fashion. Trust me on that. You'd never believe some of the stuff I had to wear on the runway."

"I bet." Jimmy gave her a quick glance, trying not to be creepy. Her plain black bathing suit from the other night on the balcony had been replaced with a red and white checked pattern that looked like something from a 50s pinup calendar. Very appropriate, especially compared to a lot of the tiny swatches of fabric women wore on the beach, but Emily looked amazing in everything she wore.

Emily sighed and rested her fingers on his arm. Jimmy stilled, afraid if he moved even slightly, she would remove her hand. The touch was tender, like when she had traced the scars on his leg at Jockey's Ridge. In those moments, Emily took down her shield, even if briefly. He struggled to breathe, feeling her fingertips trace over his skin. Even these small touches ignited all the feelings he had for her, physically and otherwise. They also made his mind race with questions.

What did the touch mean to her? Did she feel the same chemistry that made his body blaze to life? How did she feel about him? If she didn't feel anything, why was she touching him?

They sat in silence and he realized after a few minutes she had fallen asleep again, her eyes hidden behind sunglasses and her head lolling a little to one side. She must really be exhausted. He wanted to scoot his chair closer, to let her head rest on his shoulder, but knew if he did, she might wake and put her walls right back up. Instead, he sat as still as he could, relishing in the feel of her hand where it rested on his arm and the soft sleeping sounds that came from her. He could get used to this. He *wanted* to get used to this.

He dozed himself and sometime later a dog barking startled Emily awake and her hand dropped. "Sorry. Today has taken a lot out of me."

"I don't mind. I fell asleep too. It was kind of nice."

She smiled sideways at him. "Yeah, it kind of was."

"Emily!" Kim called from down the beach and Jimmy realized in the time they'd slept, the other women had packed up their towels and Beau had taken down the volleyball net. "We're heading up! We'll leave around five, okay?"

Emily waved and stood, stretching until Jimmy heard her back pop several times. "Well, I think we're going to an early dinner to send off the girls leaving tonight. Thanks for hanging with me today. Hope it wasn't too much trouble."

"You're no trouble," Jimmy said.

Emily looked him in the eye before heading back to the house. "That's where you're wrong. I'm nothing *but*."

Jimmy didn't know if she was joking or giving him some kind of warning, but trying to calm the erratic galloping of his heart, he knew it was true. Emily was trouble and he was in too deep to care.

CHAPTER TWELVE

Emily had taken charge of the grocery cart. While Kim and Sarah argued about meal plans and what they needed to buy, she put her foot up on the cart and pushed off, riding the cart down the aisle like she was a little kid. She wasn't feeling childlike, however. Just child*ish*.

The agency called that morning and left a message saying that she didn't get the print campaign. Which meant more time living at home with her parents and more time working at her ridiculous temp job. For ... what? Her life was starting to feel like it was just fading out into nothingness. This week had been a surprising bright spot with Jimmy, but he had gone back to work this morning and she missed him desperately. It was amazing how attached she felt in just a few days. What was she going to do when she left Sandover Friday? The thought made her feel sick.

As the cart sailed down the aisle, lifting her hair from the back of her neck, she tried to push thoughts of Jimmy away. She needed to focus on her future and some kind of real life plan. She wasn't lazy. The hard work that got her to New

York the first time proved that. Emily had drive, but she lacked direction and purpose. Modeling had been her life, only partly because of her mother's influence, but after the second time in New York, she couldn't bring herself to think about doing it full time. It wasn't the work of modeling so much as the lifestyle.

An older woman turned into the aisle, giving Emily a dirty look. She hopped down off the cart, searching behind her for Sarah and Kim. They were still bickering in front of the whole grain crackers.

"Ladies," Emily said. "It's food. Not a treaty for world peace. I'm going to just load up with frozen pizzas if you don't hurry up."

Kim sighed. "I was trying to be good and eat well the rest of the week because of the wedding. But I also don't want to cook. And it's Jackson's kitchen so I just feel weird. Frozen pizza it is."

"We'll get some bagged salads," Emily said. "They can help offset your guilt."

At the end of the aisle Emily turned toward the produce section, not waiting for Kim and Sarah. They were now heatedly discussing cereal and whether whole or skim milk was healthier.

As Emily neared the produce section, she saw a big wooden cart display with local fruits and vegetables. A sign talked about the history of fruit stands to the island's local economy and culture. She stopped to read and picked up a ripe tomato. It smelled so good she wanted to take a bite out of it like an apple.

"What do you think?" Jackson's voice startled her and she dropped the tomato, wincing as it hit the ground. He only smiled and bent to pick it up.

"Oh, no! Sorry. Didn't mean to murder an innocent. You

need bells or something. You're like a silent ninja. I'll take that since I ruined it."

"Don't worry about it," he said, turning it between his palms. "What do you think about the displays?"

"I stopped to read, which means that it's effective. I think it's neat."

Jackson made a face. "Neat? Okay, so you hate it."

"No, I actually mean it. Just poor word choice due to the whole you scaring me thing. I like the idea a lot."

"I'd say thanks, but it was all Mercer," Jackson said. Emily realized that a woman who looked like she was fresh out of college stood on the other side of Jackson.

Emily clutched her hand to her chest. "Do you require all employees to also undergo silent ninja training? Jeez." She reached around Jackson to offer her hand. "I'm Emily. I saw you sing at church, right? You've got some pipes."

"Thanks." Mercer shook her hand firmly but dropped it quickly, barely meeting Emily's gaze. She wasn't being rude and it didn't feel like shyness. More like, she was extra reserved.

"And you work here with Jackson?" Emily pressed. Reserved people were like a special challenge to her. She got a weird pleasure out of making people talk or cracking their shells.

"I do."

"She's the manager and handles projects like this that really help us be the store we want to be. Local. Not a chain." Jackson had notes of pride in his voice. While this had just been a grocery store to Emily, she could see and hear how important it was to him. Not just as a business, but something more.

"I think it's great," Emily said.

What she really thought was that it was depressing

someone as young as Mercer was managing a whole store and planning initiatives while Emily was still a temp. I mean, good for Mercer. Bad for Emily. She tried to shake the dark cloud out of her head.

"So, not to bring up a touchy subject, but the store seems pretty quiet. Is it just a bad time for shopping? Or is this normal?"

Jackson sighed. "No, it's too empty. We're working on that. Everyone's at the Harris Teeter up the road."

Emily looked around, noting the details that she didn't normally see in a grocery store. The one nearby customer had an employee helping her pick out peaches from another bin. The conversation seemed light and friendly. She heard laughter over the rows of fruit and veggies.

Then there was this display, which was both well-done and innovative. The idea really hitched onto the trend for farm to market and local, sustainable products without seeming like it was just jumping on the bandwagon. It seemed genuine.

"You're smart," Emily said to Mercer. "This is really good. It has the emotional component to it, but doesn't feel manipulative. Honest and, sorry for a trendy term, organic."

Mercer nodded and gave Emily a small smile. "Thanks."

She was a tough nut to crack, but Emily liked that about her. If she were staying here, Mercer would be the first friend she tried to make. Friendship with Mercer seemed like it wouldn't be easy, but would be a struggle well worth her while.

Wait—if she were staying? Why was she even thinking about friendship with Mercer? Emily would leave on Friday. She shook off the thoughts and went back to assessing the store.

"Do you guys ever partner with local restaurants or chefs?" Emily asked. She was thinking of a campaign in New York she did early on where the agency contracted with an events company to have the models show up along with other social media influencers to build buzz around a local opening.

"Let me show you our cafe," Jackson said. He was practically bouncing on his heels.

"I'm getting back to inventory," Mercer said. "Good to meet you, Emily."

"You too. Nice work in the store!"

Mercer only nodded and barely avoided colliding with Kim and Sarah as they came around the corner, balancing half a dozen frozen pizzas in their arms. "There you are," Kim said. "We need the cart. Hey, Jackson! We love your store"

"You can take over cart duty," Emily said, giving it a gentle shove in their direction. "I'm going to head over to the cafe with Jackson. Meet me there in a few? We can snag lunch or something."

As they walked amicably toward the cafe, Emily continued looking around the store, noticing the details: the neat ordering of each aisle, the hand lettered signs in various spots around the store, how each employee smiled and made eye contact. And how empty the aisles were.

The cafe was more of the same theme: bright, clean, inviting, and mostly empty. There were a few different food stations with grilled sandwiches, sushi, and other homemade food items to take home or eat in the comfortable looking seating area.

"So, what's the problem? Your store is incredible. Why isn't anyone here?"

Jackson's face was guarded. He ran a hand over his chin,

which was covered in a day or two of growth. "Great question."

"Sorry," she said. "I'm blunt. I really love it and think it's amazing. Just trying to pinpoint the disconnect."

"Do you work in marketing?"

She laughed. "Hardly. I'm now an unglorified secretary at a marketing agency. Before that I was a model. I have zero qualifications for anything."

His eyes were assessing. "That's not true. I get the sense you'd be extremely qualified for whatever you do."

The compliment filled Emily with warmth. Hardly anyone ever praised anything about her other than her looks. "Thank you."

"I don't know what the disconnect is," Jackson said. "Other than price. And the changing culture of the island. We are the oldest. The first. Family owned. Not my family, but my family bought it to keep the store intact and preserve the history. It used to matter to On Islanders. Now, price trumps everything. We can't match Harris Teeter. Plus, the island has changed. More On Islanders have moved off. Sandover is more of a tourist destination than it used to be."

Emily nodded. "That makes sense. I mean, of course. I guess I just feel like...I don't know. Price doesn't trump some things."

"Like what?" Jackson asked.

Loyalty. Luxury. Story. She may not have a degree in marketing, but she had researched and listened to a lot of podcasts on things like entrepreneurship and business. She had also picked up a lot at her temp job, despite their insistence that she answer phones and not use her brain. She had never had an opportunity to apply the things she'd picked up.

"I'm not sure," Emily said. She didn't trust the words

floating in her head. As they stood talking Emily noticed the fire engine out front by the curb.

"Hey—is the store on fire?"

Jackson followed her gaze and chuckled. "Nah. Probably Beau and Jimmy are here getting groceries. Those guys can put away the food. They come in a few times a week to stock the station."

Emily felt a thrill thinking about Jimmy here. She curled her fingers into her palm so Jackson wouldn't see them practically vibrating with excitement.

"They're nothing if not loyal," Jackson said. "Anyway, thanks for the feedback. I'd love to hear more if you have any brilliant ideas. I'll take any of them."

"Thanks." Emily was once again feeling warmed by the respect he seemed to have for her. Undeserved, but she was grateful. With a wave, Jackson disappeared deeper into the store.

Emily heard Kim and Sarah and ducked down the frozen food aisle. She wanted to find Jimmy. He was here somewhere and the pull towards him was like some primal call she couldn't ignore. She had gone three years without seeing or talking to him but now being apart for a few hours left her feeling aching and empty.

Emily found Jimmy and Beau toward the back of the store near a section of refrigerated meats. Jimmy tossed a few racks of ribs to Beau who tossed them in the cart. They worked together like a machine, not even talking, the way good friends can. With an ache, she thought about how she and Natalie used to have that kind of easy friendship. Now they were lucky if they saw each other twice a month. And it just wasn't the same. The more time she spent with Jimmy, the more Emily realized how deeply Natalie's words had cut

141

her. She had let those words build a wall between her and her best friend.

What would Natalie say when she found that Emily had spent so much time with Jimmy this week?

Pushing the thought aside, Emily took a breath and started forward. She was only here for a few more days. It was stupid to let the past or even future worries cloud this time. For now, she should stop fighting it and just go with her gut. She could worry about the consequences later.

Grabbing a tube of frozen ground beef from a nearby display, Emily crept up behind Jimmy. Beau saw her coming and she put a finger to her lips. He smiled and looked down so he wouldn't give her away. When she was right behind Jimmy, she placed the frozen tube against the back of his neck.

With a shout, Jimmy jumped and spun, almost taking her down. Emily dropped the tube of beef, which landed on her toes. The pain was instant and blinding.

She began to laugh hysterically.

"Emily?" He was looking at her like she was insane.

"My toes," she managed to gasp.

"What?" Beau joined Jimmy and they both stared at her as she laughed and wiped her eyes and clutched her foot.

"I think ... I broke my toes ... with beef."

Understanding flashed on Jimmy's face. Kneeling, he took her foot in his hand. Emily grabbed his shoulder to steady herself, loving the solid feel of him even through the stabbing pain in her foot.

"Emily," Beau said. "I don't know you well, but you sure end up on the wrong side of a lot of accidents."

She glared. "Total coincidence. Or bad luck. Maybe it's your island. It's a death trap."

Jimmy shot Beau a glance and then looked up at her with

a grin that sent her stomach flipping. "Definitely not the Island. We used to call her All-the-Attention-Emily. So much drama."

"I think your memory is broken," Emily said. "I'm so not dramatic."

"Mm-hm. The bad news is that I think you managed to break these two toes."

Her toes were killing her but not so much that she wasn't affected by his strong hands and soft touch. It was a welcome distraction. "Are they the ones who went to market or the one who went wee wee wee all the way home?"

Jimmy chuckled. "I think these are the one who got ground beef and the one who got none, actually. Which is fitting."

"Of course. What's the prescription, doc?"

He got a funny look on his face. "You need to elevate it and ice it." He held up the frozen tube of ground beef. "This would actually work."

Emily groaned. "The hair of the dog that bit me."

"More like the hair of the beef that bit you," Jimmy said. And the two of them fell into hysterics. It had been so long since she had laughed this hard or since she'd heard the sound of his laughter. Emily clutched her stomach with one hand, the other tightening on Jimmy to keep her upright. Beau stood nearby, shaking his head.

"I'm going to finish the shopping up," Beau said. "Em, you should come to lunch at the station. Jimmy can get a better look at your toes. I don't know if you need a splint or something, but he'll fix you up."

He walked away with the cart, whistling. Jimmy stood and offered Emily his arm. She wrapped her fingers around his bicep. She hadn't meant to hurt her toes and it hurt like crazy, but now she was getting to go to work with Jimmy.

Toes would heal. This would go down as a fair trade in her book.

"My lady, may I escort you to our truck?"

"If I had a dollar for every time I heard that line ..."

"You'd have a dollar?" He grinned at her.

"Yep. Just the one."

Without warning, Jimmy swooped her up in his arms, causing her to squeal in a very un-Emily fashion. He cradled her against his chest and her hands automatically went behind his neck.

"Jimmy! You can't just carry me through the store."

"I not only can, but I *am* carrying you through the store. This is faster than you're gimpy limping."

Emily giggled as he marched toward the front of the store, carrying her bridal style. Though she had protested, she did not mind at all. Emily had a lithe build, but she was not a small woman. She loved Jimmy's strength and how effortless he made it seem to carry her. She rested her head on his chest. His heartbeat raced along in his chest, making her smile. It was no match for hers, though, which felt like it had grown wings. Emily smiled and closed her eyes.

This.

This is what she wanted. Being this close. Feeling secure in his arms. She wanted Jimmy. All the uncertainty in her future still hung like a haze, except this one shining light: she wanted Jimmy in her future. Not as a friend. Not as someone who lived hours away from her.

What if he didn't feel the same way? She could sense the attraction between them, a chemistry that seemed to charge the air with electricity when they were nearby or touched. But Jimmy had always looked up to her. He probably had totally unrealistic expectations of her, the way you do with a childhood crush. What if that's all he felt for her?

She pressed her face tighter into his chest, breathing him in. Again, she was worrying too much.

Emily wished the walk to the engine was longer. For once, she didn't fight letting someone else take care of her. It was nice for once to be taken care of. To let someone else do even little things. Usually she fought to do everything on her own.

That was one of the things Hudson had said to her in his breakup speech, which he had clearly rehearsed. "You don't need me," he had said. "It's like you feel you don't need anyone. I can't get close to you. It's all surface."

Thinking of those words made her eyes sting with tears. Not because she missed Hudson, but because she wanted so badly to let that guard down with Jimmy. To need him. But she kept coming back to the fear of him not feeling the same way. Or just liking her surface, not everything underneath. Who she really was, her past—everything. Jimmy was such a good guy. Emily had a host of problems: a messed-up family, no real job or plans for the future, and things in her past she had never told anyone.

New York. The thought came to her, filling her with the usual sense of shame. Emily swallowed down the knot in her throat. She would never know how Jimmy felt if she didn't take down her walls. If he turned and ran the way every other guy did, it would destroy her. But was it worse not to try?

When he shifted to open the door, she clung tighter to him. He gave a low chuckle. "Okay, spider monkey. You're going to have to let me go if you want me to help you in."

Emily gave a dramatic sigh and loosened her grip. "A girl could get used to this. I mean, even if I didn't have busted toes, I kind of like this whole being carried around thing."

"I'm not sure you could afford my rates as a personal carrier."

"Probably not. Especially because I'd want exclusive

rights." She hadn't meant the words to come out so flirty, but there they were.

Jimmy lifted her up into one of the back seats and caged her in with a hand on each side of her thighs. His gaze was intense. If her heart had been flying before, it was now moving at light speed.

"You want exclusive rights to me, huh?"

Yes. Absolutely yes. "Um ... yes?" A flush stained her cheeks.

Jimmy stepped up on the side of the truck, crowding her in a way that she loved. She resisted the urge to grab him by the shirt and bring him closer. He lifted a hand toward her face and tucked a strand of hair behind her ear. It immediately came loose in the breeze that always seemed to be moving over the island. He moved it behind her ear again, letting his hand linger on her neck, holding her hair in place.

"I think that could be arranged. I wouldn't mind an exclusive contract with you." His voice was low and husky, doing funny things to her chest.

"Yeah?"

He made a sound that was somewhere between an affirmation of assent and a growl. They stared at each other for a long moment. Her heart had been racing, but now felt like it was slowing to a stop. His gaze fell to her lips. Without meaning to, Emily licked her lips, which suddenly felt dry under his gaze. She wanted nothing more than to close the distance between them and press her lips to his. But she couldn't make the first move. Jimmy leaned closer and her eyes closed. She felt his breath on her face and her skin tingled, every nerve ending doing a happy dance.

"There you are!"

Beau's voice shattered the moment and her eyes flew open in time to see disappointment flash across Jimmy's

146

face. He schooled his features into a smirk and gave her a wink that seemed to indicate that they'd return to this moment later. Emily's breath fell out of her in a long sigh. She hadn't realized she'd been holding it.

Beau stopped the full cart next to the engine. "How are the toes?"

"Still broken," Emily said. Jimmy moved away, starting to pile grocery bags in the front seat.

"I ran into Kim and ... Stacy? Or Sarah?"

"Sarah," Emily said.

"Sarah. Right. Do they always bicker like an old married couple?"

"Yep." Emily smiled at Beau as he handed Jimmy another bag.

"Anyway, I let them know you messed up your toes and are coming to the station with us to get fixed up and have lunch. We can return you later."

"Aren't you guys working?"

"Afternoons before the full tourist season are typically pretty slow. We've already done some drills, had an equipment check, and a workout this morning, so a little down time is okay. I mean, if all this is okay with you?"

"Sounds great." Emily's gaze shifted to Jimmy as he put the last two bags up front and shut the door. Beau spun the cart away to one of the return areas.

Smiling, Jimmy hopped up on the side of the truck and leaned close again. Emily's whole chest tightened, like an invisible corset had just been cinched up. Her lips parted and her gaze dropped to his mouth, eager to recapture that lost moment. But Jimmy only grinned and pulled the seatbelt securely around her waist. His smile widened as he closed the door and climbed over her, intentionally pressing down on her body with his weight, careful to avoid stepping on her feet.

"Oof!" Emily groaned and poked Jimmy in the side.

He laughed and flinched away, flopping down in the seat beside her. "Hey, no tickling." Jimmy buckled his seatbelt and gave Emily a smile.

"Then no squishing."

Beau hopped up front behind the wheel and turned back to look at them. "Pipe down you two. Is this your first ride in a fire truck, Emily?"

"Yep."

"I hope it doesn't disappoint." Beau turned back around and the truck rumbled to life.

"Me too," Emily whispered.

Jimmy gave her a last quick look before they pulled out of the parking lot, his eyes full of a longing that she knew was mirrored in her own. Yep. It was official. Her walls were coming crashing down, leaving her open to love, but also open to a pain she didn't want to even imagine.

CHAPTER THIRTEEN

Once they got to the station, Jimmy was surprised that Emily demanded a tour first thing. "We should fix up your toes," he said as Beau called down Whit and Robbie to help carry the groceries upstairs.

"Eh. I'm getting used to the pain. And you already told me there's not much you can do about broken toes, right?"

"Ice and elevate. Which you can't do if you're walking around." Jimmy loved that she was interested in his work and the station. But he didn't want to have to watch her hobble around in pain. She was always too tough for her own good.

She rolled her eyes. "After I see the station, I'll sit in a chair like a good girl, icing and elevating. I've never been in a fire station, if you can believe that. I want to see it."

Beau grinned as he passed by where they were arguing next to the truck. "Jimmy, just be her crutch. If need be, carry her like you did in the parking lot. She can't weigh more than a buck twenty."

He definitely wouldn't mind holding Emily in his arms.

She molded to his body perfectly. Anything to get her closer
...

"Compromise. Let me tape your toes first," Jimmy said.

He helped Emily to a seat in the truck bay and found a roll of duct tape. He knelt at her feet and propped her heel on his knee. Tenderly he began to tape the two swollen toes together.

"Really? Duct tape? I thought you were, like, trained."

"Believe it or not, I've found that this works better than the athletic or first-aid tape. Is this too tight?"

She touched his shoulder and it sent a wave of awareness through his body. "It feels good. Thank you."

Nervous, he found his mouth firing off facts. "This is called buddy taping. You may need to change it out, but it's safe to shower and everything else. If you re-tape it, I put a cotton ball in there, which will help keep your skin from getting irritated. In probably about six weeks, you won't feel it anymore. Until then, you can just do whatever activity level you're comfortable with, but for the next few days, ice and elevate. And rest."

He looked up to find that she was grinning at him. Jimmy traced his fingertips along the bottom of her foot. It should have been ticklish, but she only stared at him. "It won't work."

"What?"

"My feet aren't ticklish. Most of me isn't, actually. It takes a lot to get me to laugh."

"I didn't know that about you."

"There's probably a lot you don't know about me." Her voice was quiet and tinged with something sad. Regret? Shame?

Jimmy stroked the bottom of her foot. She may not be

ticklish, but he saw the shiver that passed through her at his touch. "How's your pain level?"

"I'm okay," she said. "I mean, it hurts. But I think I'll live. Too bad I won't get a scar."

"You do love a good scar."

"Depends on the person with the scars."

She smiled and Jimmy felt that same twisting in his gut he did every time she touched him or said anything flirty. He didn't think he was reading between the lines, but it was hard for him to think that his dream girl might actually return his feelings. It seemed too good to be true. But if Beau hadn't interrupted them earlier, he had been about to kiss her. She looked completely on board with that. The idea got heat rushing through his body. He cleared his throat and stepped back, offering her his arm.

"Shall we? You can lean on me or I'm happy to be your personal—and exclusive—carrier if you'd like."

Emily grinned as she took his arm. He loved the way it felt to have her fingers curled around his bicep. "I'll try walking. If it gets to be too much, I'll ask for help."

"Will you? Because I seem to remember an Emily who was pretty stubborn and liked to do everything herself."

"I'm working on it," she said.

Beau and Robbie came back from upstairs. "Ready for the tour?" Beau asked.

"Yep," Emily said. "Hang on." She removed her hand from Jimmy's arm and wrapped it around his waist.

He curled his arm around her shoulder. "Sure I can't carry you?"

She rolled her eyes and huffed. "Let's get moving, Crutch. Now. Show me all the things."

Robbie trailed along behind them and Jimmy wished he would go back to whatever he had been doing. He was not subtle in checking Emily out. Jimmy felt a surge of protectiveness and anger. Not that it was surprising coming from Robbie, but he hated seeing guys treat girls like objects. Especially Emily. As much as possible, he tried to position them so that he stood between Emily and Robbie.

"There's no pole?" Emily said after they left the truck bay. "I was kind of excited about the pole."

"Most stations don't have them anymore," Beau said.

"That's a shame."

"You know your way around a pole?" Robbie said this with the maximum amount of innuendo and Emily jerked.

Jimmy tightened his arm around her and he clenched his teeth so hard she could probably hear it. *I'm going to kill him.* Jimmy's thoughts were immediately rage-filled to the point he couldn't even speak. He'd felt flashes of this before when guys had openly ogled Emily, but had never heard someone make a comment like this out loud to her. Especially not someone he knew and worked with. Beau gave Jimmy a warning look and opened his mouth, but Emily was quicker.

"Make a comment like that again and you'll be intimately familiar with a pole. Because I'll be using one to knock that smirk off your face."

Her voice had a sweetness to it that didn't match her words, making them somehow more ominous. And amazing. Jimmy was still almost vibrating with anger. He was furious with Robbie and almost as angry with himself. He should have said something. He should have stood up for her instead of silently seething. Emily could obviously handle herself. She didn't seem affected, but he knew how well she kept herself guarded. Emily pulled her hand from his waist to his back, smoothing it up and down as though to soothe him. She was insulted and degraded, but she was comforting *him*. This woman ...

Robbie took a step back as Beau took one forward with a hard look on his face. "Get out of here, man. We'll talk later."

Twisting his lips into a frown, Robbie cast a glare at Emily, but darted up the stairs.

He wouldn't be the only one talking to Robbie later. But Jimmy might need a day or two so he didn't lose control. "I'm so sorry about that," Beau said. "About him. That's not okay."

"Whatever." Emily gave an eye roll and patted Jimmy's back again before returning her arm to his waist. "I'm well-versed with idiots and how to handle them. Let's finish the tour. And then I want to eat food."

"I don't know if we have enough food here to handle your appetite," Jimmy said. It was hard to joke with his anger still humming right below the surface, but he thought banter with Emily might cool him down.

"Oh, Jimmy. You always know just what to say to make a girl feel special."

He and Beau both laughed as they headed to the workout room. It was pretty decent for the size. A few treadmills, a rowing machine, and a nice set of benches and weights for squats and bench presses and all the standard things.

"So this is the ab factory where they manufacture all the six packs." Emily smacked Jimmy in the stomach. He grunted, but didn't mind her touch. Not at all.

Beau laughed. "I guess so."

Emily's hand lingered on Jimmy's stomach for a moment and sent heat flashing up and down his body. He couldn't move away since he was helping to hold her up, but he shifted slightly so that her hand went safely back around his waist until he could breathe normally again.

Emily pulled slightly away and turned so she could see his face better. He could feel the heat in his cheeks. They were probably the color of the truck. "This is new. You look embarrassed, Jimmy." She turned to Beau. "Does Jimmy not rip his shirt off any chance he can get?"

Beau grinned, obviously enjoying her teasing. "No, he does not."

"Interesting. Because the Jimmy I knew took his shirt off as much as possible in front of me, whether the situation called for it or not. It's above 75 degrees? Shirt off. Tacos for dinner? Shirt off. It's a Wednesday afternoon? Shirt off."

"Is that so?" Beau said, chuckling. "Well, Jimmy. What do you have to say about that?"

"It was a long time ago," Jimmy said. "I was an idiot back then."

"Just back then?" Beau raised his eyebrows and Jimmy snorted. "So we don't need to worry about you ripping off your shirt anymore?"

"Unless we're at the beach. Then all bets—and shirts— are off. For now, you're safe."

Emily laughed and he turned them both so he could help her hobble out of the gym. He loved the fact that he could make her laugh. Her laughter sounded like life to him. Life and light and unbridled joy. He couldn't help smiling in return. His cheeks almost hurt from how much laughing and smiling they'd done over the past few days.

His smile faded and his breath caught as Emily leaned closer to him and spoke in a voice only Jimmy could hear. "Just so we're clear, I don't always like to be safe."

He couldn't keep a goofy grin from his face. Her closeness and the words with their hint of promise made his heart leap in his chest. A tiny sliver of doubt worked its way through his happy cocoon. Because as much as he wanted to trust whatever was happening between them, it felt in so many ways like a repeat of the past.

Her lips twisted in a smirk, like she knew just what effect she had on him. She probably did. Was it sincere? Or was she toying with him—again?

She nudged him with her hip and he tried to swallow down his doubts. "Come on, Crutch. Let's move."

Jimmy loved having Emily watch him cook. Not that making ribs was that big of a deal, but to impress her—he wasn't even denying it—he made homemade BBQ sauce rather than just using the bottle in the fridge. Beau winked, but didn't say anything. Emily's moans about how good the sauce was when they sat down to eat made it totally worth the extra effort.

"Let me get this straight. You cook now," Emily said, wiping sauce from her chin. "You're a fireman and you cook. Why hasn't some On Island single lady snatched you up and made you put a ring on it?"

Beau almost choked on his laughter. "They keep trying."

Jimmy shot him a look. That wasn't exactly true, though there had been a few different girls that he had dated before Amber. All relationships ended about the same way —long before they became what he would call relationships. "I'm pretty busy," Jimmy said. "And the island's pretty small."

"What he means to say, I think," Beau said, "is that none of the ladies knocking on his door have been the perfect lady." He gave a pointed grin at Emily and then carried right along. "So, Emily, tell me about modeling. You did like the whole thing in New York, huh? Was it all the stereotypes you hear about modeling?"

She made a face. "I'm assuming you mean a bunch of

mean skinny girls eating lettuce and having drama over the same jobs."

He laughed. "Something like that."

"It was just like that. Well, not all the girls were awful. I liked at least two of the other models I met. And most of us eat. I think 90% of models just got the genetic jackpot. It's honestly just too hard to *try* to stay that skinny if it's not natural. I knew some girls that worked to stay that thin. They were completely miserable." She patted her flat stomach. "I'm all genes."

"No kidding." Beau nodded to her plate, where only the bones were left from a half-rack of ribs.

Emily smiled. "Yeah. I did eat less then, but basically still weigh about the same. I have an insane metabolism. I'm grateful for it, don't get me wrong. Eating is fun. But it's a weird job to have where your body basically is your instrument or tool or whatever. Writers have laptops. Carpenters have hammers. Models have their body. You *are* the job. It starts to feel like you're not much more than an object. You get good at dissociating."

Emily's voice got quieter as she spoke and Jimmy felt his protectiveness surging. She had never opened up that much about modeling to him and he was starting to see why. Jimmy was glad Beau kept asking questions. He'd always been curious about her time in New York and whether she really liked modeling. She'd always referred to it flippantly in the past, like it was no big deal that she had been inside the pages of magazines like *Vogue*.

Emily continued while arranging the bones on her plate into neat rows. "It's so strange to walk into a room and have strangers examine every part of you and talk about you like you aren't there. Like you don't feel anything about the words they're saying. And they ... touch you. Putting clothes on, taking them off. Measuring, pinning, adjusting. It's like you aren't even there at all. You just live in your head while your body is somewhere separate."

"That sounds really weird," Jimmy said. "And hard."

"And not very healthy," Beau said.

"You get used to it." Emily shrugged. "Which isn't always the best thing. Sometimes the lines are really blurry between appreciation and objectification. And sometimes there are hard lines that get crossed when they shouldn't."

She trailed off, a look in her eyes like she had left the room. Beau gave Jimmy a look that he knew mirrored his own. Concern. What specifically had happened to her in New York? He'd always assumed it just didn't work out and she was embarrassed. But he got the uncomfortable sense that something had happened there. Something big. Not just the things that she was saying, which sounded like they could take a lasting emotional toll.

"Em?" Jimmy touched her hand lightly. She jumped a little. "I didn't realize New York was so hard for you. I'm sorry."

"It wasn't." She licked her lips, then whispered, "The first time anyway."

He stared at her. "You went twice?" He remembered now that she mentioned "the first time" when they were playing foosball. The remark had just passed over him until now. Natalie hadn't told him.

She looked guarded now. "I did."

"When?"

She hesitated. "Right after Natalie's wedding."

The table was quiet. Beau met Jimmy's eyes again and frowned. The atmosphere in the room had shifted. Emily was hiding something. A big hurt. Beau didn't ask any more questions and Jimmy couldn't. Not yet. She seemed willing to talk, almost like she wanted to, but they could both sense her pain. For once, she wasn't hiding everything behind a wall of sassy comebacks and sarcasm. Just as soon as Jimmy had the thought, Emily shook her head and smiled, trying to arrange her features into the normal, happy mask. It didn't quite work.

"That's all the woes you need to hear about the challenging job of modeling. Sorry I kind of blathered on about it. Modeling is pretty ridiculous. I mean, you don't need a brain to do it. Or strength, like y'all. It's not even a character thing. You either look the part or don't and you can either pose or not. It's a stupid profession. Foosball was definitely the best thing I got out of New York."

"Foosball?" Beau asked. He had adjusted quickly to the lightness Emily was trying to force back into the conversation.

Jimmy smiled. "She beat me in several games Sunday. By a lot. Her goalie shot is epic."

"Too bad there's no professional foosball circuit," Emily said. "I'd clean up. They'd never see me coming."

"Speaking of cleaning up, I'll do dishes since you cooked," Beau said.

He scooped up the plates before Jimmy or Emily could protest. They sat across from each other for a moment or two.

"There's one more part of the station we didn't show you yet." Jimmy stood and held out his hand. "There are stairs, but I can carry you up."

She took it and stood, still hobbling slightly. "If you must. I usually limit my being carried to once per day, but I'll make an exception. Just for you."

"How are the toes feeling?"

"Like they're broken."

"I've got some aspirin. Do you want some?"

"That would be lovely. Is this last part of the station somewhere I can elevate it? Some guy told me ice and elevate."

He grinned. "Hang here. I'll get you ice and aspirin."

"I'm not going anywhere," Emily said.

But as Jimmy jogged back to the bunk room, his thoughts were on the days of this week, slipping away. Friday, Emily *was* going somewhere: back home. This time with her felt so fleeting. And yet, so weighty, like if he didn't take the risk to bring up what was happening between them, all would be lost again.

"No pressure," he muttered to himself, grabbing a bottle of pain relievers. "No pressure at all."

CHAPTER FOURTEEN

Emily didn't care where Jimmy was taking her, only that he was carrying her again. A little sigh escaped her as he had picked her up. She hoped he didn't hear it, but the flicker of a smile on his face told her that he had. So much for being subtle. Breaking her toes was the best luck she'd had in ages. It gave her an easy excuse to be near him and to need his help—something she hated asking for. It was maybe the first time in her life that Emily liked feeling needy.

After their lunch, where she'd said more than she meant to, Emily wanted nothing more than to be in Jimmy's arms. She hated talking about New York and modeling. Years ago, she had come up with a series of quick responses when people asked her about either, things that didn't make her have to really think about them. But somehow, Beau had drawn out more from her. She knew that she needed to talk to Jimmy about it, but the words were hard to find. Clutching his shoulders, she said a silent prayer asking for strength and for the right words.

And for Jimmy not to see her differently if she opened up.

"Going up," Jimmy said at the bottom of a set of stairs. It was in a back hallway of the second floor, leading to the roof, she guessed.

"Are you sure you can manage me? I'm not a tiny person."

Jimmy chuckled. "Do I need to take my shirt off to remind you of my strength?"

Yes, please. The thought of it sent her heart racing.

"Are you reconnecting with the Jimmy of days past?" she said.

"Maybe you're bringing him back. Is that bad?"

"I like a little bit of old Jimmy mixed with new Jimmy. Both are nice."

"Nice, huh? Ouch."

"Nice isn't a bad word."

"I'd prefer awesome. Great. Amazing. Strong. Dashingly handsome."

She laughed. "Okay. Those too."

He grinned. A shimmer of attraction seemed to hang in the air between them. He had to feel it too. Emily bit her lip. They reached the top of the stairs, but he didn't put her down yet. Awkwardly, he managed to open the door leading to the roof.

"Here we are," he said. "It's not much, but it's got a great view."

He continued carrying her across the rooftop, which was empty save a seating area with wrought-iron furniture and worn cushions. One of those canvas overhead tents stood on metal poles around the area, shading the chairs.

"We tried camping chairs up here, but they blew away in a storm. We picked up some old furniture that's heavier. Not the most comfortable, but it's okay."

"You can see the ocean," Emily said. "I love it."

Jimmy settled her down on one end of a small couch. She hated the moment he put her down. He pulled one of the chairs over to prop up her foot and then sat down right next to her and put an arm around her shoulders. Her stomach was a mess of fluttery feelings. She leaned into him, trying to channel the bravery she had prayed for as he carried her up.

They sat comfortably for a few minutes, looking out over the ocean in the distance. She stole a glance at him. He looked down and met her gaze, smiling, but she couldn't hold his eyes and looked back out over the ocean.

"You've changed," Emily said. "More than just not taking your shirt off every five seconds."

He chuckled. "Yeah? How so? Good or bad?"

"You used to be a little cocky. Now you're more...confident."

"I was pretty cocky, wasn't I?" He smiled.

"It was cute. Not like the big-headed pride some people have, but more that whole teenage boy thing where you think you're a super hero."

"How does confidence look on me, then? Am I still cute?"

She turned to look at him. He asked lightly, but she could sense that it was a real question. Their faces were so close that she instinctively pulled back a little. Though what she really wanted was to lean closer and kiss him. She studied his face and his cheeks grew pink. Now he looked away first.

"Confidence looks very good on you," she said quietly.

He smiled, but still looked away from her. It felt like they were both resisting an inevitable pull. A good kind of tension hung in the air between them—electric and filled with anticipation. The realization made her equal parts nervous and excited.

She leaned her head against his chest, looking out over the water. This was the perfect time to talk to him about

New York. The logical part of her brain, the one that hadn't been able to call a therapist after, but had Googled helpful sites, knew that what happened wasn't her fault. Jimmy was too decent of a guy to blame her.

But the doubts kept questioning: if he knew, would he still want her?

He cleared his throat. "So, how's work going? You've mentioned getting a job a couple times this week. You were joking, but it made me wonder."

"My job totally sucks. I'm a temp. I thought I could turn it into something more permanent, get my foot in the door with digital marketing, but they aren't interested in me."

"I'm sorry. Are you going to stay there for a while? Or find another temp job?"

"I don't know what to do. I have very few skills that translate into a paying career. And I have nothing that I really want to do. I feel kinda stuck, J."

"J?"

"You need a new nickname. New you, new nickname."

He smiled. "Okay. I like it. Anything that gets you to stop thinking of the younger, cockier version of Jimmy."

"He wasn't so bad. But Jimmy now, aka J, is pretty great."

Lame. The coolness and control she usually felt when it came to guys was gone. She cared way too much what Jimmy thought of her now. The way her whole body shivered as his fingertip grazed over the bare skin of her arm made that even more clear.

"Can I ask you a question?" he said.

"You just did. But you can ask another." She held her breath, somehow knowing what was coming and steeling herself for it. When they were downstairs with Beau, she had caught the glances they gave each other while she talked. She knew he wouldn't let it go. It wasn't in his nature. She was equal parts relieved and terrified when he gave her an easy way to talk about it.

"Did something happen in New York?" She stiffened and fought the urge to pull away. "Don't answer if it's not something you want to talk about. I don't want to pry or make you talk about something you aren't comfortable talking about. Or maybe I'm wrong. I mean, I kind of kept up with you through Natalie and didn't hear anything. It's just that in talking about it, you sounded so ... lost."

I was. I am. Her mouth was suddenly bone-dry. She swallowed and closed her eyes to hold in the tears. All the moisture from her mouth had gone straight there. New York was something she had tried to forget. Like that would be possible. But at least she hadn't been thinking about it in years. This week, for whatever reason, it kept bobbing to the surface. Maybe because she reconnected with Jimmy. And he was the reason she went back to New York in the first place. Ultimately, it was her fault for rejecting him. But when he ran, she had too.

She wished she hadn't said so much at lunch so they could be talking about something else right now. Like the weather. As much as she knew that she didn't want her past being a secret between them, she also didn't want to have this conversation. Ever.

He waited, but Emily couldn't find the words. What she should say or what she should leave out. Fear gnawed at her stomach, replacing the butterflies that had been there minutes before. It swallowed them whole.

He squeezed her shoulder. "Emily, forget I asked. Really. We haven't talked in years. I don't have a right to start asking personal stuff."

"It's fine." Emily swiped away the tears before they fell, hoping it wasn't obvious that she was crying. She turned slightly and pulled away, shrugging out from under his arm. "You don't need to be sorry. It was my fault. Everything."

Jimmy leaving. New York. The end of their friendship.

The pause in the conversation grew around them, making the ocean sounds swell. No, wait—that wasn't the ocean. It was the sound of the road down below, the ebb and flow of cars, not the tides.

Stupid phrases rolled through her mind as she agonized over what to say, song lyrics and phrases that her mind turned to fit the situation.

To tell or not to tell, that is the question.

He loves me, he loves me not.

Will he stay or will he go?

She didn't know how Jimmy would react or what he would think of her. But she knew that if she wanted a chance with him, a real chance at a real something, she needed to take down her walls. And New York was the biggest one.

Her voice surprised her, as though some subconscious part of her made the choice to speak.

"I was working with a different agency the second time I want to New York. Not as reputable. I was older. Less...fresh, they said. I had to go with whoever would take me."

Jimmy took her hand, lacing his fingers through hers. She looked down at their hands, studying them. She had no feeling from the touch, like her nerve endings were dead.

"We did events sometimes. Just got paid to show up, be beautiful. Party decorations. Things." Bitterness marred her voice and she watched Jimmy squeeze her hand even tighter.

"This time, though, it was...more than that. It sounded like a normal job. I mean, I didn't have any red flags. I should have, though. I think I was just distracted and desperate. They sent three of us to a private party in a loft. Not a big party. Ten men? Eight? I don't know how many. Much older men. No other women. No wives, girlfriends, anything. Just ... us."

She cleared her throat. He traced her palm with his thumb. She could see the movement, but still the feeling did not register. Instead, she remembered the feelings she had that night as they moved through her, starting with unease, confusion, bone-deep fear, and finally full-blown panic.

The sounds of the party were still clear. They'd been playing rap music, which made her smirk at first: old white guys listening to Jay-Z. It only took a few minutes for her to lose the smirk. The bass so loud it was hard to hear. Not that any of the men were interested in conversation.

She remembered hearing the cork popping on expensive champagne bottles. One of the men sprayed it on Denise, the youngest of the three models. Emily had felt alarm go up. Denise's eyes had gone wide, but they were professionals. She turned it to laughter. They were there to be pretty. Their job was to smile and be objects of desire.

It took less than ten minutes for everything to spin out of control. For it to become totally clear how far the idea of being objects would go.

Parts of the night were as clear as if they happened the night before: a man pressing his lips onto Emily's, smelling of cigars. The feeling of someone else, grabbing her butt from behind. Struggling in what felt like a sea of hands and arms and bodies. A champagne glass clinking against her teeth as someone tried to force her to drink. The sound of Denise's screams. Then there was a wave of memories like a fog. Things she couldn't or didn't want to see clearly.

There in the heat of almost-summer, with the gorgeous beach as the backdrop, Emily felt a cold spreading in her skin. She began to shake. A tremble at first, but then uncontrollable quivering, her knees knocking and her teeth chattering.

"Emily, can I … can I hold you?" Jimmy asked.

She could not look at him, but nodded.

Gently, Jimmy picked her up and cradled her in his lap, the same way he'd carried her twice today. Her arms went around his neck and he pulled her close. Her cheek rested on his chest. Within a moment or two, the shaking stopped.

He kissed the top of her head. "Emily, you don't have to finish. I'm sorry I didn't realize when I asked—"

"No," she said. "I need to say it. I need you to know."

And I need to know that you'll still want me after I do.

She took a breath, trying to push the images from her mind and just recite the facts. "They hired us as escorts. Hookers. I don't know if the agency knew or not because I never went back to them, but I'm pretty sure they did know. Based on how much they were paid, what our cut was supposed to be. And how particular they were about what we wore and which girls went on the call.

"I was the oldest. Denise was seventeen and Alicia twenty. It got out of control so fast. I was able to get us out. Not soon enough. But at least we got out before…too much happened."

"Emily."

She felt his breath on her cheek and he kissed her head once, twice, three times. She both loved and loathed his comfort, the same way she loved and loathed herself.

The memory of fear rose up like nausea and she tried to swallow it down. Denise screaming, on and on. A hand yanking her hair. Her dress ripping. Hands on her body. Hips grinding painfully into hers. Someone trying to pull her dress off her body. Fingertips digging into her upper thighs, reaching up her dress.

There was the memory of a champagne bottle swinging in her hand. The sound as it made contact with someone's skull. A groan of pain, a curse, a threat.

Swinging again and again. Glass breaking and pain in her ankle. Falling.

Angry shouts. More cursing.

And then she was running down flights of stairs practically dragging Denise and Alicia. Denise never stopped screaming, the whole way down. There had been blood. The slit in Denise's dress had been ripped up, reaching all the way to her waist. Her underwear was gone, leaving her hipbone jutting through the tear.

Emily's brain couldn't process that. She had to get them out. Part of her strained to hear if anyone was following, while she rushed them all toward the lowest floor and the red gleam of an Exit sign.

A drop of wetness brought her back to this moment, to this roof with Jimmy. He was crying. She looked up at him, his face twisted with the effort to hold back. In all the years and all the things she'd seen him through, she had never seen him cry. Not even in the hospital with his shattered legs.

The sight of it was what she needed to pull her from that night and firmly root her on this rooftop. The nightmare was over. The sun shone and the waves crashed and this beautiful man loved her no matter what. Why she had been afraid of his reaction, she didn't know.

Actually, she did know why. She had read about the way assault victims carry guilt around with them, even if they know it wasn't their fault. Just like that scene in the old movie with Matt Damon where the guy keeps saying that it wasn't his fault until he broke down. She knew it wasn't her fault. She knew Jimmy wouldn't think that. But still, at her core, she felt like it *was* her fault. She could have and should have known better or left sooner.

Even more, Emily felt like she was tainted. As though what those men did without consent was a reflection on her own moral character. Their hands on her body had left stains that she couldn't wash away. This had been her internal battle for the past few years. Now? She could at least close the door partway. Telling someone—not just anyone, but Jimmy—was a massive step toward healing.

Emily reached up and brushed away a tear from his cheek.

He struggled to speak with a steady voice. "Were you— are you—okay?"

Emily's voice felt stronger now. The power that night held on her had faded, or at least dimmed.

"I mean they don't really have levels of sexual assault, right?" Her voice sounded more bitter than she meant it to. "There's rape and then there's … a lot of other things. I guess on a scale of terrible versus just awful, it was a few steps above just awful. It could have been worse. I did get this." Emily lifted her hair back from her face. She could feel the scar, just beyond her hairline. Hidden enough that most people didn't notice the four-inch long line.

She remembered the punch across her jaw that made her crumple to the floor. The neat sting of the glass on her face. Sticky blood running down her cheek, her neck, and into her dress.

"My first and only stitches. Usually I like scars. They build character. This one, though, this one doesn't. It's just a sad reminder of a lot of stupid choices."

He traced the scar with his fingertip. And then he bent to kiss it. Jimmy was kissing her face. His lips were soft and warm. Even in this moment, where she laid her heart bare and talked about being assaulted, his lips set her aflame. Her lips felt completely bereft, longing for a kiss that never came. Emily had to close her eyes until he pulled away.

"Emily, whatever choices you made, this was not your fault. Not any tiny bit your fault. Did you have any help after? Any counseling?"

"You're the only one I've told. I made sure Denise and Alicia were safe. Used my emergency credit card and bought new clothes. Got stitches at urgent care. Took a bus from Port Authority home. I stayed in a Motel 6 until everything healed on my face so no one would know."

She didn't eat for three days. Drank the minibar dry. She hadn't had a drop of alcohol since.

The whole time she was in the hotel room, she watched golf on mute. She hated golf. But it was so bright and green. Everything looked beautiful and controlled and peaceful. The polite clapping and neat polo shirts tucked into belted khaki pants calmed her. She didn't tell Jimmy these things.

Or how she had to keep her body from shaking when she got home and her mother lost it about Emily quitting. She had zoned out during the lecture, sitting on her hands, but caught the basic gist: she was a disappointment, a quitter, a failure, a coward. If she wasn't a model, what did she have left? Average high school grades, no college degree or experience. Emily had tried to let the words bounce off, but they were the secret fears she had about herself. Other than her looks, what did she have?

Her eyes burned and Jimmy's arms tightened around her again. He pressed another kiss to her forehead. The gift of his touch knocked her mother's words right out of her head. They weren't gone, but lost some of their power. Emily still had so many regrets, ones that wouldn't ever leave her. She should have suspected something about that call. She should have protected the other girls better. She should have reported it or reported the agency. Probably both. She never should have gone back to New York. And the one that stood out above all the others: she should have been honest about her feelings for Jimmy.

"I shouldn't have done it."

"You didn't know what would happen when you went there. You can't blame yourself."

Emily licked her lips. Her words were shaky. "No, I mean, I shouldn't have blown you off at Natalie's wedding."

Jimmy stiffened. Emily was crying harder now. Silently, but her whole body shook with it. Without his firm grip on her, she might have shaken right down to the floor. Honesty was hard. She felt weak, like she had just opened herself up to pain that she couldn't imagine. If Jimmy hurt her, it wouldn't be because he meant to. She could feel his tenderness in the way his fingers brushed over her skin and his lips had pressed into her hair. But he might not still feel for her the way he had. Until she knew that for certain, she would feel like her chest was cracked open, waiting to swell with joy or to be crushed with sadness.

"Why are you bringing that night up now?" Jimmy's voice was measured, but she could hear the hurt and anger, just below the surface.

Of course he was hurt. She had done that to him. Emily pushed her face closer to his chest. Less because she wanted comfort and more because she wanted to hide. "I ran to New York after you ran here. And you ran because of me. Because I hurt you."

Jimmy didn't speak and in a brief moment of panic Emily realized that she might have read this all wrong. Maybe he didn't leave just because of her. She might be completely self-centered, thinking all of his decisions revolved around her.

The thought froze her heart as she waited for him to say something.

Gently, Jimmy took her by the shoulders and pulled her away. For a moment, she thought her fear was realized until he tipped her chin up with his fingers so she had to look at him. Emily couldn't bear his fierce expression. She covered her face with her hands. He tried to pull them away, but she shook him off.

"Emily, look at me."

"I can't," she whispered. She felt like a stick house that had been blown in with one gust, or like the balcony from a few nights ago, shattered and splintered in pieces.

"Em, please." The tenderness in his voice coaxed her to open her eyes. He tugged at her hands again and this time she let him. Her face felt raw and swollen from crying. Jimmy held her hands in his, twining their fingers together. She wanted to revel in his touch, but her fears and doubts were too big. "Look at me."

His eyes were still intense, the blue that of a stormy sky. But there was softness there too. Before he could speak, she took her hand from his and placed it gently over his lips.

"I'm so sorry, Jimmy. About everything. I feel like my life is just one bad choice after another. I hate that I messed things up and hurt you. I screwed it all up, ruined what we had. We didn't talk for three years, Jimmy. Three years. That's on me. It's not okay. We lost our friendship. And ... everything. Now I can't seem to fix things in my life. It's all a mess. I'm struggling with depression or anxiety or ... I don't know. Just struggling. I'm floating and lost."

He wiped the tears from her cheeks. She closed her eyes at the brush of his fingertips over her face, but opened them again when he cupped his big hands around her jaw.

"A lot has happened. Yeah, you hurt me. But honestly? I

don't think I would have been the man you needed back then. If something had happened between us romantically, I would have found a way to screw it up. I might have lost you forever. We're here now. It's crazy when you think about it—how it happened. Beau said something to me about God's plans..."

"He said something to me too. 'You go nowhere by accident,' I think. Right?"

He smiled and the tightness in her chest eased. "Right. I'm so sorry about New York. I can't wrap my head around how that might be a part of God's plans. If I could have done anything to prevent that from happening to you, I would have. But I do know you can't blame yourself. I'm really glad that we are where we are right now. This rooftop, this moment. But I'm sorry about what happened on the journey here. If you want to blame anyone, you should blame me. I never should have opened my mouth that night. I think I knew that you didn't feel the same way. I never should have pushed when you didn't have feelings—"

"I did feel the same way." Emily didn't mean to say the words, but she did. Their eyes locked. He looked completely taken aback. Shocked, but then a flicker of something else. Hope.

"You did?"

"I did. I wasn't sure and I was scared. Confused. Unsure. But I did. I was just too cowardly to do anything about it." Emily's mouth twisted. Everything felt cheesy and dumb and also way too vulnerable. But Jimmy's eyes had grown brighter, the storm in them calming to a smooth, cloudless sky.

"How I felt ..." Jimmy paused and swallowed heavily. "I still feel the same. Time and distance? They only made me more sure when I saw you how I felt. The question that's been driving me crazy is: how do you feel about me?"

It wasn't lost on Emily that Jimmy was intimating that he still had feelings, but hadn't specifically said what he felt. Similarly, she found herself fumbling over the words in her mind. "I ..."

I *like you* like you.

I really like you.

I care about you.

I'm attracted to you.

I like you more than a friend.

I love you.

She sucked in a breath. The last one was how she really felt. It was the only one that fully rang true. But she couldn't say that. Not after that conversation. Not first. Not if she wasn't completely sure that he felt the same way.

Despite asking the question, Jimmy didn't seem particularly concerned about the answer. Or maybe he sensed her response. It was probably written all over her face. Instead of waiting, Jimmy tilted his head forward.

His lips were so close to hers. Was he going to kiss her? The current of attraction between them felt like the moments before a big storm, when lightning skittered across the sky to flash a warning.

Emily's heartbeat was like a drum in her ears.

It was strange to think of kissing him right now, that she would even want to after talking about the assault in New York. But this was not that. Emily felt freed after telling him. With Jimmy, she knew that she was safe. She was loved. Even if he hadn't said the words out loud yet.

The sound of the ocean and of cars cruising by faded into white noise. Emily was hyperaware of every place her body touched his. Her eyes were fixated on his lips, slightly parted, inching closer. Her breathing picked up. She felt his chest rise and fall faster.

It was too late for worry or second guessing.

His lips brushed against hers so softly that she sighed. He smiled against her mouth. And then they were laughing and kissing—the most amazing and ridiculous and joy-filled kiss of her life. It wasn't romantic or tender or all-consuming passion, but more like relief. The kiss released the years of tension between them.

Emily wound her hands around his neck and pulled him closer, the smile fading as passion did take over. The years of waiting now turning hungry and burning. His fingertips moved over her jaw and neck, making her shudder as their mouths moved in the perfect dance. She could feel the promise in it. Her body reacted as though she was dry kindling and he had just taken a torch to her. This kiss was everything. It felt like hope and a future. Jimmy felt like home.

Suddenly an alarm rang through the building and the speakers on the roof. Emily pulled away. Jimmy stiffened and closed his eyes, blowing out in frustration. But when he opened his eyes, he grinned. "I want to be mad, but I can't. Because I've been waiting what feels like my whole life to kiss you, Emily."

Her smile was so wide that it felt like the muscles in her face were cramping. He stood suddenly before she could respond. "I've got to go. I hate that I do, but I do. I'll carry you back down. Can someone come pick you up?"

"I'll be fine. I'll text Kim or someone."

"We'll finish this later, okay?" His eyes fixed on hers before he pressed a soft kiss against her lips. He was smiling as he pulled away.

"Later. Sure." Her voice sounded strangled and breathy. It

was all she could do not to grab him by the neck again and bring him back to her lips.

"Later." He grinned and hoisted her up into his arms.

Emily savored the feel of being lifted in his arms. She resisted the urge to run her hands up the back of his neck into his hair. As he carried her down the stairs again, picking his way carefully with her nestled into his chest, she repeated one word to herself.

Later.

Later.

Later.

CHAPTER FIFTEEN

When they got back to the station after a call that was essentially someone burning dinner, Emily was gone. Jimmy had hoped she would be sitting in the kitchen where he left her, even though he had told her to leave. She had left one note on a napkin in the middle of the kitchen island. It read: LATER, with a crooked heart scrawled next to it. Jimmy couldn't stop a grin from spreading over his face.

"I take it you guys had a good talk," Beau said, smiling.

Talk, kiss, everything. It still made Jimmy's gut clench to think about what Emily had gone through in New York. The sound of shame in her voice gave him a visceral reaction. He ached for her, but had a raging fury toward the men involved and the agency that sent her. The weight of her secret seemed to lift as she said the words out loud.

He wanted to give Emily every assurance he could that she was safe. More than anything, he wanted to keep her protected and to let her know that she was loved. She had been through a lot and was still going through something.

He couldn't believe how strong she was to hide all this and try to battle through it on her own. Not for a minute did Jimmy think he could somehow "fix" her. But he wanted to be with her while she worked through what she needed to. Today felt like a first step. Not just for her to heal, but for the two of them.

He could still feel her lips against his. They had both been smiling and laughing, at least as the kiss started. Not a Hollywood kiss, but real and perfect.

"Yes. It's unfinished, but it was a start. A really great start."

"I'm so happy for you. Just think of the story you'll have."

Jimmy could only nod, a smile still on his face. He was having trouble believing it still. His dream girl. His lifetime crush. No—his lifetime love. He hadn't said those words yet, but he didn't want to hold back. *Later*, he thought, tucking the napkin note into his back pocket. Something like adrenaline rushed through him, a nervous energy that he knew wouldn't subside until *later* became right now. He shot her a quick text:

J: When can I see you?

She responded almost immediately.

E: Not soon enough. When are you done with your shift?
J: Tomorrow morning. Early.
E: How early? In case you forgot, I don't do early.
J: I remember. ;) I'll be there when you wake up.
E: If I wake up and you're watching me sleep, it will be creepy. Not romantic. Just so we're clear.
J: Noted. See you…
J: …LATER

E: Later ;)

Waiting was going to kill him. Even though he should take a nap, Jimmy found himself in the weight room, trying to burn off the nervous energy with a workout. The endorphins kept him in a happy place but did little to turn down the volume on his excess energy. He took a shower and decided to call Natalie. She had watched Jimmy moon over Emily for years and wouldn't believe that he might finally get the girl. He didn't want to say too much in case he jinxed it, but he felt an urge to tell his sister before Emily did.

Natalie's voice sounded cheerful but strained when she answered. "Jimmy, hey."

"Hey, sis! How's it going?"

"Pretty well. I'm exhausted. So, you know—normal mom life."

"Where's my favorite niece?"

"Napping. That's the only reason I answered the phone. Otherwise it's just too hard to carry on a conversation. How are things at the beach?"

"They're good. Very, very good. I wanted to invite you to come down this week for a night or two. Bring Scarlet. Jeremy if he's not working. You keep saying you will, but this week is especially good."

"Not that I mind a little poke and prod to visit my favorite brother—"

"*Only* brother."

"Only *and* favorite brother, right. But any particular reason you sound so eager to see me?"

"The weather's really great." He smiled, teasing this out.

"Sure. The weather. And? I can hear it in your voice. What's going on?"

181

"The craziest thing happened this weekend. Well, several insane things. First: Emily's here."

There was a brief pause on the line. "My Emily?"

He chuckled. "One and the same." Softer, he said, "Maybe soon *my* Emily."

"What?! Jimmy, back up. What's going on? Why is Emily there? And you're seeing her? I thought she broke your heart and that's why you disappeared."

"Yeah, that's part of why I left. It's a long story. Let me start with how we ran into each other. You won't believe this."

"I can't believe she didn't tell me she was going down there," Natalie said. She didn't even sound like she was listening to him. "How long has she been there?"

"She got here on Friday night. Focus, Nat. I'm trying to tell you."

"Sorry. I'm just a little ... well. Anyway. Go on. This has got to be good."

Jimmy launched into the story of the balcony rescue. Even thinking back on it made him nervous all over again. Until he got to the part where he got Emily on the ladder just before the whole balcony went down. He couldn't help grinning at that part of the story, but didn't share all the details. Like how Emily had clung to him on the ladder afterward for long moments and the way his feelings came rushing back over him like a rogue wave. Natalie interrupted only with a few questions throughout, mostly staying silent.

When he was done, there was a long pause. Jimmy pulled the phone away from his ear and looked at it, wondering if the call had dropped. "Nat?"

"Yeah, sorry. So, Emily is there. She almost died and you saved her life. And now you're hanging out and she's sleeping in your bed?"

He chuckled. "Not with me in it, but yeah, that about sums it up." The thought of Emily in his bed still got him all tied up in knots.

"How does Amber feel about that?"

Her voice sounded accusing and Jimmy furrowed his brow. His sister usually had his back. She was his champion and acted too often like the protector he didn't really need. He didn't understand why she was acting like this now, though. He'd expected her to be laughing and happy. To see the way God orchestrated this whole thing to bring Emily back into his life. Instead, he felt like he was on the defensive.

"I'm not seeing Amber anymore," he said.

Natalie was too quiet. When she spoke, her voice sounded hard and cool "Did you break up with her because of Emily? Because I talked to you two weeks ago and you were dating."

"We weren't ever dating. We went on dates. It wasn't official. I told her that this weekend."

"After Emily got there?"

"Yeah, but like I said—"

Natalie said his name like a groan. "Jimmy. Emily is my best friend. You know I love her. But I have watched her break the hearts of guy after guy after guy. For years. And I watched you get torn up over her and move to another *state* when she hurt you. I feel like you *just* got over her and moved on. Don't fall right back into this unrequited love thing. Please. Why go back to that? She doesn't even live down there. She's never going to settle down. Definitely not with you."

"Not with me. You don't think I'm good enough for Emily? Is that it?"

"Just stop. Jimmy. Clearly, I think you're the most amazing person. I think you deserve better."

"That's pretty cold to say about your best friend."

"I love Emily. I do. She just goes through a lot of guys. And she always saw you as a little brother."

Jimmy sucked in a breath, feeling like he had taken a punch to the gut. Even though he could still feel Emily's lips against his, Natalie's words were the embodiment of his fears and doubts. She was wrong, but it still hurt. It deflated his joy and caused a crumbling in the confidence that had felt so solid a few hours before. He clenched his jaw, drawing air slowly into his chest. He wouldn't let these worries rob him of this. Doubt was not going to creep in and poison his relationship with Emily. He simply wouldn't let it. He had to fight for this love, the one he had waited so long for.

Natalie spoke before he could, her voice softer than it had been before. "I'm sorry. I know I'm being harsh. Emily cares about you, but she doesn't feel the same way you do. She never has. I just don't want to see you get hurt."

"Things can change. A lot has happened over the past few years. She and I had a conversation about this, Nat. We talked about all of this. And we kissed."

"You kissed her? Or she kissed you?"

Why did Natalie sound like this was hard to believe? Why was she pushing so hard against this? Jimmy sighed. "You're really going to give me the third degree about this, aren't you? We kissed each other. It was mutual and very—"

"Stop! That's enough. I don't want details. Ew."

Jimmy smirked. "Well, you certainly sounded like you did. I don't want to feel like I have to prove this to you. I'm an adult. She's an adult. Honestly, I thought you'd be happy. She's your best friend. Marrying her would be bringing your best friend into the family."

"You're already talking about marriage?" Her voice was practically a shriek.

"No, we haven't talked about it. But I am thinking about it. I love her." The words seemed to gain strength just from being spoken out loud. They were no less true, but they felt more powerful. "I love Emily. I want to marry her. But it's early. We just talked about this like two hours ago. How about you give me a break, be a little happy for me, and come down to the beach and see for yourself."

Natalie sighed into the phone. "Wow. Okay."

"Okay, you'll come?"

"I need to talk to Jeremy, obviously. But Scarlet and I don't have any plans. I love the beach. We both miss you."

Jimmy smiled. He was about to say something about how it wasn't so hard to be open-minded and accepting, but Natalie kept going.

"Look, I know you; I know Emily. I love you both. I still think this is a bad idea. You're going to get your heart broken. Again."

Jimmy rolled his eyes. "You know, having an older sibling is overrated."

"You love me."

He did. But if it came down to it and she kept pushing this and putting doubts in his head, he would choose Emily. Hopefully she wouldn't press him to make that kind of a choice. A thought struck him that made the center of his chest feel cold. Would Natalie say these same kinds of thing to Emily about him? Would she really try to drive a wedge between them?

"I'm so happy that you're coming. But come with an open mind. Don't think you're going to change my mind. And don't try to change hers. Okay? Promise me you aren't going to get in the middle."

"I'll do my best. You just need to understand that I'm looking out for you. Just like I always have."

"You know that I'm not a kid anymore, right?" he said.

"Exactly. So don't go back to your childhood crush."

He groaned. "I'm hanging up now before I take back my invitation."

They hung up and he texted her the address to Jackson's house. She responded that she'd let him know her plans once Jeremy got home from work and they had a chance to talk. He sat for a long time after, staring at the phone in his hand, wishing the conversation had gone differently. He'd been so excited about Emily and about inviting Natalie to come down. Maybe it was a big mistake.

Even as he tried to tell himself that Natalie was wrong, a sliver of dread unfurled in the pit of his stomach. Maybe he had hoped too soon.

CHAPTER SIXTEEN

Emily sat on the couch, popping cheese balls in her mouth, listening to the other women discuss the finer points of pedicures. She could not have made herself fake interest. After being gone with Jimmy for a few hours—Jimmy!!—she felt like she needed to put in group time. Even if her heart was elsewhere, which it most certainly was. Both her heart and her mind were wherever Jimmy was with his strong arms and eyes that truly saw her and his mouth that made her toes curl, except for the broken ones.

She had an ice pack on her toes and her phone balanced on her thigh, obsessively glancing at it, waiting for more texts from Jimmy. They'd already texted a few times since she left, but it wasn't enough. She wanted—no, *needed*—more. She felt like a starving woman. What would be enough? She didn't know.

Every so often doubts pricked her happiness. Nothing new, but the same old worries about Jimmy being too young or Natalie's brother, both of which she could mostly set aside, and then there was the big one: What if she wasn't enough for him?

Jimmy was the ultimate catch, truly. No, he wasn't perfect. Perfection was impossible and would have been boring. He was light and fun and trustworthy and so very good looking. Emily had dated a lot of guys, but she had never felt so safe and also so heated in another man's arms. He deserved the best. Emily, on the other hand, seemed like a catch. But her past boyfriends had all cashed in on the return policy. She could almost imagine what they would write on a slip of paper, explaining why they were sending her back: Item not as expected. Broken. Should have read the reviews before purchasing. Disappointing.

She shivered on the couch and Kim tossed her a blanket. She wasn't cold, but made a show of putting it over her bare legs. After coming back from the station, she hadn't told the girls what happened. They'd all been distracted by her broken toes anyway. Of all the things Emily struggled with, her biggest weakness was being vulnerable. She could walk a runway at a fashion show or stand practically naked in a room while other people dressed her, no problem. Talking about what happened in New York? Telling Jimmy how she felt about him? Terrifying.

Sitting still wasn't working, so she jumped up and hobbled to the kitchen. Her toes weren't so bad now with the duct tape. She would probably be walking fine in a few days. As she stuck the ice pack back in the freezer, she shook her head at the cups and plates and bowls scattered everywhere. She sighed and started to clean. She didn't want Jackson coming back home to see his beautiful house trashed.

Moving with purpose helped her keep the thoughts and worry under check. She felt equal parts elated and terrified. She wanted to get in her car and drive back to the station, throwing herself in Jimmy's arms like a desperate woman. And yet her sense of self-preservation kept screaming at her to get back in the car and drive far, far away. Pronto.

That was an instinct she was going to ignore. She wouldn't run from Jimmy. Not again. She could do this whole being vulnerable thing. Her other relationships didn't work because they weren't the right fit, not because there was something inherently wrong with Emily.

Was there something wrong with her?

Nope. She would not give into those feelings or fears. And she would not run. Her life had been a disaster since she locked up her feelings, lied to Jimmy about them, and ran. Running didn't do any good. You always had to come back and face whatever it was you ran from, or it would come find you. If this thing with Jimmy worked, it would be amazing. *They* could be amazing. Together.

Emily looked up at the sound of footsteps in the kitchen. Jackson leaned against the fridge, giving her a kind smile. "Thanks for doing that. Need help?"

"Oh, hey. No thanks. I've got this." Emily looked around, realizing that she was almost done. While stewing about her feelings, she'd tossed all the red cups, wiped down the counters, and loaded almost everything in the dishwasher. She held up a plate. "Last one."

"Well, I appreciate it."

"The least we could do is not leave your place looking like a frat house on a Sunday morning."

He snorted. "This is a little better than a frat house. I've seen my share back in the day." He lowered his voice. "I have to say I am a little shocked how much mess a group of civilized ladies could create."

"We're not so civilized. And clearly, our group is missing someone with type-A tendencies and a neat streak."

EMMA ST. CLAIR

"That's okay. I do have a service that comes every week. I asked them to put off for a few days and come after you leave."

"That's a good plan. It really was nice of you to take us in."

"It wasn't *nice*. It's the least I could do after you almost died on one of my properties. I'm still sorry about that."

Emily rolled her eyes. "I'm not going to sue you, Jackson. I think we already established that. I'm very much alive and well. Mostly well." She waved her injured foot at him. Her toes were starting to throb a little she realized. Probably time to sit down.

"What happened to your toes?"

"Oh—long story. I think two of them are broken. Jimmy taped them up for me. It happened in your store, actually. A frozen beef accident. I might sue you for that."

"Hm. I somehow don't think that case would be as strong."

"Maybe not. Oh, well. Maybe I'll just beg you for a job instead."

Emily hadn't planned to say those words. She had been thinking about the store, off and on when she wasn't replaying the moment when Jimmy's lips met hers. That kept her brain tied up most of the afternoon. But she liked solving problems and so Bohn's had popped into her head at random times. But she didn't mean to ask Jackson for a job.

Even as she said it, Emily realized how much she liked the idea. A job at Jackson's store. A relationship with Jimmy. A fresh start and a new future.

"A job?" Jackson didn't look horrified, so that was a good sign. He rubbed a hand over his jaw. "Depends on the position. Are you really looking for something?"

"I am. I could be." Emily put the last dish in the dishwasher and wiped her hands on her shirt. "I've been thinking about how to get more people in the door."

"You and me both. It's been a constant problem. As for jobs, there are always cashiers and baggers moving in and out. But for people looking for more permanent, high-paying positions, there aren't many. The store is in a bit of ... a precarious place financially. Hiring someone on a salary basis would be more of a bit of a stretch. Unless they could bring something to the table that could help with that precarious position. Do you have a special set of skills that would help a struggling grocery store?"

She grinned. "Nothing like Liam Neeson's special skills. Some experience at a marketing firm. I'm a temp and they won't let me near campaigns, but I've picked up a lot just watching. Branding and social media—mostly Instagram. Not a lot of on-paper experience that would make a nice resume."

She told herself that these weren't untrue. Not fully, anyway. She had seen a lot of marketing campaigns cross her desk in the past few months at her temp job. And until she realized that she felt fake doing them, Emily had worked one-on-one with brands, creating sponsored content on Instagram. A few of her friends from the modeling world had sought out her help with their social media. She hadn't gotten paid or anything, but she knew that was an actual thing people paid for in the online space. It was another idea she toyed around with, but announcing herself as some kind of coach or expert made her feel strange.

Jackson smiled. "Write up a proposal. Nothing formal or fancy. I don't need a resume. Just some ideas for what could get things moving in the store. Can you do that?"

Emily's heart sped up. He was giving her a chance. For a real job that she could actually see herself enjoying. One that would mean moving here to Sandover.

"I'll get it to you before I leave Friday." Her phone buzzed in her pocket.

Jackson nodded. "I'll look forward to it."

He headed into his room as she pulled out her phone, her heart beating way too irrationally fast. A potential job. Here. Getting out of her parents' house, finally. There was a text from Jimmy. Emily chewed at her lip. Would this freak Jimmy out? They had kissed just hours ago and now she was thinking about moving here for him? No sense telling him yet.

J: I've got a surprise!

J: Guess who's coming tomorrow?

E: Yo mama?

J: Ha. Nope. But close. Two of our favorite people.

J: Hint—one is highly likely to eat sand.

Emily felt her heart sink. Natalie and Scarlet. What had Jimmy told Natalie?

Truth be told, she'd been waiting for some kind of shoe to drop. This was the shoe. It hit her square in the gut with the force of a steel-toed boot. What was Natalie going to say about this new development? One that happened without Emily so much as telling her best friend she was going to Sandover. Now she was here and something was happening with her and Jimmy. She could only imagine what Natalie might say.

She wouldn't have to wonder for long, because her phone began to ring in her hand. Natalie was calling. Probably to tell Emily to stay away from Jimmy. She got up and went downstairs to Jimmy's room, where she closed the door and took several deep breaths. She wouldn't let Natalie make the choice for her this time. If she'd been honest the last time, maybe they wouldn't be in this situation. Or, who knows, maybe Natalie never would have approved of her best friend dating her little brother.

Emily forced cheerfulness into her voice. "Hey, you! How's it going?"

"It's good." Natalie already had a tone. "But I hear things are pretty exciting where you are?"

Emily's heart was pounding. Why did she care so much what Natalie thought? Would she still really care if Emily and Jimmy got together? She wasn't Jimmy's mother or Emily's keeper.

She forced out a small chuckle. "I guess you talked to Jimmy? He told you about how he gallantly saved me from certain death and all that jazz, huh?"

"I just got off the phone with him a few minutes ago. I was a little shocked, to say the least. Why didn't *you* tell me? I didn't even know you were going down there."

"I thought I told you about this months ago. It's for Kim's bachelorette thing."

"I remember hearing about that, but not that you were going to Sandover. I would have remembered. You know, since Jimmy lives there."

Natalie still had a tone, but she hadn't outright said whether Jimmy had told her that they were in a relationship. Were they in a relationship? The fire alarm had interrupted before they had time to actually talk about it. Should she tell Natalie? What was there to say? I realized I love your brother and we made out on a rooftop and now I'm thinking of moving here? Natalie would give her a hard time about that no matter what guy she was talking about. Maybe Jimmy hadn't said anything other than the fact that Emily was here.

"I wasn't planning to see Jimmy. He showed up in a very

dramatic way. Thankfully. Because otherwise I might be a pancake right now."

Natalie sighed. "I'm really glad you're okay. That must have been terrifying."

It had been. With the distraction of Jimmy, Emily hadn't thought much about her near-death experience. But talking about it now made her stomach churn. "Yeah, it made for an exciting start to the week. Not the kind of excitement we'd planned."

"So now you're, like, staying in his house?"

"Yeah, me and the girls. Plus Jimmy and his roommates, Jackson and Beau. The whole thing is a little nutty."

Natalie's voice brightened a bit. "I hope you're prepared for more craziness. I'm coming down tomorrow with Scarlet!"

Emily made a squealing sound of excitement, thankful Jimmy's text had given her enough warning to prepare. "My favorite god-daughter! And my BFF!" She lowered her voice. "Seriously, you are so much more fun than these girls. I mean, they're fine. But anyway. That will be great."

"I'm a little nervous about how Scarlet will do in the house. You know how she is."

"Yep—super active and a regular climbing monkey. There are lots of stairs. But it's a guy's house, so there aren't a ton of breakable things lying around. It's pretty sparse as far as décor. Not a lot of vases to smash. We'll keep an eye on her. I mean, between you and me and Jimmy, she'll be totally fine."

"I can only stay a night, so it should be fine. I'll be there tomorrow right after lunch." She paused. "Hopefully we can talk sometime while I'm there. Maybe before Jimmy gets off work."

Emily couldn't swallow. Talk. Right. The way they talked in the bathroom the night of Natalie's wedding. She shoved aside the sick feeling in her stomach. "Fun! I can't wait to catch up."

Natalie was quiet for a minute. "Okay, well I'm going to get ready. You wouldn't believe the amount of things you have to pack to travel with a toddler for just one night. It's insane."

"Well, text me when you get close and I'll come help you carry things up." Stacy had moved to a different bedroom when some of the other girls left. She and Emily almost had a standoff about keeping Jimmy's room, but Emily wouldn't budge. "We've been staying in Jimmy's room, so now you and me and Scarlet can share."

"You're staying in Jimmy's room, huh?" Natalie didn't sound surprised. There was an edge in her voice.

"Not with Jimmy. I mean, obviously. The guys are all staying upstairs in Jackson's room. We all just grabbed beds wherever we could."

"Hm. Okay. Well, I'll see you tomorrow."

"See you!"

Emily stared at the phone in her hand. The whole conversation felt off. Emily knew part of it was the fact that she and Natalie had drifted a little bit in the last few years. But it also felt like Jimmy was right between them, sending tension radiating through their relationship. They both knew it and both talked around it. If Natalie wanted "to talk," the tension would get out in the open sooner than later.

Natalie would just have to understand. Maybe Natalie and Jimmy could hash it out and Emily could stay out of it. Jimmy definitely would have a problem with his sister trying to get involved. He probably didn't know Natalie had done just that at the wedding and would be furious when he found out. If he found out. Emily wasn't about to tell him. This

EMMA ST. CLAIR

whole thing could get messy, which was the last thing Emily wanted.

The bottom line was that Natalie would have to get over whatever objections she had, if she still had them. Because this time, Emily wasn't running—or walking—away.

Her feelings for Jimmy wrapped securely around her heart like strong arms, but also managed to feel like an explosion of fireworks in her chest. Especially when she thought about the moment on Jockey's Ridge when they talked about almost losing each other. Touching his scars. Waking up next to him in the chair on the beach, his smile dazzling her. Telling him about New York and feeling the weight of that memory lift.

The way he carried her in his arms like she weighed nothing.

The smell of him on his bed sheets.

The solid feel of his body against hers on the ladder after he had pulled her to safety.

Feeling raw desire as he moved closer, about to kiss her.

The soft warmth of his lips against hers.

All of these tiny and large moments from this week—had it only been a week?—added up to one thing: She still loved Jimmy. But not as a brother or a close friend or any of those other kinds.

She loved Jimmy. Full stop.

For the first time in years, Emily felt hopeful. The dying embers of her dreams for the future had been tended. Now the smallest curl of flame was being fanned into a flame of something warm, good, and bright.

Before joining the others upstairs, Emily pulled out her laptop and began working on a proposal for Jackson. One more step toward a future that she could almost taste.

CHAPTER SEVENTEEN

Emily slept fitfully. If she had dreams, she did not remember them. When she stretched and dragged herself out of bed, she felt like she had been running all night long. Not surprising, given her high levels of excitement and nerves. She was going to see Jimmy again today—yay! The thought of his smile and the way his blue eyes always drank her in had her stomach doing funny things. But she was also going to see Natalie—yikes. Maybe. It could be totally fine. Three years had passed since Natalie told her to stay away from Jimmy. Circumstances were different now. Natalie might surprise her with support, but their phone conversation didn't inspire confidence. Emily needed to be ready to choose Jimmy over her best friend. The very thought hurt.

She found texts from Natalie and from Jimmy waiting on her phone.

N: Leaving in a few! Can you make sure there's space for me to set up Scarlet's travel crib?

N: And maybe if there are any breakable things within reach or things she'd destroy, could you move them? She's a terror. See you in a few hours!!

N: Yay!

The thought of seeing Scarlet took the edge off Emily's nerves. She loved that tiny firecracker and didn't see her often enough. While she read Jimmy's texts, she picked up the room a bit, moving anything that was toddler-height. She had forgotten about her toes until she first put her feet on the floor. They were tender, but not that bad. She wasn't sure how long to leave the duct tape on, but she could ask Jimmy later.

J: I'm home but it was a long night. Napping in Jackson's room. Will try to get up before Natalie gets here. No promises.

J: Oh and also ... later. ;)

Emily had hoped that "later" would mean before Natalie got there. Being with Jimmy would give her that bolster of confidence she needed to get through this—whatever "this" turned out to be. Things with Jimmy seemed like a dream, really—a few days ago, they hadn't been speaking. Now she was thinking thoughts about a future and using the word love, at least in her thoughts. But it still felt so new and fragile. If it was any other relationship, any other guy, maybe it wouldn't last through Natalie's disapproval. But this would. Emily touched her lips, remembering the feel of Jimmy's kiss and the promises it made her. They would move through this. Soon it would be a memory they laughed about, how they had to convince the best friend and sister to get on board with their relationship.

"Em!" Kim gave Emily a one-armed hug as she made it to the top level, looking for coffee. And, obviously Jimmy.

"Let's take it down a few notches to morning volume, please. You're speaking to an uncaffeinated person."

Kim giggled. "Sorry."

Sarah handed Emily a mug of coffee. "Want to go thrifting with us? We thought we'd go before anyone else is up."

Thrifting would be a great way to distract herself. Especially if Jimmy would be sleeping after a late night. "Sure, as long as we're back before Natalie gets here with Scarlet."

Emily's nose felt itchy from all the dust by the second thrift store they hit. There were tables full of costume jewelry and racks of clothes that looked like they were pulled straight from some grandma's closet. A grandma who loved sparkly dresses and sweaters with flowers and kittens on them. It must have been hard to clean sequined formal dresses because when she moved them along the rack, Emily had a sneezing attack.

"Can we find something a little more this century?" Emily said, sneezing again. "I think I'm allergic to history."

Kim put down a gold clutch. "We passed a place a mile back that looked cool. I think it was called Classy & Trashy?"

"Sounds perfect for us," Emily said.

The store was bigger and brighter, with a good selection of new and used things. Old doors stood beside new local paintings. Emily found a table of postcards people had sent over the past fifty years. She read through a few, which she found fascinating, even though most of the notes were just boring *wish you were here* kind of things. Postcards didn't have a lot of room for story.

Kim found a recovered ottoman with a nautical print that she wanted for her new apartment. She and Sarah fought about whether or not it would fit in the back of the car on the way home. Emily wandered away from their fighting and found a table of necklaces that reminded her of Jimmy. It was definitely more of a guy's necklace, though Emily would have also worn it. Two thin strips of dark brown leather held a single silver coin with some kind of inscription she couldn't read.

"That's a doubloon," the store owner said, coming up beside Emily. "Well, a replica. Pieces of eight were the common currency back in the high times of piracy. The real coins are typically worth a few hundred apiece. A local artist makes these in the same fashion."

Emily traced the front of the coin, which had been intentionally weathered to look antique. She remembered Jimmy talking at Jockey's Ridge about local pirate stories. "It's really neat."

"I've got some other varieties up front with more dainty chains and some with beads if you'd like something more feminine."

"This is perfect. I'll take it."

The woman wrapped it in a square of folded tissue paper. "Need a bag?"

"No thanks," Emily said. She put the tissue-wrapped necklace in her purse, carefully zipping it into an interior pocket. Sarah and Kim met her at the register, the ottoman— and its argument—left in the back corner. Sarah had picked out a hand-painted sign for her kitchen that read: As for Me and My House, We Will Serve Tacos.

Kim held up two large metal drawer pulls. One shaped like an octopus and the other like an anchor. "Which do you think Ethan would like more?"

Emily plucked another choice out of the bin: a busty mermaid with a shell bikini. She wiggled her eyebrows at

Kim. "Honestly? I think most guys might prefer the mermaid. But otherwise, maybe the octopus?"

Kim giggled and put back the anchor. "Can you imagine a dresser with those mermaids on every drawer?"

"Or a kitchen with mermaids on the cabinets?" Sarah said.

The two of them laughed as Kim counted out the correct number of drawer pulls for whatever piece of furniture she had at home.

After the cool of the store, the parking lot seemed incredibly hot and bright. Emily took the necklace out of her purse and traced the front of the doubloon as they walked to the car. It had been an impulse buy. Probably a silly one. She felt nervous thinking about giving it to Jimmy. Was it too soon for gifts? She knew Jimmy would love it and could picture it around his neck. Picturing him unwrapping the necklace gave her an extra bounce in her step. She couldn't wait to see his face.

When they got back from shopping, Jackson's jeep was gone and the other guys seemed to be asleep still. Must have been a rough call late that night for them. Stacy, Kim, and Sarah headed down to the beach, but Emily stayed at the house, cleaning and making enough noise hopefully to wake Jimmy. Maybe that was a little desperate, but she didn't really care. He must have needed the rest. But she needed to see him.

When she pressed her ear to Jackson's bedroom door, she heard light snoring and a white noise machine. If Jimmy had been alone in there, she might have gone in and woken him up. Just the idea of a sleep-tousled Jimmy made her feel all giddy. But Beau's car was downstairs, which meant he was probably in there too. Emily just kept cleaning loudly, trying to brace herself for whatever Natalie brought with her.

Her phone buzzed in the pocket of her cutoffs.

N: Here! Finally. This place is gorgeous.
E: Right? Be right down to help carry bags and my favorite little person.

Emily took deep breaths as she made her way down the flights of stairs, toes aching a bit from all the walking that morning. *This is your best friend. You're fine. She's fine. It's all fine.*

Too bad pep talks didn't work. Emily kept giving them anyway, but this one for sure seemed pretty useless. Her nerves were all singing like live wires and her knees felt shaky. Not a good start.

Natalie was already unbuckling Scarlet from the car seat when Emily got downstairs. She was grateful for the adorable distraction of her goddaughter.

"Scarlet! How's my favorite big girl!" Emily said.

"Emwe! Emwe!" Scarlet shouted from her car seat, pumping her chubby legs and fists as Natalie lifted her out.

Emily laughed and clapped her hands. "Hand that big girl right to me! Hey, Scarlet! Aren't you looking ready for the beach! Love your dress. So pretty."

Scarlet pointed to her cotton dress with flamingos on it. "Mean-go. Mean-go."

"Yes, flamingo! That's a big word!" Emily turned to Natalie then. "She's talking so much now!"

Natalie looked exhausted and hardly made eye contact, pulling bags out of the car. "Better. She's still a little behind apparently, but people keep saying as long as she has more words by the time she turns two, it's fine. Otherwise, I guess the state offers speech therapy, which stresses me out."

"Oh, this girl will be perfectly fine." Emily tapped Scarlet on the nose. "She's brilliant, just like her aunt."

"Well, hopefully she'll start running her mouth like her brilliant aunt too. In a good way."

Emily pointed a finger at Natalie. "You may regret saying that soon. Anyway, good to see you, bestie. I was so excited to see this little lady that I didn't give you a hug."

She perched Scarlet on her left hip and gave Natalie a side hug with her free arm.

"Good to see you too," Natalie said. "Though this drive about killed me. I haven't really done a trip this long without Jeremy to help. He's so good with Scarlet. Things are just easier with him around."

"He's a great dad," Emily said. "But I'm here now, so just relax. I mean it. Jimmy and I—uh, I mean, I'll be helping lots. So chill and try to enjoy."

Did Natalie's eyes narrow when she said "Jimmy and I"? Or was that just squinting because of the sun?

"I don't think I know how to chill anymore," Natalie said. "I'm already stressed thinking of this house with so many stairs and then there's the ocean and drowning … "

"Whoa whoa whoa! Let me stop you right there. We are going to have a perfectly fine time and Scarlet will be safe and sound. I'll take her upstairs if you want to bring up just what you need for now. Make Jimmy carry the rest later. Just get what you need for the beach now. Our room is on the first floor."

Emily hadn't meant to bring up Jimmy again. She felt her stomach drop when his name left her lips for the second time. She wished she could pull it right back in her mouth.

Natalie pursed her lips and looked like she was going to say something. Emily spun away toward the stairs with Scarlet and called over her shoulder. This shouldn't be so awkward. Why did Natalie have to make it harder? She tried to push away all the negative thoughts and let her focus stay on the tiny red-headed person perched on her hip.

Pressing a kiss to Scarlet's head, Emily whispered, "You think I'm good enough, right?"

Scarlet's response was good enough, even if she didn't understand. "Emwe good. Emwe good."

Fifteen minutes later Natalie and Emily were in their bathing suits and had wrangled Scarlet into a swim diaper and some kind of suit with a flotation device built in. Emily had Scarlet on her hip again while Natalie carried about five bags over the dunes to the beach. The other girls had come up from the beach for lunch just as Emily and Natalie got to the beach.

Kim made a beeline for Scarlet. "Your daughter is so adorable! Oh my goodness I want kids so bad."

"Thanks," Natalie said, that mama pride in her voice.

Once they picked a spot near but not too near the water, Emily set Scarlet down. The little girl started waddling after a seagull. "This suit looks kind of like the snowsuit the kid had on in that Christmas movie," Emily said. Natalie looked at her blankly. "You know, where he fell down and couldn't get up because his coat was too puffy?"

"It will keep her from drowning," Natalie snapped.

"Hey—I wasn't being critical. I feel much safer knowing she has a built-in flotation thingy. Just an observation."

Natalie didn't say anything, but went after Scarlet, who was still chasing the bird, sighing heavily. Apparently traveling with a kid was way more work than Emily had ever considered. Natalie seemed more stressed than she'd last seen her, exhausted and worn. Hopefully time in the sun and surf would lighten her mood. When would Jimmy wake up? Her own efforts to lighten up the mood or help Natalie seemed to make things worse. Jimmy always had that way of brightening things. Hopefully it would still work, even with the weird tension coming from Natalie that Emily so far was ignoring.

"Wada wada!" Scarlet pointed to the ocean.

"That's right! Water. That's the ocean. O-cean," Emily said.

"She can't say ocean," Natalie said. "She doesn't know that word yet."

Emily turned to look at her and held Natalie's gaze. "Hey, listen. Are you okay? I feel like I can't say or do anything right now without you taking my head off. I'm not being critical. Of her or of you. I'm just trying to help you if you'll let me. I had plans to enjoy this day."

"I'm fine."

She wasn't fine. Emily stared at her for a moment, her look saying it all. Natalie burst into tears, dropping the bags and covering her eyes.

"Okay, I'm not fine," she said through her sobs.

Emily wanted to hug her and to ask what was going on, but Scarlet began wind-milling her arms and reaching toward the ocean.

"Wawa wawa wawa!" she shouted, struggling in Emily's arms.

"Hang on, girl. We'll get there. Listen—I'm going to go take Scarlet to the ocean. Set up a chair or towel and just chill. Okay? I want to talk, but I think we may have to wait a few. I've got this for now. Take a breather. Hit pause on this conversation."

Natalie sniffed. "Okay. I'm sorry."

"Stop apologizing. You're a great mom and you're doing fine. I'm here, so just chill. Cry, sit, sleep, whatever. I've got this little wild woman."

Emily set Scarlet down and held out her hand. Scarlet took her finger in her chubby fist and began an awkward walk-run toward the waves. She tripped and fell in the sand, but did not cry.

"Need help?" Emily held out a hand.

"No!" Scarlet yelled, slapping Emily's hand away.

"Well, you got that word down."

Scarlet paused as she hit the wet sand where her feet began sinking slightly. She stepped back. Emily watched with wonder. You could almost see the wheels turning in the little girl's head as she tried to figure out what to do with the damp sand. Emily wiggled her toes down into the sand beside her. A bigger wave broke and sent a thin, foamy wash of water up over their feet. Scarlet squealed, raising her arms to Emily to be picked up.

Emily laughed and hoisted her out of the water. "Wet. That's the ocean. Wet."

"Wet," Scarlet said.

"That's right! Perfect." Something about hearing her word repeated on this tiny person's lips made Emily's heart soar. She was the furthest thing from a maternal woman, but with Scarlet, everything changed. Finally, she understood what women meant when they talked about feeling their ovaries ache. Being around Scarlet, holding her, watching her go from the tiny infant she remembered awkwardly holding in the hospital with Natalie to this spitfire of a toddler—it gave her an insane amount of joy. More than she could have imagined.

Emily wanted this. She wanted it bad. The family, the kids, the whole thing.

With Jimmy?

Definitely with Jimmy. She couldn't picture it with anyone else. Somehow she knew he would be the perfect Dad, making up for whatever mistakes Emily would make as a mom. The realization that she was even thinking about this seriously short-circuited her thoughts. Was she even ready for a serious relationship? Would she be good at being married? Being a mom?

Helping with Scarlet was one thing, but being a full-time mom ... totally different. Natalie had the whole zombie look down pat. Could Emily really handle that?

Scarlet watched the waves come rolling in and Emily watched Scarlet. Emily loved this age. Much more than the baby stage, when it was hard to tell what Scarlet wanted unless she was crying. Maybe she didn't have a ton of words yet, but you could see her thinking about the world. It was life-giving to watch. Yeah, maybe it would make the exhaustion and zombie-mom thing worth it.

She remembered the first few months when Scarlet was born. Emily practically lived at Natalie's house. Natalie really struggled at first, then hit a stride, then struggled again. It seemed like an ebb and flow based on things you couldn't control, like teething or fevers or Scarlet learning to climb out of her crib at thirteen months. Even with someone as great as Jeremy supporting and being there, Emily could visibly see the stress of it all. If Emily ever did become a mom, she had a much better sense of the joys and the struggles after watching Natalie go through it.

"Is that my favorite niece?"

Jimmy's voice startled Emily. She couldn't help but smile at his wide grin and Scarlet's squeals. The little girl reached for Jimmy. "Mimi! Mimi!"

Emily laughed. "Mimi? Isn't that a grandma name?" His

body pressed into hers as she passed Scarlet to him. His muscular chest and abs and ... oh man. She stepped away, cheeks flushing. She'd seen Jimmy shirtless before. Just the other day. But that was before they'd become ... whatever it was they were now. They still hadn't finished that whole conversation, though the kiss definitely meant they were something more than old friends even if they hadn't made things official. Now seeing Jimmy shirtless felt totally different. Thankfully, he didn't seem to notice her ogling.

Jimmy covered Scarlet's cheeks in kisses as she giggled. "She can't say a J yet. Only a confident manly man can handle being called Mimi. I like it."

Scarlet reached for Emily again. She moved closer to Jimmy, totally aware that somewhere behind them, Natalie's laser focus was on them. Scarlet wanted to stay in Jimmy's arms, but also to hold Emily's hand. Emily looked at Jimmy. Her heart was near to bursting with the mix of emotions standing so close, seeing him hold Scarlet with such ease and such joy. It was like seeing a glimpse of a future. Maybe her future. *Their* future.

"This suits you," Emily said.

"What?" Jimmy tilted his head.

"Being an uncle. Or ... a dad."

He grinned and met her eyes. When she looked at him, all she saw was love. Love—and what felt like a question. Or an offer. Her heart felt like it was going to beat out of her chest. She could see a life with him, almost like it was rolling out before her in her mind. The feeling of joy and protection and kindness and love. Children. Exhaustion. Joy. Chaos. Love.

Suddenly she was reminded that Natalie was probably still watching them right now. Emily glanced behind them. Yep. Natalie sat up very straight on a beach towel, watching the two of them with her daughter, a stiffness in her shoulders. Emily stepped away from Jimmy, dropping Scarlet's hand.

Scarlet began wriggling in Jimmy's arms. "Dow. Dow," she said.

"Down? Okay, you got it, big girl."

He set her down in the wet sand. Scarlet reached for Emily's hand as another wave washed over their feet. Emily met Jimmy's eyes again over Scarlet's head. He grinned and she felt her stomach twist. A bigger wave splashed Scarlet and she reached for Jimmy, who hoisted her up in the air, spinning her around.

"I've got this," he said. "You and Natalie never get to hang out. Go! You guys sit, talk, whatever girls do."

"Okay." Emily hesitated, but Jimmy waved her on.

"Later," he said, giving her a wink. "Go!"

"Go go!" Scarlet repeated.

"Okay, but only because Scarlet says so." Emily tried to throw him a teasing look, but she hoped he couldn't see through the forcedness of it. She walked back to Natalie, feeling the nerves start to sing again now that she didn't have the distraction or buffer of Scarlet. It was such a foreign feeling. *Poker face,* she told herself. *Put on your poker face. It's just your best friend.* She plopped down on a towel next to Natalie. "Hey. Feeling better?"

Natalie nodded and sighed. With her sunglasses on, it was hard to read her features. "Sorry about that. I've just been really struggling lately. Scarlet is so busy. I feel like I can't take a shower or eat a meal or even just sit for five seconds. She cried half the drive down and I kept having to stop and get her out of the car seat and then put her back in the car seat ... Maybe this was a mistake coming down here without Jeremy to help."

Emily touched her best friend's leg. "I'm sorry about the

drive. You're doing really great. It's hard. You've got me to help. And Jimmy."

Natalie turned to look her full in the face. Emily felt heat rising in her cheeks and turned back toward the ocean, where Jimmy chased Scarlet along the water's edge. "Em, what are you doing? With Jimmy?"

Emily watched Jimmy pick Scarlet up in his arms. He was smiling and laughing and Emily couldn't help smiling at the two of them. Her heart swelled in her chest and she thought suddenly of the Grinch, whose heart grew three sizes. She wanted to giggle, but Natalie's intense gaze stopped her. She had lifted her sunglasses so Emily couldn't avoid her eyes.

"I like Jimmy." Emily's voice was too quiet. The words not enough. "I really like Jimmy." Better. Emily licked her lips. This time, the words came out a whisper. "I think I love him."

"You what? You *love* him?"

The silence stretched out as they both watched Jimmy playing with Scarlet along the water's edge. He was incredible. He was the best. Emily stared out at the ocean in front of her. The words were true, whether Natalie accepted them or not. "I do. Very much. It took a while for me to admit this even to myself. I'm terrified of what it means. Doesn't make it less true. I don't want to screw this up. And I want you to approve of whatever this is."

Emily finally turned to look at Natalie, surprised to find that her best friend was crying. Her mouth fell open. "Natalie!"

Natalie sniffed and covered her face. "I'm sorry. This isn't about you. I mean, kind of it is, but it's more."

Emily froze for a moment, then sighed and leaned over to wrap her arms around her friend. Her own eyes burned. Natalie thought it was that bad she and Jimmy liked each other? She could have handled anger and prepared for that. Tears and sadness were a whole other thing. She tried to ignore the slice of pain through her gut.

"Is it me? You don't think I'm good enough for him?"

Natalie jerked her head back and the fierceness in her eyes shocked Emily. "What? No!" She sighed. "I'm messing this all up. I'm pregnant."

Now Emily jerked back. A smile hit her face until Natalie started crying harder. "Hey, hey. You're okay. What's going on? Are you ... not happy?"

"I'm just a giant ball of hormones. And I feel sick. And Scarlet's so hard. I feel like I'm failing at this mom thing and now I'm making you feel bad about Jimmy and making this all about me. I'm sorry, Emily."

Emily squeezed her tighter. Natalie had put her head down on her bent knees. Relief flooded through her. Natalie was pregnant. Which amped up her hormones and likely her moods. Maybe the tension she felt had less to do with Natalie disapproving and more to do with being pregnant.

"You are a fantastic mom. Seriously. It looks so hard and you are just doing great. Scarlet's amazing and that's all you and Jeremy. You're both great. You made one amazing human and you'll have another. It will be great. I'm sorry you're feeling like this, though. Can I do anything?"

Natalie sniffed. "I'm sorry. Thank you."

They sat for a few minutes, the sound of Scarlet's squeals making them both smile as Jimmy chased her along the shoreline. "So, me and Jimmy ..." Emily started, just as Natalie said, "About Jimmy ..." They both laughed and Emily waited for Natalie to finish.

"I owe you an apology. Probably a few. I shouldn't have butted in at the wedding. I was stressed out then too and, if I'm being honest, I was afraid you'd break him."

211

"Which kind of happened anyway."

Natalie sighed. "Yeah. It did."

"But I think maybe we weren't ready for each other then."

"Did you like him back then too?"

"Yeah, I did. But I was scared. Even more scared than I am now, which is still pretty scared. I'd seen him so long as a brother. When that started to change, it shook things up. You gave me an easy out. It wasn't just your fault. And I think honestly, he's in a better place now than he was then. Sandover suits him."

"It does." Natalie turned to look at Emily. "So do you."

"Thanks. It's been a rough road, but I think God put us right where he wanted us. I wasn't ready a few years ago. He still was young. We were in such different places. If I had acted on something then, I think it would have crashed and burned. But now ..."

"Now he's grown up."

Emily smirked. "He has. Very much so." Emily gazed at Jimmy picked Scarlet up, the muscles in his back flexing.

Natalie swatted her arm. "Ew, Emily. That's my brother!"

Emily threw back her head and laughed. "Even from an aesthetic appreciation, you've got to admit that your brother is a hottie. His muscles have muscles."

"I heard the piano player at church once call him a beefcake." Natalie giggled.

"Ms. Edwards? Isn't she like eighty-five? Beefcake. But I guess the description does fit ..."

They both began laughing so hard that they didn't notice Jimmy approaching until he stood in front of them, blocking out the sun.

"What fits?" Jimmy asked. Scarlet wiggled in his arms, reaching for Emily.

"Uh, your swimsuit," Natalie said.

Emily began to laugh even harder and stood, letting Scarlet lead her by the hand back to the water. "Wawa! WAWA!"

"Want me to come with you?" Natalie asked. "I can take her."

"Nope. I got this. Rest. Enjoy."

"I'll join you," Jimmy said.

"Nope. It's brother-sister bonding o'clock," Natalie said. "I think we need to chat. If that's okay, Em?"

"Perfect." She felt much better about this now that she knew Natalie approved. Maybe she was also going to break the pregnancy announcement to her brother.

Scarlet let go of her hand and did her best waddle-run to the water's edge. A fat seagull stood watching nearby. It only took a few seconds before Scarlet was off, chasing the bird, and Emily was off, chasing Scarlet. They played this game for what felt like forever, but was probably just ten minutes. When Scarlet finally ran for Natalie and climbed in her lap, Emily collapsed on a towel next to Jimmy.

"Okay, motherhood is exhausting. Scarlet's the best kid in the world, but I don't know how you do this every day."

Natalie gave a smug grin and flicked her eyes to Jimmy. "It's especially hard now that I'm pregnant."

Emily watched Jimmy's face. It took a minute, then he broke into a huge grin. "Wait—what? Sis! Really?" He wrapped both Natalie and Scarlet in a big hug and they squealed.

Emily watched, contentment spreading its warm fingers in her chest. This. This was going to be her life, even more than before. It had been so much easier than she had thought.

"I can't wait to be an uncle times two. Congrats."

"Thanks," Natalie said. "I'll be happy when I stop feeling

so horrible. I mean, I'm not barfing all the time, but I'm just exhausted. And irrationally angry."

"Angry? You?" Jimmy hoisted Emily over his lap to shield himself from Natalie as she swung at him.

"Hey! No fair! I didn't do anything!" Emily giggled. She loved how Jimmy could so easily just pick her up. Even if it meant getting in the middle of a sibling fight.

Natalie stood, brushing sand off her bottom. "My turn with Scarlet. Thank you both so much for helping her. I mean it. It's so nice to have an extra set of hands. This was a good idea, me coming down. For more reasons than one." Scarlet was off and Natalie scrambled after her toward the water's edge and more birds.

Emily was still halfway in Jimmy's lap. He set her down fully on the sand next to him and wrapped a strong arm around her shoulders, pulling her close to his chest. He smelled like a mix of sunscreen and whatever deodorant he wore. It was intoxicating and she inhaled deeply.

Jimmy tilted his head to look down at her. "Did you just sniff me?"

"Maybe. You got a problem with that?"

"Nope." He pulled her tighter. Emily didn't even mind the feel of sand against her skin where their bodies touched. The dang sand. She'd have to get used to it if she was really considering a move here. A small price to pay for moments like this, she thought, sighing.

As though he could read her thoughts, Jimmy said, "I know you hate the sand and all, but do you ever think you could live somewhere like this?"

Emily could hear what he was really asking underneath the question. She thought about telling him she was working on a proposal for Jackson, but wanted to surprise him. If it worked out, anyway. "I think maybe I could. For the right reasons."

She looked up at Jimmy, meeting his deep blue gaze. Their faces were just inches apart. The blood felt like it was rushing madly through her body. His eyes were intense and she dropped her gaze, right to his lips. Then back up to his eyes. They needed to talk, but she also wanted a repeat of the toe-curling kiss from earlier.

"What kind of reason would you need?" He stroked a hand across her cheek. She could feel that touch in every part of her body.

She swallowed. Her voice, when it came out, was husky and low. "I think I would need a permanent reason," she said. "One that would keep me here for good."

"A for better or worse kind of reason?" he whispered.

"Something like that."

Jimmy leaned forward and she closed her eyes. His breath feathered over her cheek, sending a shudder down her spine. His hand was in her hair now, fingertips near the back of her neck. She realized she was holding her breath.

He closed the last distance between them until their lips met. As his mouth moved over hers, warm and soft, Emily knew that she already had all the reasons she needed to stay. Truth was, she never wanted to leave. For once, everything in her life seemed to be lining up.

Why did that give her the tiniest sense of worry?

CHAPTER EIGHTEEN

Getting Emily alone for a conversation was becoming almost like a joke. But getting less funny with every passing moment. Because Jimmy could see the moments he had left with her this week disappearing like sand down the hourglass. Kissing was great. Knowing that Natalie approved felt good. But the two of them needed to talk about this. Even if Jimmy wasn't sure exactly what to say. Was it too soon to ask Emily to move here? To give her a reason to move here? The thought made sweat start to bead on his forehead. Whether out of fear or excitement, he wasn't sure.

He was saying normal things, doing normal things, but underneath it all, he felt like his body was humming with electricity. Everything in him felt pulled toward her, as though even his skin was aware of where she was in a room and inclined in that direction. All he wanted was to be alone with her. Instead, they were all grilling out and the house was loud with people.

"Jimmy, I think that's enough on the tomatoes." Natalie leaned a hip against the kitchen counter.

He shook his head and looked down to realize that he had cut through more tomatoes than there were people there for dinner. Even with the addition of Natalie, Scarlet, and Jackson's fiancée, Jenna. He gave her a rueful grin and set the knife in the sink. "Guess I was a little distracted."

Natalie turned her gaze knowingly across the room where Emily had Scarlet in her lap, reading her a book. "I'm really happy for you. Sorry for being a little slow to get on board. I'd blame the hormones, but part of it was that I'm overprotective. It's a big sister thing."

"As long as you're on board now, we're all good. I mean, she's your best friend, so it seems like this should be like your dream come true."

"It is. I mean, a little weird since I don't want to have to hear about, you know, any details at all about you guys romantically."

"Like I'd want to share. Gross."

Natalie rolled her eyes. "Girls talk. Normally. Emily and I will just have to figure a way around that. It's fine." She started stacking the slices of tomato on a platter that someone had set out. She whispered when she spoke next. "I also just know how much you liked Emily. For so long. And I was worried she might break your heart."

"But you're not still worried, right?"

Turning, Natalie touched Jimmy's arm. The concern in her eyes made him nervous. "No, but it still makes me a little bit nervous. You know I love Emily. But she's kind of a flake. She's had a lot of boyfriends. No steady job. I kept telling her to go back to school, but after she spent all that money doing the training to be a dental hygienist and couldn't handle putting her hands in other people's mouths. Anyway. She's flighty."

Jimmy clenched his jaw. "You're wrong about her. She's been your best friend for what—fifteen years?"

Natalie sighed. "You're right. I'm sorry. I love you both. If it doesn't work out, that would just suck."

"Thanks for the vote of confidence, sis. In both me and Emily." He couldn't keep the bitter edge from his voice. Natalie wrapped her arms around his waist. He patted her back as she squeezed him. She always found a way to soften him up.

"I'm sorry, Jimmy. I've voiced my concerns and I do approve. I just want it to work out, you know."

"Trust me. I do too. Now stop worrying. You gave your stamp of approval. Too late to take it back, sis." He spoke lightly, though his feelings were anything but.

"Just as long as you're careful."

He tightened his arms around her. "Natalie," he said in a warning tone. The truth was, he was over this conversation. She needed to let it go. Things were different with Emily now. But Natalie's words had stirred up the doubts, making his thoughts feel cloudy and less certain. He had already been through these thoughts when he first saw Emily on Sandover. He took Beau's advice to take the risk and things were good. The last thing he wanted was to be thinking again about them. Thinking about it made his gut churn. He shook his head, like that could dislodge the tiny doubts.

Emily wasn't going to break his heart this time. She wasn't going to run, even if she had to leave Friday. He hoped that tonight they could finally talk and he could convince her to come back to Sandover. Permanently. Jimmy was already thinking rings and vows and honeymoons and kids. He knew it was a lot, but that's how he felt. This was all he had wanted for so many years. Remembering how much she hurt him in the past wasn't going to do anything to benefit the relationship now. Jimmy didn't realize how tightly he was squeezing Natalie.

"Oof. I think you're squishing my innards. And the baby."

Jimmy let her go and looked over, where Emily was looking at them both. Natalie smiled and bumped her hip into his. Jimmy grinned and bumped her back. A little harder than he meant to and she took a few steps and ran into Jackson, who was precariously balancing a tray of burgers. One of the burgers on the edge splatted onto the floor.

"Jimmy! Sorry, Jackson." Natalie picked up the burger and tossed it in the trash.

"We can stand to lose one. I think I went a little overboard with the burgers," Jackson said.

"Are we feeding the 5000? Sorry—child of a pastor jokes. Don't pretend like you don't have that same humor, sis," Jimmy said, as Natalie groaned.

Everyone gathered in the kitchen. Emily stood next to Jimmy, her hip just barely resting against his, lighting that whole side of his body on fire. Jenna, Jackson's fiancée was there, grinning up at him. Jimmy loved the way Jackson lit up when he was around her. They were both almost forty, but acted like a couple of lovey-dovey teenagers around each other, goofy and happy. Jimmy wanted that too.

"Who's got the blessing?" Jackson asked.

"I'll do it," Beau said. "Where I come from, we hold hands."

Natalie stood beside Jimmy with Scarlet in her arms. Jimmy held out his hand and Scarlet grabbed his finger. On his other side, he took Emily's hand, trying to keep his fingers still when all they wanted to was to move, touching and exploring every part of her hand. He squeezed once and she squeezed back.

Beau said the blessing, ending with: "And all God's people said?"

"Amen!" a chorus of voices said.

"Men!" Scarlet echoed, and they all laughed.

Stacy had gone out to dinner with Robbie, and without them, the mood in the house seemed lighter. Natalie helped round things out and Scarlet kept people laughing. Throughout the meal at Jackson's long dining table, Emily kept her leg touching Jimmy's. Halfway through dinner, he slipped his foot out of his flip flops and trapped her feet. Emily turned her head and gave him a sideways smile.

Natalie took Scarlet down to give her a bath before bed while everyone else lingered around the table. Jackson's fiancée Jenna told embarrassing stories about Jackson in high school, making them all laugh.

"So, it wasn't love at first sight, then?" Kim put her hand over her heart. "I love hearing people's love stories."

Jackson made a face and then grinned at Jenna. "Maybe you should tell them about when you started falling for me."

Jenna grinned. "Oh, I see—time for you to embarrass me now?"

"It's only fair."

Jenna rolled her eyes. "Fine. He and I were riding in that elevator over there—" She pointed to the tiny elevator over by the stairs. "—and I opened the door while it was moving. Not my finest move. We were stuck for like an hour. Beau and Jimmy had to rescue us."

"It was very romantic," Jackson said.

"And sweaty."

Jimmy put his arm around Emily as they settled in for the whole story. He loved watching Jackson in love. He felt like he and Emily were destined for the same kind of future, the same kind of stories. *Remember the time you almost died when that balcony collapsed?*

Maybe too soon for that one. He still felt nauseated thinking about how precarious it had been. But one day, he felt more and more certain that they would have their own story of how God brought them together, over the years and despite everything. The fleeting doubts he felt were nothing more than that.

"How did you know?" Emily's voice startled Jimmy back to the conversation. "I mean, it sounds like you guys kind of had that love-hate thing going strong."

Jackson and Jenna exchanged a glance. He gestured to her. "I think I kind of knew forever. Or hoped. Little different for Jenna."

Under the table, Jimmy squeezed Emily's hand. This didn't sound so unlike their story.

"I think sometimes you have to dig a little below the surface. Jax is more than just a pretty face." Jenna smirked as Jackson groaned and shook his head.

"I'm not pretty."

"You kinda are," Beau stage-whispered, and everyone laughed. Under the table, Emily clutched Jimmy's hand tighter, like she was holding on for dear life. He squeezed her fingers.

"It's about character," Jenna continued. "What's underneath is what lasts. The more I got to know Jackson, the more I knew that he was the kind of man I could trust. Sorry, this is sounding a little cheesy."

Kim leaned on her elbows. "No, it's perfect. And you're so right. What's that verse—beauty is fleeting?"

Jackson leaned closer to Jenna, putting a hand on the back of her neck. "While this woman is as beautiful as she was when she was eighteen—" Jenna rolled her eyes at this. "—she's right. Her heart is what gives her real beauty." Now Jenna blushed as Jackson kissed her cheek.

Jimmy put his lips to Emily's ear and spoke so only she could hear. "Sounds like us." He let his lips linger on the curve of her ear, just long enough to note that a shiver went through her. She gave him a small smile, then pulled her hand away from his, taking a long sip of water.

After dinner, Jimmy offered to do the dishes, his usual job around the house. Jackson and Jenna left hand in hand for a walk on the beach, while Kim and Sarah argued about movie choices. Beau had taken a phone call out on the balcony. Emily stood beside him without being asked, loading the plates and cups in the dishwasher. Every so often Jimmy flicked soapy water her way and she would fling some right back. He loved that Emily gave as good as she got. She didn't have much to say, which was unlike her, and seemed lost in thought.

"You okay?"

"Yep. Just thinking."

"Looks like some serious thinking." She gave a tight smile but didn't look at him. "I'm here if you want to turn the thinking into talking. I wondered if maybe we could take a walk on the beach after this. I've been wanting to talk to you for like two days now. If you can handle more sand."

"Sounds good."

Jimmy was about to press her a little more but decided to wait. She had started to close down sometime during dinner, but he couldn't think of a reason why. Maybe it was the overwhelm of the week finally catching up to her. She had almost died, been rescued, reunited with Jimmy, broken her toes, kissed him for the first time, and more. It was a lot. Plus, she hadn't slept much. Yeah, that kind of week could cause anyone to break.

Turning off the sink, Jimmy leaned close and pressed a kiss to Emily's temple. "You know I think you're amazing, right?"

"Thanks." Again, her small smile didn't seem to reach her eyes.

Jimmy put a hand on the small of her back, feeling the urge to have her close, just as Natalie brought Scarlet up. She still had damp hair and pink cheeks from the bath. "Someone wants to say goodnight!" Natalie said.

Scarlet wrapped her arms around Jimmy's neck. She gave him a wet kiss on the cheek and he laughed. "Nigh nigh."

He kissed her on the forehead and handed her back to Natalie. "Night, my sweet girl."

Scarlet reached for Emily next. The sight of her snuggling Scarlet close into her neck made Jimmy's chest feel full. Emily was so beautiful. In the morning, at night, in the photos he'd seen of her modeling, when she had no makeup on her face at all—always gorgeous. But nothing was more beautiful to him than Emily holding Scarlet close. Even now, with her expression shuttered and her eyes a little haunted.

His heart clenched, wanting to smooth away the lines creasing her forehead. The caveman part of him wanted to toss her over his shoulder and claim her, promising her forever. But seeing her so worn down, Jimmy knew he should probably hold back a bit. Maybe not make giant declarations of love or telling her that he was already thinking of moving her here and marrying her. That might be too much for her to handle with how worn she looked.

After Natalie disappeared down the stairs, Jimmy leaned back against the counter. She shut the dishwasher with a satisfying click and smiled at him. He could see the effort that smile took as he studied her face.

"We don't have to walk if you don't want."

She blinked. "Do you ... not want to?"

"You just look like you could use some rest. It's been a long week and you've been through a lot."

She murmured an agreement, but her face only looked more closed. Jimmy tugged gently on a strand of her hair. "Your choice. Movie? Walk on the beach?"

Emily opened her mouth to answer just as Beau rushed in from the balcony. "Jimmy! We've got to go. There's a fire at one of the storefronts just Off Island. They need backup."

Jimmy turned to Emily with an apology, but she surprised him by pressing a quick kiss against his lips. She smiled and squeezed his arm. "Be careful, okay?"

He kissed her forehead. "Always. Guess we'll get back to this conversation ..."

At the same time, they smiled and said, "Later."

CHAPTER NINETEEN

Emily had been wiping down counters in Jackson's kitchen when he and Jenna returned. He smiled before ducking into his room. "You know that you don't need to keep cleaning, right?"

"I don't mind. It relaxes me." *Especially when I'm trying to hide a giant internal freak-out from people who know me way too well.* Thankfully, Natalie was still trying to wrestle Scarlet into sleep and Jimmy was off on a call. While she had been worried to see him go, part of her needed the relief from trying to keep it together.

"As long as you know that you don't have to." He kissed Jenna on the cheek. "I've got to send a few emails about a shipment that I forgot. Be right back."

Jenna sat down at a stool across the counter. Emily tried not to stiffen up, wiping down the same area that she'd been over three times. "So, you and Jimmy?"

"Yep." *Maybe. Probably.* Earlier, that would have been a quick affirmative, backed by a sense of confidence that had evaporated over dinner, hearing about Jenna and Jackson's adorable love story.

Emily knew, logically, that she was being ridiculous. But it felt like Jenna had opened up her brain, removed all the trigger words, and then she and Jackson had used them all. Character, underneath the surface, beauty from the heart—all those things that guys seemed to find lacking in her over and over again. How long until Jimmy was giving her the same breakup line? Her fingers trembled and she gripped the counter.

Because of her usual confidence, no one suspected the punishing way Emily's insecurities sometimes battered her. Usually she could press them back into place, but every so often, they washed over her like a tsunami wave. The last time this happened had been the hotel room after New York, where she hid long enough to be able to walk around without anyone seeing the way she crumbled inside. No one, not even Natalie, would suspect the way these self-doubts could sometimes manage to take her completely off her feet. It was like one tiny thread of doubt, one worry, sometimes had the power to unravel the whole fabric of her life.

Did it have to be now? Over Jimmy? For almost a whole day, she had felt peaceful, even giddy about the relationship. Only a few words had managed to take her down to her knees. And she knew that if she talked to anyone about it, they'd just brush off her concerns. She could hear what they'd say, because she had tried telling herself the same things.

She was making a big deal over nothing. Jimmy loved her. He knew her as well as anyone since they'd grown up together. She'd shared her darkest moments with him and he didn't go running away. Whatever other guys had found lacking in her, things were different with Jimmy. The way he looked at her with utter adoration just proved it.

So why couldn't she silence the whispers in her head that she wasn't enough?

Why did she keep hearing her parents' disappointment in her?

Why did she hear all the breakup speeches over the past few years playing like a reel in her mind?

Emily's toes throbbed and she grimaced. Jenna noticed and pointed to the stool next to her. "Want to sit? Jax said you broke your toes at the store."

Grunting, Emily sat down, thankful for the distraction of conversation. Her thoughts were too loud. "I did. Frozen rolls of ground beef are way harder than you'd think."

Jenna laughed. "I bet. Wow. Well, I just wanted to say that it's great to see you and Jimmy together. I heard you guys have a similar story to us?"

"Something like that." Emily bit her lip. It was more like their story than she wanted to admit. She found herself tongue-tied, torn between asking Jenna questions about her relationship with Jackson and wanting to escape the conversation altogether. She should probably just join the other girls watching a movie nearby. But Stacy had come back, presumably after Robbie got called in with Beau and Jimmy, and Emily didn't think her walls could stand whatever daggers Stacy threw tonight.

"I've never seen him so happy. I say that like I know him well. It hasn't been that long. But he, Beau, and Jax are inseparable. Jimmy and Beau really helped Jackson become the man he is, the one I fell in love with. You probably already know how amazing he is."

Yep. Way too good for me. Grief shot through her like she

had already lost him, followed by a wave of self-loathing for letting the dark thoughts win. "He really is a great guy."

"I don't know you well, but to win someone like him, I'm sure you're pretty great yourself."

The kind words almost pushed Emily to tears and she bit her lip, trying to hold back the emotion clawing its way to the surface. She was not going to fall apart here. Footsteps on the stairs saved her as Natalie practically dragged herself to the top. She looked exhausted and rested her head on Emily's shoulder. "Scarlet is going to kill me with this whole bedtime thing. It's like an Olympic event. Now I'm so tired I want to sleep and it's not even nine."

Emily patted her back. "There, there. You're doing great. Today you kept a tiny human alive for another day."

"Can I hire you to be my personal cheerleader? Motherhood doesn't come with a lot of accolades. I could use someone following me around just telling me I'm going to make it through the day."

"Yes, I could do that. Starting tomorrow."

Jenna hopped up from her stool as Jackson emerged from his bedroom. Briefly, Emily saw the mattresses strewn across the floor in his room from where Beau and Jimmy slept. She really needed to turn her thoughts outward. Here she was, letting the dark worries fill her, when those two guys were out fighting an actual fire. For the first time since dinner, Emily felt her head clear a little bit.

"And then there were two," Emily said with a smile.

Natalie glanced over to the couch, then lowered her voice. "You want to watch the movie with them?"

Emily made a face. She didn't want to be a gossip, but Natalie knew that she and Stacy didn't get along. "Nah. We could go out or something, but I'm not feeling energetic and you look beat. I mean, beautiful, obviously, but beat."

Natalie rolled her eyes. "Yeah, right." She yawned. "I'm sorry. I'm not much fun these days."

"Psh. Totally untrue. But you're doing double duty with a wee baby inside and a wild one outside. When are you due? I didn't even ask earlier. I'm sorry!"

"Late December."

"Aw, a Christmas baby!"

Natalie yawned again. "I hate to do this, but I need to bail. I may not be able to stay awake on the drive home in the morning if I don't. And Scarlet gets up so stinking early. Sorry in advance."

"How about this? I'll get up with her. You sleep in."

Natalie's eyes went wide. "Seriously? You'd do that? "

"I don't care. Sleep is for the weak," Emily said.

"Are you still saying that? Sleep is good for you. Studies show that you live longer and have better skin and—"

"Hm. I think I changed my mind."

Natalie hopped off the stool and hugged Emily. "Thank you."

After watching the end of the movie and checking her phone obsessively for updates from Jimmy, Emily quietly made her way into the room downstairs. Natalie had a noise-maker on, the sound of a storm covering over Scarlet's small snores. Emily tried to get in bed without waking Natalie, but she shifted and rolled over as Emily pulled the covers up.

Natalie's arm flopped against Emily and then she pulled it back. "Sorry." She didn't sound fully awake.

Emily smiled in the dark. "Don't get handsy now. I'm taken."

"For now, anyway. They never last long." Natalie's voice trailed off and her breathing evened out.

She wasn't even awake, Emily tried to tell herself. It didn't even sound like Natalie remembered it was Jimmy, not some other random guy. But awake or not, the words sliced right through to Emily's heart and woke up those dark whispers she'd been pushing back for the last hour. She tried to think of Bible verses that would counter her self-doubt and over-whelm, but the only ones that came to mind were David talking about being cast out in darkness.

~

True to her word, Emily got up with Scarlet when she stirred around 6:15. "I got this," she whispered to Natalie, who was already sitting up. "Go back to sleep."

She took Scarlet up to the top floor with the diaper bag, changed her, and let her eat frozen waffles at the table. She was going to heat them up, but Scarlet grabbed one out of her hand and started munching away.

"You're going to break your teeth!" Emily said. But she tried one and they weren't that hard. "Hm. I think you're onto something, kid. This isn't so bad."

Scarlet left pieces of waffle trailing behind her as she ate, flitting around the room pointing at different things and babbling. Some words Emily could pick out easily. Like, "Netflix," when she pointed at the TV. That one made her laugh.

The first chance she got, she checked her phone. Jimmy had texted her at 4:07.

J: Just got home, safe and sound. Will probably sleep til 10 or so. Later. ;)

Later. She smiled at the word, which had become sort of their word in the last few days. The dark cloud that had hung over her dissipated in the morning light. She had been so stupid to worry and let her mind get away from her like that. No more of that dramatic nonsense. Today was a new day and she only had a few left with Jimmy.

He still wasn't up when Natalie climbed to the top of the stairs, still yawning. "Tag," Natalie said. "Go take a shower or something. I'll take Scarlet. Thank you! That was refreshing. Though I dreamed I turned into a toothbrush, which was mildly disconcerting."

Emily wondered if Natalie remembered what she'd said when Emily came to bed. Probably not. That made it easier for Emily to let it go too. "I think you need more sleep."

"Maybe. It's also the pregnancy hormones. Crazy dreams. Did Jimmy get back?"

"He's here but sleeping. When are you guys leaving? Are you sure you can't stay?"

"Yeah—one night of travel with baby is about all I can handle. Even with you and Jimmy helping. I'll leave around noon. I wanted to hit the beach again."

"Sounds great! I want a shower and I'll be ready in just a few."

Emily loved Scarlet, but she enjoyed the few minutes under the hot spray of a shower. The day had barely started and she was exhausted. While Emily got dressed, her thoughts slid back to Jimmy. They still needed to talk about what was next. It was like they were teetering on the edge of something and it was giving her vertigo. She wanted to feel the security of solid commitment from him, through words, not just her best guesses and the amazing kisses they'd shared.

If he didn't object and Emily could land a job working for Jackson or something else, she'd move here next week. But did he want to move that fast? Was she the only one dreaming of a wedding? She had started thinking of kids' names and how they needed to register for one of those stand mixers everyone gets and no one uses. Yellow. They would get a yellow one.

Emily lay back in Jimmy's bed in just her towel. It still smelled like him, but it was fading. She could smell her own shampoo and Natalie's perfume now too. She turned a pillow over, pressing it into her face and inhaling deep. There he was.

"You were an idiot to worry," she said, out loud and grinning. "This is real. This is happening."

Hearing Scarlet's squeals upstairs and the thudding of heavy footsteps, Emily threw on clothes over a bathing suit. The same black one that she wore when Jimmy rescued her from the balcony. He *rescued* her. She would keep this bathing suit, put it in a box or maybe one of those frames you can hang on the wall. This was the suit she was wearing when everything started again. It was worth remembering. Maybe she should go back to the house they'd originally stayed in, snag a piece of the broken balcony. She could frame them together.

Later.

After a few hours on the beach, Emily and Jimmy stood on the driveway, waving and blowing kisses to Scarlet and Natalie—but, honestly, mostly to Scarlet. As soon as the car was gone, his arm around her shoulder turned into two arms picking her up and throwing her over his shoulder. She slapped at his back, but truthfully, she loved feeling his strength.

"Jimmy!" she was laughing and squealing and her hair was in her mouth. "What are you doing?"

He set her down in front of him and brushed her hair from her face, grinning. "I guess I didn't really have a plan. I've just always wanted to do that. I've also always wanted to do this."

With a hand on either side of her face, he leaned in and kissed her. Softly, then with a passion that told her everything he hadn't said yet because they still hadn't had THE conversation. She felt the hairs on her head tingling at their roots while her heart rammed against her chest like it was trying to escape.

It didn't matter that they were in the middle of the driveway in the middle of the day. It didn't matter that they hadn't said the words that needed saying yet. His kiss smoothed away her doubts and brought light to the darkness.

She stood there, kissing her Jimmy, until a car drove by and someone shouted, "Get a room!" out the window.

Then and only then they pulled away, both laughing. She let him take her hand and they started toward the beach. Her toe slowed her down and so he threw her over his shoulder again. He only dropped her hand to take off the shirt he wore over his bathing suit. She took the cue and dropped her shirt in the sand, but it took longer to wiggle out of her cutoffs, so she walked behind him to the ocean, watching the muscles in his back tense with every step until he spun around and caught her just at the point of waves breaking.

She kissed him this time, hoping that her lips did as good a job of telling him everything she felt. After what could have been five minutes or four hours, they broke apart, both smiling. Her lips felt raw but good. So good.

"So," she said. "This is what being in love is like?"

His eyes widened at her words and his smile took over his whole face. He kissed her, once, then pulled close so their foreheads were touching. "Yes, this is what being in love is like. I'm glad you finally decided to join me, because it's much better when the person you love loves you back."

She felt a thrill move through her at his words and grabbed his neck to pull him in for another kiss. But his arms were lifting her again and before she realized what he was doing, he tossed her into the waves.

Sputtering and laughing, she came up for air, tasting the salt on her lips and the sting of water in her nose. *"James!"*

"That," he said, striding toward her in the water, "Is for not loving me back sooner."

After hours of playing in the sun and surf and still somehow not having the conversation, Emily found herself in the shower again. Jimmy had to go help Jackson move something at one of the rental houses, but had promised to take her to dinner where they'd finally talk. It seemed more like going through the motions, since they'd spent the afternoon laughing, kissing, and tossing around the L word.

The nice thing about the sand and stickiness of the beach was how refreshing it felt washing all of it off. When she emerged feeling new, her skin still warm, Emily put on a simple black sundress. It was comfortable but also showed off her legs. Jimmy had made it very clear that he really liked her legs.

Natalie and Scarlet had left the room looking a little disheveled. As she bent down to put on her strappy sandals, Emily spotted a stuffed animal of Scarlet's under the bed next to an open book. She grabbed both and realized almost immediately that it wasn't a book, but Jimmy's journal. Curiosity itched over her skin. It wasn't snooping if she just glanced at the open page while she moved it back to the bedside table, right? It was hardly more than peeking. It's not like she did this on purpose, which would be worse. Emily glanced down at the open page.

It was a list, dated a few months ago. Her heart started beating faster and she found herself smiling at the title at the top of the page in his blocky handwriting: THINGS I WANT IN A WIFE.

She smiled and bit her lip. *Let's see how I do,* she thought, scanning the list.

Christian
    Makes me laugh
    Beautiful
    Wants kids
    Isn't money-obsessed
    Likes the beach

Mentally she gave herself a check-mark for most of the list, other than the beach. Though the beach was growing on her.

She skimmed the list, ready to close the book. Until her eyes fell on the last thing on the list. It was in all caps, so she didn't know why her eye wasn't drawn there first.

Her breath caught and her eyes stung immediately with hot tears. It felt like her heart shriveled up and went cold. The darkness she thought she'd shoved down into the corner of her soul covered her so fast that for a moment, she felt like the whole room went black.

All the hope and giddy feelings and thoughts of the future

died in one swift moment with two words, the last thing on the list:

NOT EMILY

Maybe it was written months ago. It probably stemmed from his hurt over what happened at the wedding. Things were different now. Logically, she knew that. But this journal was a window to Jimmy's private thoughts. It was his truth.

And the truth was that he hadn't wanted to marry her just a few months ago. So much that he added her name to a list of things he wanted in a wife. Not her. Not Emily.

Emily didn't realize she was grinding her teeth until she heard the sound. She unclenched her jaw, a shuddery sigh moving through her. Emily closed the journal, trying to push back the sick feeling rising in her gut. It only took her a minute to decide that she was leaving and another five to get her bag and run out to the car. She may have had a list of flaws a mile long, but she could say this about herself: she could make a quick decision when the situation demanded it and not look back once.

CHAPTER TWENTY

"Can't you drive any faster?" Jimmy said, his legs nervously bouncing up and down in the passenger seat of Beau's car. It had been only an hour, but he had a date with Emily. Every hour away felt like more. And every hour brought him closer to the end of the week when she had to leave. If he was being really honest, there was also a small part of him that expected Emily to bolt. Natalie hadn't been completely right that Emily was a flake. But maybe just a little right. That's what scared him.

Strong and courageous. Those were the words Jimmy needed still, apparently, when it came to dating the most beautiful woman he'd ever known. Burning buildings and beautiful women. It worked both places. Honestly? Emily was more terrifying. And as much as her kisses and her looks and their time the last few days made him sure, until they sat across from each other and he said the kinds of words that needed to be said, he would feel like the bottom might fall out.

He'd always hated that phrase "lock that down" about women and marriage. It sounded so ... crass. Impersonal.

Until now. Now? He was absolutely about locking that down and throwing away the key. But if he was being honest, it felt less like locking Emily down and more like handing her the keys. She already owned him. Always had.

Beau smiled. "A little eager to get back?" Jimmy just rolled his eyes and Beau kept going. "You can thank me anytime you want."

"For what, exactly?"

"The good advice that you should stop trying to run from Emily and just let things happen."

"Oh, you'd like to think you're the matchmaker."

"Aren't I?"

"We had years of history leading up to this moment. You just gave me a gentle nudge. Thanks for that."

Beau snorted. "Yeah, okay, Mr. Terrified to Even Talk to Her. If you want to say it was a nudge, fine. I'm just happy to see you happy. I assume this crazy look on your face is happy, right?"

"Happy doesn't begin to describe it. I feel … complete. I mean, this is it. She's it. She always has been, but now that she sees me the same way." He shook his head. "I can't even believe it. And yet it seems so right. Like we've been together for our whole lives, not just twenty-four hours."

"Be honest," Beau said. "Are you counting the hours?"

"Dang straight. And every one is better than the last. So stop driving like a grandma and get me back to my woman. I have words to say. And until I say them, I'm going to feel equal parts excited and terrified."

Beau glanced at him. "You haven't had The Talk yet?"

"We keep getting interrupted," Jimmy said. "Which is maybe good because I feel like yesterday I would have just asked her to be my girlfriend. But now …"

They were at a stop light, but Beau hit the brakes way

harder than he needed to. Jimmy grabbed the console. "What?"

"Dude. Calm down. You're not going to propose today ... right?"

"No way. I've got to ask her dad first. And probably she should officially be my girlfriend first. So, I'll ask that, then I'll ask if she wants to move here, then I'll ask her dad—"

"Move here?" Beau had a huge smile on his face.

"Yep. I'm going to ask that." His heart pounded thinking about it. But he was going to do this.

Beau shook his head. "Okay. I've just got to say this. You are an inspiration. I'm going to do it. I'm going to ask Mercer out. For real this time. If you can go from pining after your lifelong love to asking her to move cities for you in a week, then I can do anything."

Jimmy wanted to say something to Beau about this, but all those thoughts were gone when they pulled up to Jackson's house. Emily's car was gone. Jimmy felt the first edge of panic in his stomach. There were a lot of reasons her car could be gone. One of the other girls might have borrowed it. Maybe Emily made a coffee run or wanted to buy a new dress to wear for dinner.

But his immediate thought, of course, was that she ran. Almost like he'd been waiting for it to happen, for him to blink and realize it had all been a dream.

She wouldn't, though. He left her an hour ago and she could barely stop kissing him to let him walk down the stairs. He made himself get out of the car slowly. He wouldn't panic. He wouldn't run up the stairs and search the house.

"She probably just went out for something," Beau said. His words made the sweat start on Jimmy's forehead. It meant that Beau either sensed Jimmy's panic or had the thought himself that Emily might have gone.

"Yeah, probably." He took the stairs two at a time.

Outside his closed door, he paused, as though he knew what to expect. When he opened it to find her bags gone and his bed made, he knew. A darkness passed over his eyes briefly and he grabbed onto the doorframe to steady himself. The fear that he'd kept gated let loose into full-blown panic and despair. Still, he ran through the house, calling her name and looking in rooms for her purse and bag.

"She left." Stacy sat on the couch on the top floor, legs stretched out, reading a fashion magazine.

"Oh?" She was the last person Jimmy wanted to talk to, but she held information in front of him, a dangling carrot. He disliked her even more for it.

He heard Beau make it up to the top floor. Jackson came out of his room. They both stood behind him, not saying anything. Why didn't they say anything?

"Where did she go, Stacy?" He kept his voice level and calm.

"Back to Richmond, I guess. She took all her bags with her. Left about half an hour ago in quite a hurry." She didn't look up from the magazine she was reading. But he could hear in her tone the pleasure she was taking and would have bet money that she had something to do with it. He would have asked her if she knew why, but had a very strong feeling that he wouldn't get the right answer. So he didn't ask.

He turned away from her and went to the kitchen, keeping his back turned to Beau and Jackson as well. He dialed her number. Voicemail. "Hey, Em. I got back and you're gone. Did you leave? Stacy said you went back to Richmond, but I'd rather hear from you. Call me. It's, uh, Jimmy."

He sent a text next.

J: I'm confused and trying not to freak out. Did you go back home?
J: Please call me.

He jumped as a hand closed over his shoulder. He expected Beau, but it was Jackson. "Hey, you okay?"

He nodded. Faster than he should have, convincing no one, least of all himself. "Yeah, fine. I'm sure it's nothing. A misunderstanding or something."

Jackson glanced at Stacy on the couch, who was clearly listening, though she made every appearance of reading the magazine. He pushed Jimmy toward the master bedroom. Beau closed the door behind them. Jimmy sank down in the floor beside the bed.

"It's not happening again, right? She's not blowing me off. Is she?" The full force of his fear and panic hit him like a punch to the gut. "Did I misread this? We didn't have the talk, but we talked around it. And she said the word 'love.' She kissed me. How could she run? Why?"

"I don't know what's going on," Beau said. "Don't make a guess. You don't know. I just know that she looked like you hung the moon an hour ago. If she bolted, something happened. And it would be good to find out what if possible. Before you do anything crazy."

"I'm fine."

"Sure you are," Beau said. "You're great."

Silence descended on the room for a few minutes. Or more. Jackson paced the room. Jimmy tried not to think. At all. None of his thoughts were any good.

Jackson stopped pacing and sat down on the floor in front

of Jimmy. "Emily asked me about jobs the other day. Jobs at Bohn's, specifically."

Jimmy's head snapped to attention. "She was thinking about moving here?" Beau put a hand on his shoulder.

"Maybe she's just scared?" Beau said. "I mean, that could be it. She's got a commitment problem, right? And you're younger and her best friend's brother. Maybe that's still an issue even if she didn't want to say it."

Jimmy stood up. His voice sounded flat and colorless. Just like everything around him. "It doesn't matter. Thanks, but it just doesn't. I mean, she left. The end. Who cares why? It's done. And I'm just that idiot who loved her and put it all on the line. Again." Jackson and Beau both started to speak, but he held up a hand. "Not now."

Jimmy gathered his things together in the duffle bag he'd brought up from his room downstairs. "Might as well move back to my room now that it's empty."

Back in his room, there was no sign Emily had been there. Until he got in bed and smelled her on his sheets. Only then did he fully break down, hoping the pillow that smelled just like Emily was enough to drown the sounds from the rest of the house.

CHAPTER TWENTY-ONE

Five days. That's how long Emily had been back from
Sandover. How long it had been since she ran from
Jimmy. Even the thought of his name hurt. Every
few minutes she caught herself rubbing absently at the top of
her chest, like she could ease the ache inside. She stared at
the crossed-off days on her desk calendar, tracing her finger
over the days a week ago when things had looked amazing
and beautiful, even if just for a moment.

Work was terrible, but the days spent at home were
worse. Her thoughts had too much time to play and her mom
had too many opportunities to criticize her. It wasn't hard to
see where a lot of Emily's worries and self-destructive
thoughts came from. Her mother gave them voice. Or maybe
her mother had a way of sensing what Emily was most sensi-
tive about so she could pick apart those things out loud. Just
over the weekend her mother brought up her failure as a
model, her going-nowhere temp job, and her string of
doomed relationships. Along with her comments about

Emily staying in pajamas, not showering, and eating only cereal for days.

"Your hair is starting to look brown," her mother had said, wrinkling her nose. "Maybe time for shampoo?"

She wasn't wrong. About any of it, really. But hearing it didn't make any of it better. She only felt more stuck.

Escape had been so close. For a tiny blip of time, she had hope. Thoughts of a future. With Jimmy. Too bad he didn't want a future with her.

Now the quiet thoughts were the ones that told her she was being ridiculous and emotional. That she shouldn't have let those words on a page speak for Jimmy. They shouldn't have the power to negate all the things he had said and the way he looked at her. He couldn't fake the emotion in his kisses. She should have asked him about the entry and let him explain.

But it hurt too much to open herself up to these quiet, perhaps very rational and very right, thoughts. Nope. This level of hurt was far too much. And it was just the beginning of a relationship. An unofficial relationship when it came down to it. What would happen if they actually tried this, if she moved there, and something went wrong? That thought made panic claw at her throat. It made her stay in Richmond, trying to ignore her mother and get through a job she hated.

Mr. Anderson gave her a stack of papers to file and things to catch up on. Though he'd given her such a hard time about taking a week off, it only took that day to catch up on tasks she had missed. She didn't even care about the mindless work because being home was worse. She slept all weekend, moving from her bed to the couch, ignoring her mother's pursed lips and sighs. Her phone rang and texts came through, but she ignored Kim and Natalie. Jimmy stopped texting the day she left. She deleted them and the voicemail he left. The sound of his voice made her sob. She hated crying.

She wondered if he had told Natalie yet. Emily couldn't bring herself to do it. Their friendship might really be over this time if Jimmy said that she had left. Emily wasn't going to tell anyone about the journal—certainly not his sister. It was humiliating and defeating. Natalie had been right all along.

She wasn't enough. Not for her parents. Not for Jimmy.

Yesterday morning, when she should have been at church, her mother came and stood at the foot of her bed. "Everything okay?"

Emily hadn't moved from her spot. Her mother had no maternal bones in her body, so this wasn't a real check-up. Emily could have said anything at all and her mother wouldn't care. "Just dandy."

"Well, that's good. Your father and I have been talking. I think it's time for us to cut the cord."

"Time for you to kick me out, huh?"

Her mother had sighed but didn't correct her. "I think it's long past time, don't you? Maybe this will be what you need to get you thinking seriously about your future and your career."

"What career?"

"I don't know," her mother had said. "Since you threw your viable and respectable one out the window when you left New York."

Emily had rolled her eyes. "Thanks, Mother. You really know how to motivate a girl."

Just before her mother closed the door, she'd said, "Two weeks. That should give you enough time."

Clearly her mother didn't understand how things like

leases worked or how difficult it was to find a roommate at a random time of the year.

Emily sat at her desk at work, staring at the computer screen, trying to think of tasks, since Mr. Anderson wouldn't give her real work to do. She had taken care of all the scheduling and filing. The inbox was at zero. Her little corner of the office was immaculate. She was bored and bored was bad for her brain.

She had tried to talk to Mr. Anderson that morning about an idea she had for one of the brands they were working with, but he simply stared at her. "You answer phones," he'd said. Emily resisted the urge to give him a sarcastic salute when she left his office.

With all her tasks done and the phones silent, she hit a dangerous stretch where she had time to think. She cleaned the microwave in the break room—not her job—and made a fresh pot of coffee—also not her job.

She had to do something to stop obsessing over the words from Jimmy's journal. Seeing his true feelings, written in the one space where you tell the truth: of all the things he wanted in a wife, he did not want her. For the first time in her life, she had truly opened up and taken a risk. And it didn't pay off.

It was hard to reconcile this with how he'd been with her. The look in his eyes when she told him about New York. The way he held her so close. His laughter, his kisses. Everything seemed so ... right. But she couldn't shake those words and how deeply they hurt her: NOT EMILY.

She knew that he had written those words because she hurt him. He was trying to get over her. She had told him she wasn't interested. That's probably all it was: hurt. Anger.

But seeing those words there on paper made all the doubts

she'd had about him come rushing back in a flood. She could see his face and the love in his eyes, then she would see those words on the page. Those two words touched on all her fears and insecurities in a way nothing else could. Surely by now he had realized that Emily had seen the journal. But still, he hadn't called.

Needing something to move her mind past this, she started searching for apartments and rooms for rent around Richmond. None of her friends needed roommates—not that she wanted to live with any of them. Everything was so expensive. Especially when this job was still not secured long term. They had made no mention of bringing her on full-time. It probably made way more financial sense for them to keep her on as a temp. Not that she wanted to work here anyway. She thought, not for the first time, about the proposal she had started for Jackson, still sitting unfinished on her computer.

Hesitating, she did a search for rentals on Sandover. Even opening up the page made her heart beat faster, like she was doing something she shouldn't. Her stomach fell. Prices there were even more expensive. It was a beach island and all.

Why was she torturing herself? She wasn't going to move there the way things were with Jimmy. And yet the idea of moving to Sandover and starting over had taken root in her. She could imagine a new life there: Hope Church on Sundays, working for Jackson, hanging out with Mercer and Beau and ... Jimmy. It didn't work without him. And she had ruined it.

She had to find something to do. Now. She needed a challenge. Some kind of problem to solve. She knew of one, but it involved taking her hurt from Jimmy and stuffing it. If she was good at anything, it was filing hurts away. Gritting her teeth, Emily opened up her proposal for Jackson. The cursor blinked on the page before her.

She pushed Jimmy out of her thoughts and tried to focus on how to save a certain grocery store from going under. Even if she wouldn't be the one there to help put the plan in place.

She worked through her lunch hour and much of the afternoon when she didn't have phone calls or copies to make. Emily sat back at her desk and looked over the finished proposal. She had seen enough of these cross her desk that she knew the proper template, even if hers was a little light on some aspects. Particularly, her experience and successes. Her plan involved a combination of a rebrand capitalizing on Mercer's Bohn's Local initiative and use of media, both traditional and in the social media sphere. Bohn's had a steep fight ahead and this might not be enough to bring things around. But it was a good, solid plan. A plan that she wanted to present in person.

It would require a long drive and a whole lot more bravery. And an actual conversation with Jimmy. One she should have had before leaving him with no explanation. She was ashamed of her behavior. Being hurt didn't give her enough excuse to hurt him back. Even if she still came away broken, she needed to apologize and to ask him about the journal. To see his face when he told her the truth, whether it was those words in the journal or what she had seen in his eyes when he looked at her and felt when he kissed her.

Running was stupid. She was tired of it.

"What are you working on?" her boss stepped up behind her and Emily jumped.

"Oh, just—it's nothing." Emily closed Word, glad she had already sent herself a copy.

He frowned. "No personal projects on company time."

She stood up. "I guess I quit then."

"What?"

Emily stepped around him and walked to the door, where she turned to face him again. "This is way less dramatic than I imagined. Aren't you going to yell?"

"I don't understand what's happening. Where are you going? Why?"

"It's time to stop running. And that starts by walking— walking right out the door."

He stood there gaping as she left. It was far less satisfying than in the movies, but she still had a giant grin on her face as she left.

Five days. Jimmy had been walking around with the taste of bitterness in his mouth for five days. When he woke up every morning, it was to realize again that Emily was gone. Not just gone. She had left him. She made him believe they had something special, that he was special and then disappeared. It was so much worse than Natalie's wedding. He felt like he'd lost half of himself.

He worked and ate and watched TV and worked out. He held conversations and did all the things that he did in a typical week. He breathed and slept and tried to hold conversations. They went on a call and put out the biggest fire he'd faced in an old storage unit. There was no rush at the end, no sense of accomplishment. Everything was washed out and gray, like he was seeing through a veil.

Another break from work and he wished he could go back, pick up some extra shifts. These long, empty days were endless. A hurricane was in the Atlantic, getting closer to hitting the coast. While reports were still unclear exactly where it would make landfall or how big it was, the fire crews were all on call. He didn't want to hope for a big storm to ride out, but at least it was something to do. He and Beau had helped Jackson put the storm shutters down on the house. Jackson had been busy at Bohn's, trying to keep things like bread, milk, and ice on hand. They helped there when they could, loading and unloading extra shipments of essentials and delivering to people with limited mobility.

Now Jimmy lay in his bed, which no longer smelled like Emily. That first night, he'd gotten up after he finished crying and did a load of laundry to wash the smell away. He went for a run on the beach while it was drying, not trusting himself to be in the house. Barefoot, he had pounded across the sand in the darkness and ended the run with a quick swim, returning sticky and tired, the endorphins that usually kicked in doing nothing for his mood. When he came home, showered, and made his bed again, he immediately regretted washing the sheets. He missed her scent.

He should go run tonight before the weather got too bad, but he couldn't bring himself to get out of bed. Sighing, he picked his Bible up, but he didn't want to open it. He wasn't ready to be comforted or work through what he was feeling. Maybe he was angry with God—he didn't want to think too hard about any of it. Beau had tried to talk to him about it earlier, but Jimmy told him to give him a few days and left Jackson and Beau upstairs watching a baseball game. They both hated baseball, so he knew it was for him.

Setting the Bible back down, he picked up his journal. He wasn't ready to talk, but he could write. He filled the first page with his blocky print writing, but when he turned the page to write on the back, it was lumpy under his pen, like something was stuck between the pages underneath.

Jimmy flipped back and a page opened easily. What was

this? A necklace he'd never seen before was tucked into the journal. A leather strap with a coin on it—a doubloon. It took him a moment to understand.

Only one person might have thought to get him a necklace related to pirates. Pain shot through his chest. He palmed the necklace, blinking back tears. When had she gotten this? And why was it in his journal?

Only then did he notice the page it was on: the list of qualities he'd wanted in a wife. He remembered writing it on a night six months ago. Not for the first time, he had been trying to convince himself to get over Emily after so much time had passed. His eyes traveled down the page and his breath stilled as he saw the last words he had written, "NOT EMILY," and then the one word below it, not in his handwriting:

later

No. No—Emily couldn't have seen this page. But obviously, she had.

Pounding up the stairs with the journal in his hand he stood in front of Beau and Jackson. He pushed the open journal at them across the coffee table.

"I know why she left." Silent tears rolled down his face and didn't care that they saw. Pacing the room, he tugged at his hair, needing to feel the sting of pain.

They both leaned forward and looked at the journal. Beau sucked in a breath. Then they turned their faces to him, both reflecting the same combination of pity and sorrow.

"Wow." Jackson sat back on the couch.

"Why didn't she just ask me about it? She should have

given me a chance to explain rather than just running off, assuming the worst."

"Maybe so," Beau said. "But this is pretty personal. You literally wrote down that you didn't want to marry her. Specifically. I might run too."

"How can I fix this? Can I fix this?" Jimmy whispered. "Tell me what to do."

Jackson leaned back on the couch. Beau closed the book. "Why did you write that?" His voice was curious, not accusing.

"I wanted to get over her. It was a bad night, for whatever reason. I felt hurt still. And mad. I mean, obviously, I don't feel that way. It's the opposite. It was just part of me trying to get over her. The truth is that I want to marry her. Only her."

Jimmy sank down on a chair across from Beau and Jackson, the baseball game still playing behind him on the television. Someone scored and the crowds cheered. Jackson turned off the TV.

"You have to earn her trust again," Jackson said. "And earning trust can sometimes be a slow battle. You take it inch by inch."

"But sometimes you can take it by storm," Beau said. "Jackson, you did that when you surprised Jenna fixing up that rental house just for her. That was a big gesture."

"That's true. We had some slow build and have more work to do, but that big moment told her a lot. It was the start of trust, I think. Of her giving me a chance."

Beau closed the journal. "Jimmy, you should go to her. Right now. Go to her and show her what you really feel. Tell her, but also show her."

Jimmy nodded. "I'll go. But what about the storm? Don't you need me here?"

Beau shook his head. "Latest reports make it look more like we'll get the dirty side. Wind, but a lot of rain. It's slowed down, too. Voluntary evacs, but I doubt it will be more than that. Flooding on the roads, but less storm surge and not as much wind."

"You're okay if I go?"

"Go get your girl," Beau said.

CHAPTER TWENTY-TWO

When Emily's mother answered the door, Jimmy's nerves hit him full force. He had only met Emily's parents once, at Natalie's high-school graduation when he'd been finishing up freshman year. He remembered being confused at how someone wild and funny and kind like Emily grew up with such wealthy, uptight parents. Then again, she had spent most of middle and high school at his house, with his family. She didn't say much about her home life, other than the fact that her dad was always busy with work and her mother with committee work, whatever that meant.

The house was easily twice as big as his parents' and in a much nicer neighborhood off River Road. It was almost as intimidating as Emily's mother in some kind of fancy skirt and jacket with big pearls around her neck. Especially when she checked him out from head to toe. *Yuck.*

He cleared his throat and shifted uncomfortably. "Hi, Mrs. Whitfield. I don't know if you remember me. I'm Jimmy, Natalie's brother."

Recognition flashed in her eyes. "Oh yes of course. Are you here for Emily? Because she left a bit earlier. I'm not sure when she's coming back. She had an overnight bag with her. Said maybe she'd be back in a few days. Hard to pin her down." She pursed her lips.

He had driven almost four hours for nothing. The grand gesture now felt more like poor planning. But seeing her wasn't the full plan. "Oh. You don't know where?"

She smiled and gave a small laugh. "She's a big girl. I don't keep up with her plans. I've got a very busy schedule."

"Who is it, dear?" The door opened wider and Emily's father stood in the doorway. Filled the doorway was more like it. He was enormous.

Jimmy swallowed his panic and stuck out a hand, willing it to remain steady. "Jimmy Echols, sir."

"Natalie's brother," her mother said. "You know—Emily's best friend?"

"Yes, of course. You're the baseball player, right? Full ride to … somewhere. I remember hearing about you. Played football myself. But I can respect an athlete."

"Actually, I ended up not playing ball due to an injury. I'm a firefighter now. I live in North Carolina. I'd love to come in and talk with you both if you don't mind. Sorry for not calling first."

They led him inside their home. It looked like the opposite of somewhere Emily would live: everything decorated professionally, nothing out of place. Obviously expensive. He hadn't realized how wealthy Emily's family was. Hopefully that wasn't something that mattered to her. His salary would never come close to providing a life like this for her.

His mouth felt dry suddenly. He should have worn something nicer than a polo shirt and shorts. "Water?" Mrs. Whitfield asked as they sat down in a formal living room.

"Yes, please," Jimmy said.

Mr. Whitfield crossed one ankle over his knee and sat back, watching Jimmy. He seemed to be enjoying his discomfort. Jimmy tried to make and hold eye contact, but it was impossible. Emily's father was simply too intimidating. He looked around the room instead, seeing a portrait of Mr. and Mrs. Whitfield and some other photographs. Only one showed Emily. It was clearly from her early modeling days. Her face looked younger, almost too young for the amount of makeup she had on. She was beautiful, but didn't look happy standing in a rose garden wearing a silvery dress.

"Here's your water," Mrs. Whitfield said, handing Jimmy what looked like a wine glass with sparkling water.

"Thank you." He set the glass down on the coffee table in front of him and leaned forward toward the Whitfields, who faced him in matching upholstered wingback chairs.

Jimmy took a breath. "I came today because I wanted to talk with you about Emily. Obviously, you don't know me very well. But I've known and loved Emily for years. We reconnected recently and I wanted to ask your permission to marry her."

The last words had come out way faster than he meant to. But he closed his mouth to keep him from trying to ramble on or explain. He had stopped by the house to get advice from his dad first, who was thrilled.

"You'll be tempted to just go on and on," he said. "To ramble until they respond. Don't. Say what you want, then wait. Even if it feels scary or awkward."

So Jimmy waited, doing his best to look like he wasn't terrified.

The Whitfields exchanged a look, then Mrs. Whitfield laughed. "Well, this is somewhat of a relief."

"You've got excellent timing, Jimmy," Mr. Whitfield said.

"We just told Emily that she has two weeks to find a new place to live."

Jimmy frowned. "Wait—so, yes? You're okay with me marrying her?"

"I'll help you load up her things in the truck right now," Mr. Whitfield said. "You do have a house she could move into, I assume? Or an apartment?"

"Well, we won't be living together before we get married."

Mrs. Whitfield laughed again. They weren't actual laughs, but the imitation of a laugh, when someone doesn't really find anything funny. "You don't need to pretend in front of us. We know how it is these days. Truly, we're happy to have her out of the house."

Jimmy cleared his throat. "I want to marry her, but not live with her before we're married."

They didn't seem to hear him and only seemed more than happy to get her out of the house. This was such a foreign concept to Jimmy, growing up as he did. Not simply the idea that her parents would have been fine with them living together, but more with the fact that they didn't seem to care what she did. Jimmy's dad had prepped him for all the questions that Emily's parents might ask—the same things he'd asked of Jeremy.

"He'll probably want to know about your job and if you can provide. Where you'll live after you get married. Maybe even why you love his daughter and how you intend to cherish her."

Mr. Whitfield asked none of these questions. In fact, Mrs. Whitfield was now talking about how they planned to turn Emily's room into a guest room. He nodded along, but inside, he wanted to scream at them. Didn't they care about their amazing, beautiful, smart daughter?

He understood, finally and clearly, why she never mentioned much about her family. It was obvious just how little they cared about her. He remembered all the nights she ate dinner with their family, lingering so late that it was often bedtime before she went home. His parents and Natalie never questioned it, but maybe they knew what he now did: her home life wasn't abusive or neglectful, but it was far from nourishing.

Jimmy felt a sudden and overwhelming need to protect Emily. To provide something like a home to her, one filled with love. He wanted to cherish her and to help her understand just how incredible and valued she was. Spending a few minutes in her home helped him understand Emily more than he ever had. He could even see why she left.

He wanted to give her more. A grander vision for family. Love.

Standing, Jimmy walked over to Emily's father and extended his hand again. He would still respect them, even if he couldn't stand them right now. "Thank you, sir," he said. "I promise that I will take care of your daughter and love her the way she deserves."

If she would still have him. And that was the big question.

Would she?

Emily sat across from Jackson in his small office, watching his face. Mercer stood just behind him, reading over his shoulder. He passed the proposal back to her and she read more closely, nodding.

She couldn't remember the last time she felt this nervous. With modeling, there weren't nerves. Even doing runway, it was like she was somewhere else, not present with the body walking out from behind the curtain. Other than the very first time, when she had all the normal fears about tripping or her clothes somehow falling off. After that, no nerves.

But this was something she'd put her heart into. She cared. As she had with Jimmy, she had put herself out there. It felt risky and completely uncomfortable. And also exhilarating. It felt like the start of something new. She squirmed in her seat, fidgeting with the armrests.

Jackson had been shocked to see her when she walked into Bohn's. "What are you doing here? You know we're under voluntary evacuation," he said to her when she walked up to him in the store.

Honestly, she had no idea. The weather was the last thing on her mind and she'd listened to playlists on the whole drive, not radio. The weather and tone of Sandover had completely changed in the five days since she left, so a hurricane made sense. The sky was ominous and the waves rough and dangerous. A steady line of cars had been leaving the island as she came on, prepared this time with money for the toll.

Mercer handed the paper back to Jackson and smiled at Emily. "It's smart. I like it." And these words gave Emily so much joy.

Jackson stared at Emily across the desk as though he had a million questions he wanted to ask, but wasn't going to. "I don't fully trust some of these ideas. Which is more a testament to the fact that I'm older than you are. Marketing has changed a lot, even in the past few years with social media. It's always changing and I don't keep up. If anything could work right now, it's ideas like this. Because none of mine have been working. I'd love to draw up a salary package that works for you. When could you start?"

"Today," she said. "Or, maybe after this whole hurricane business. I just need to move my stuff down. And find a place to live." And apologize to Jimmy.

"I could use a roommate," Mercer said.

Emily blinked at her, surprised. "Really?"

Mercer nodded. "I've got two bedrooms but one that's storage. It's mostly empty. I could use the money."

"Is your salary not enough?" Jackson asked, turning to Mercer. "I don't want you struggling."

She waved him off. "It's not that. I'm saving up."

For what, she didn't say. Emily again thought about how this chick was going to be a challenge. She held things close to the vest, to put it mildly. When she did open up, Emily knew it would be totally worth it.

Emily grinned. "I'd love that. Thanks."

"You don't need to see it first?" Mercer asked.

"Nope. Trust me—whatever it's like, I've lived in worse." Anything would be better than her parents' giant prison of a house. She pointed at Jackson. "Don't tell Jimmy. He and I need to talk first. There's a slight chance that … I won't say yes to the job and the apartment."

If Jimmy told her to get lost, she would. The island wasn't big enough for her to stay if he wouldn't forgive her. She wouldn't encroach on the life he'd built.

Jackson seemed to understand what she didn't say. "I won't tell him about the job."

Emily didn't miss his specific words. "Did you already tell him I was here?"

"I may have sent him a text. Sorry. He's not here though."

"Where is he? Shouldn't he be on hurricane duty or something?"

Jackson looked over her shoulder rather than meeting her

eyes. "Uh, I'm not at liberty to say. But I think Richmond."
He smiled.

"Why Richmond?"

"You'll have to ask him when he gets back."

Was everything okay with Natalie? The baby? Maybe he was just visiting his parents or something to get away from the hurricane. Though she always thought firemen would be helping out with natural disasters. "Huh. Okay. Well, I better go. Thank you, Jackson. And Mercer."

Before leaving, she plugged Mercer's phone number into her phone. "I'll be back in a few days. Hopefully. Need to take care of things at home."

"Sounds great," Jackson said. "Though maybe you should stay? Just considering the weather?"

Emily waved him off. "I'll be fine."

The rain still hadn't started in earnest, but the winds had gotten scary and it was almost totally dark out, even though sunset was still an hour or two off. Emily could see lightning flashing within the ominous low clouds. It didn't scare her. She loved storms and wished she could be on the third floor of Jackson's house to just watch it roll in.

Before getting in her car, she sent Jimmy a text.

E: Can we talk?
E: Heard you're in Richmond. I'll be there in a few hours. Long story.

A long story that she really hoped had a happy ending. She was still hurt and angry. But after talking with Jackson about her proposal, she felt even more sure that leaving like she did wasn't mature or fair. Jimmy needed a chance to explain the private words she never would have seen if Stacy hadn't left them out.

Only in person, looking into his eyes, would she be sure of their past and their future. And if he didn't want a future with her, she would leave. Jackson could handle her plan or not. Mercer could survive without a roommate. And she would find somewhere to move in two weeks, even without a job. Maybe she could be Scarlet's nanny in exchange for room and board. Heck, Big Jim and Natalie's mom would probably let her move in with them if it came to down to that or sleeping in her car.

Emily waited to see if he'd respond before she started the drive back to Richmond, feeling slightly desperate as she stared at the phone screen. Though she didn't want to talk until they could do it in person, a text from him would be a tiny fragment of hope to hold onto. She waited five minutes and then knew she needed to get going if she wanted to avoid the storm.

She pulled out and headed for the bridge. The long line of cars had dissipated and there were only a few leaving the island now. The water in the sound below, which had been so calm and flat when she had come the week before, now roiled and rushed with the fury of the impending storm.

As Emily passed the toll booth and began the winding drive home, one lone car came toward the island. Only when it passed by and she saw the car, she realized it was Jimmy. Without even checking her mirrors, she did a U-turn in the middle of the road, ignoring the car honking behind her. She accelerated toward the toll booth. She needed to catch Jimmy before he got through the toll booth. She planned ahead this time, but had given the woman her only two dollars as she drove onto the island. Why it was even open right now, she didn't know. The same little woman sat behind the window. She should be barricaded in her house or evacuated off the island right now.

EMMA ST. CLAIR

Before she could pull up behind him and flag him down, Jimmy's car pulled onto the bridge and the red and white striped barrier lowered, blocking her off. Emily flashed her headlights, honking her horn.

"Two dollars for toll," Greta said.

Emily didn't argue, but jumped from the car and began to run, waving her arms. Running in this weather and while still nursing broken toes was stupid. They throbbed with every step, probably setting her back in recovery. But she had abandoned the rational, thinking part of her brain a few minutes before.

She wasn't fast, but there was still time for Jimmy to see her in the rearview mirror—if he only looked.

"Jimmy!" She shouted, the wind whipping around her.

She gave up running and jumped up and down, waving her arms. "Jimmy!"

Just when she was about to turn around and walk defeated back to the car, Emily saw brake lights. The car lurched to a stop. The white reverse lights came on as he began backing toward her. She limped towards him, unable to run anymore. He stopped about twenty feet away and he jumped out of the car. She stopped running and he stood there, staring at her. But only for a moment.

Then they were both running as the skies opened up in full right over them. In the few seconds it took for him to wrap her up in his arms, they were soaked to the skin.

How had she ever doubted him? No matter what those words on the paper said and how deeply they touched on her insecurities, Jimmy had always been and was now *hers*.

The rain was almost deafening as it pounded them and the bridge. Jimmy put his face close to her ear to speak.

"I'm so sorry Emily. I'm so very sorry. Those words—I didn't mean them and should never have written them. I was

266

so hurt and was trying to force myself to get over you so I could just function. After Natalie's wedding, I was crushed. I thought I had no chance with you, ever. I was trying to convince myself to have closure because you didn't want me."

"I want you," she said, close to his ear. "I really, really do."

They were drenched but smiling like they didn't even notice. Her hair was plastered to her cheeks and neck. Jimmy did not loosen his grip on her. Tears mixed with the rain running down her cheeks.

"I love you, Emily." He pulled back so their faces were inches apart. "I know I haven't even gotten a chance to ask you to be my girlfriend yet, but things with us haven't been on a normal relationship track."

Emily began to laugh, tossing her head back and feeling rain in her mouth. Relief soaked through her, as real as the rain. "You can say that again. I love you too."

He pulled away and searched her face, rubbing the rain from his eyes. Then he dropped to a knee, his blond hair dark and wet hanging over his face. His eyes blinked against the onslaught of rain. She could not breathe as he took her hands. Was he ... ?

"I hope you don't mind if I skip a step. Or a lot of steps. I love you. I've loved you for so long. I want a future with you. You ARE the list of what I want in a wife. Only you. Will you marry me?"

Her chest contracted with such intensity of feelings that she couldn't speak. She dropped down with him and wrapped her arms around Jimmy, putting her lips to his ear. "I love you, Jimmy. I don't mind skipping all the steps. This has been years in the making. You've known me better than almost anyone and I've known you the same. We aren't falling into something new, but stepping into something known. We can do it our way. It's our story. Yes. I will marry you. Maybe not today? But yes. And soon. Please?"

He laughed and kissed her. The kiss was wet and messy and filled with their laughter and rain running down their faces.

And then he pressed the ring into her palm. She hadn't even noticed it, but had only been looking in his eyes. A single round diamond in a platinum setting. It was beautiful. Simple, perfect, everything. She wasn't the type of girl to go ring shopping, but if she had, this is what she would have picked. Simple and beautiful, no fuss. How had he done this so quickly?

"You may not be able to see in this rain, but look inside the band."

Emily dipped her head to block the rain slightly and turned the ring to see the inscription. He'd had two words engraved there, where they would forever rest next to her skin:

ONLY EMILY

The two words filled her with a joy that had her kissing him all over again, first with laughter and then with such a passion that she wouldn't have been able to keep her feet had she been standing.

A loud boom of thunder shook the sky and pulled them apart. He took her hand and stood, pulling her to her feet. "You can't drive in this. Let's get your car and go to Jackson's. We can ride out the storm there. Okay?"

"I'd love nothing more than to weather this storm with

my fiancé," she said. And with another kiss, he pulled her to his car. "I don't have money for the toll."

"Of course you didn't," he said, grinning. "You drive mine and I'll take yours and pay. I did wonder why you were running after me when I spotted you in the rearview. But it worked out in the end, didn't it?"

"The most romantic proposal ever."

"Certainly the wettest." He hesitated. "You don't mind that we skipped the whole boyfriend/girlfriend part of the relationship?"

She grinned at him. "Boyfriends are overrated. And I can't seem to keep them. Happy to skip right to the fiancé part."

He smiled back then waved her on. "Go! I'll be right behind you."

Emily didn't drive until Greta raised the barrier and Jimmy was right behind her. She never wanted to be out of his sight again.

EPILOGUE

"Emily? Are you in there?" Natalie's voice sounded dull through the closed door.

"No," Emily called. But as she spoke, her shoulder brushed up against empty wire hangers, which rattled along the metal rod. Why did the church have a closet in the bride's room anyway?

The door flew open, revealing a very pregnant Natalie in a red bridesmaid gown. A furious pregnant Natalie.

Emily giggled. "You're a vision in red, darling."

"Don't get me started on how I look nine months pregnant in a bridesmaid dress."

"Hey, I let you pick and you picked red."

"It's two weeks until Christmas. Red makes sense. And it's the least you could do having a wedding when I'm about to pop." Natalie shook her head. "Stop distracting me! Why are you hiding in there? You'll wrinkle your dress. More importantly, you are supposed to be walking down an aisle in fifteen minutes. And if you think I'm going to let you leave my brother again ... "

Emily stepped forward from the back of the shallow closet, which smelled of mothballs. She gripped Natalie's arms and leaned forward until their foreheads were touching. She stood just inside the doorway, her best friend just outside.

"I am not going to leave Jimmy. Not now. Not ever."

Natalie relaxed, visibly. "Then what? What's got you scared? Why are you hiding in there?"

"I just needed a moment. Or two."

Emily closed her eyes, still smelling the moth balls, but also cinnamon. For months now, Natalie had been chewing cinnamon gum and cinnamon candies and even sucking on cinnamon sticks. She said it was the only thing that kept the morning—or all-day—sickness at bay.

The smell was comforting to Emily. She would probably forever think of wedding plans when she smelled cinnamon. Because Ripley, her wedding coordinator On Island, was much more of a drill sergeant than wedding planner, Emily avoided her and made frequent trips to Richmond to plan with Natalie and her mom.

It frustrated Ripley and made things a little more complicated, but Emily longed to have people beside her who cared. Her mother didn't want to have much to do with the planning after Emily refused to get married in Richmond. Her mother didn't care if it wasn't at the right church with Emily in the right dress with the right photographer and have the ceremony at the right country club. She was lucky her parents were still giving her a budget, even if it was a fraction of what they would have paid if she did it their way. Totally worth it.

Emily was lucky. Some people married into a complicated family they didn't like. Jimmy's family already felt like her own.

Family. That was the thing that had her in the closet. Was she really ready for this?

Emily held out her palms near Natalie's belly. "Can I?"

"You know you don't have to ask. I only mind when it's strangers. Especially dudes."

Emily put her hands against Natalie's belly, taut under the satin. "I still can't believe random dudes try to touch your belly."

"You wouldn't believe how many," Natalie said. For a moment they stood like that. Natalie circled her hands loosely around Emily's wrists. "She kicking you?"

"Not right now. I wish she would."

"You need a good kick, Emily?" Natalie said the words, lightly, but it was a real question.

Emily didn't answer, feeling the warmth of Natalie's belly as it filled her hands. Her fingers had been trembling all day, but she felt a sheer strength and power standing here with her palms inches from a tiny life tucked away inside. She wasn't nervous. There was not one thing she doubted about her love for Jimmy.

It was more the seriousness of the occasion. The finality of vows and rings and I dos. She knew that Jimmy was it for her. But he came from a stable family, filled with love. Whether he knew it or not, he studied at the feet of an incredible relationship. Not that her parents were abusive or even neglectful, but there was nothing about their marriage to emulate, except the fact that they stayed in it. The more she planned and talked wedding and marriage details, the more Emily felt ill-equipped. What if she wasn't good at being a wife? With her baggage and her tendency to run, she feared an imminent doom.

Ripley poked her head inside the bride's room. "It's almost time. Your dad is waiting for you, Emily."

273

"Okay," Emily said. "Just another minute."

"You have thirty seconds. I'll be standing right outside the door."

Emily sighed as Ripley closed the door. "I'm almost as excited to be done dealing with her as I am excited to marry your brother. You heard her—thirty seconds. Let's move out."

"Wait. I just want to say one more thing," Natalie said. "You aren't going to be like them. You and Jimmy. It's not the same as your parents. Not even close. Whatever else you do and whether you have kids or don't have kids, you two love each other and will create a home that's filled with love."

"I know."

"Do you?" Natalie looked at her with such intensity that Emily wanted to look away, but couldn't.

"How can you know that for sure? How do you know that I'm not going to screw this up?"

"Because you aren't them," Natalie said. "You aren't like them and Jimmy isn't either. And you both have God, which changes everything. You don't need to be afraid, Em. It's going to be amazing. Not perfect, but amazing."

And then, like a tiny punch against the drum of Natalie's belly, something pressed against her right palm. Emily grinned, feeling tears in her eyes. "There it was. I felt it. She's feisty. And strong."

Natalie smiled back. "Like her Aunt Emily. Almost officially her aunt."

Something about that kick scattered the doubts that had been buzzing around her like flies. She had a man to marry.

"Let's go make this official. Shall we, sister?"

Natalie gave Emily a quick hug, the baby bump pressing into her. Emily met her father in the hallway and smiled as she hooked her arm through his.

They waited a few feet away and out of sight from the guests inside the doors. Ripley released her two bridesmaids —Natalie and Mercer—one by one, then closed the doors. She motioned for Emily and her father to move in front of the doors.

Even with the sanctuary doors closed, the sound of the string quartet filled the hallway. This was one decision she let her mother make and Emily was glad. The notes were bright and soothing at the same time. Ripley stood next to the doors, waiting for the change in music that would announce the right time for Emily to walk through.

Emily felt stiff standing next to her father. This was more affection than she'd seen in a long time from him, which was pretty sad. He stared straight ahead. He hadn't said that she looked beautiful or that he was proud of her. She didn't want to let this thought cloud her day.

Emily couldn't change him, but she could change herself. She knew he loved her, even if his love looked different than what she had always hoped for.

She leaned in and kissed him on the cheek. "I love you, Daddy."

He smiled down at her. "I know. I love you too, Little Bird."

He hadn't called her that since she was so young. She had all but forgotten about the nickname. And hearing it, somehow, gave her strength. It was like the strength she'd gotten from holding onto Natalie's belly, feeling that tiny but powerful movement underneath.

Just as Ripley put her hand on the doors to open them, Emily closed her eyes.

She knew already the look that Jimmy would have on his face. It was the same way he had looked at her for the past ten years, like she was the love of his life.

It was about time she returned the favor.

The doors swung wide to the sanctuary. Emily opened her eyes to her future: Jimmy standing at the end of the aisle with a huge smile on his face and tears in his eyes. The room was full, but as Emily gazed in, there was only one person she really saw.

Only Jimmy.

THE END

WHAT TO READ NEXT

The Billionaire Surprise Series
The Billionaire Love Match
The Billionaire Benefactor
The Billionaire Land Baron
The Billionaire's Masquerade Ball
The Billionaire's Secret Heir

Sandover Island Sweet Romance Series
Sandover Beach Memories
Sandover Beach Week
Sandover Beach Melodies
Sandover Beach Christmas

Not So Bad Boy Sweet Romance Series
Managing the Rock Star
Forgiving the Football Player
Winning the Cowboy
Taming the Cowboy's Twin

A NOTE FROM EMMA

I'm writing this note as I finish updating *Sandover Beach Week* in June of 2019. Last year, I released Jimmy and Emily's story after having so many people ask for it. My debut novel, *Cold Feet, Hot Summer,* told Natalie's story, but Jimmy and Emily stole the show for a lot of readers. (If you haven't read it, you can now read it for free when you sign up for my weekly emails!)

I've always loved Emily, but I think she was a little harder to relate to in the first version of this book. Coming back to her, I softened her a bit and expounded more on her back story and struggles. I relate to her in that I don't always feel like the RIGHT Christian woman. I'm a little sarcastic in my humor. I'm a little more boisterous and goofy. I've also struggled with depression and love late-night waffles. If you've ever felt like you didn't quite belong, I thought Emily might be someone you could relate to as well.

I like to share real-life stories that inspired what I write. When my husband and I were dating, I opened his Bible once to find a notecard where he had written qualities he wanted in a wife. There was one big one that I didn't fit and couldn't change. Rational or not, it CRUSHED me. (I'm not sharing, as it's a little personal, but just know my husband is a great guy and this wasn't anything bad on his list OR bad about me. Just a reality of something he wanted that I didn't fit.)

They say that it takes ten compliments to off-set one negative remark. I found that to be extra true when it came to this list of my husband's. He assured me that he loved me and the list was just something he made years before, long before we met. But it was really tough at the time to get over. I could imagine for Emily, finding that note in Jimmy's journal would have felt the same way. Even if logically, she could guess why he wrote it or knew that he didn't mean it. Some hurts just go right to our center, whether it's rational or not, and that's what the journal did for her, just as it did for me.

I want to say a bit about what happened to Emily in New York. As a woman, I've experienced a range of violent and offensive behavior from men. Maybe you have too. These stories matter. It can be easy, whether you went through something large or something small, not to speak up. To hide our shame and feel guilty and wonder what we could have done differently. I hope that if you are struggling to deal with an event in your past or present, you can find help. And if you didn't know this, Jesus in the Bible promises to take away our guilt. That applies to guilt over things we intentionally did wrong, but he also can heal us from things that weren't our fault, but made us feel dirty or unlovable. (Ephesians 2:1-10 is a great place to read about that.)

Know that you are not alone. If you need help, the Assaulted Women's Helpline is available seven days a week, twenty-four hours a day. Find out more on their website: http://www.awhl.org/

For my research on firefighters, I spoke with McKenna Sinclair, who was a firefighter and wrote The Odyssey of the Phoenix. I'm sure I don't fully have every detail accurate, so if you've worked in a station and I missed some things, I'm sorry!! You can always reach out and let me know. As an author, I do my best to research and then use what I need to make the story work, which may mean some artistic license.

Thank you so much for reading! If you liked this book, there are a few ways that you can support me as an author.

- Leave a review!
- Buy more books!
- Tell a friend! Word of mouth sells more things than ads. Period. You can send them to my Amazon page with all my books.

You can also join my free Facebook group: http://facebook.com/groups/emmastclair. I often have bonus scenes in there and sometimes we just chat about other reads or our favorite ice cream flavors.

-Emma

Made in the USA
San Bernardino, CA
07 July 2020

75019964R00175